H

My Family of Hicks

by Scot Rogers

First Edition: June 2025

ISBN: 979-8-9889579-9-7

For all the souls I have met along the way.
Thank you.

HICKS AMERICA
We Feed the World the Best

Our Mission

Since 1800, when two brothers founded the Hicks Trading Post to provide the best value in goods and services, our family has upheld a steadfast commitment to quality, integrity, and community. Over 225 years later, that founding principle remains at the heart of everything we do. In 2007, Hicks America proudly began the next chapter of our legacy—bringing healthy, natural foods to the table through regeneratively grown agriculture. Today, we continue to grow with purpose, offering organic produce, dairy products, and free-range farming that reflect our enduring promise: to feed the world the best.

Contents

My Family of Hicks

Ho Ho … Ahem

Known as "Santa Baby" from the reality TV disaster *Campground Swingers*, Stuart Michaels was a sight to behold—tall, lean, and rocking a neatly trimmed white beard that made him look like a young, sexy Kris Kringle who did Pilates instead of cookies. His electric-blue eyes twinkled with mischief, and his reputation was even shinier. As a self-proclaimed sex addict, he had single-handedly turned the show's amusement park into an NC-17-rated smut wonderland, conquering as many adult female *and male* campers as he could—pushing the spectacle into a #1 smash on a leading streaming service.

So, when Stuart strutted into Betty's rehab facility, fresh off a six-month bender and ready to get clean-*ish* during the production's break through January, he was immediately drawn to Winston Clarke. But Win was consumed with writing the next Great American Novel and was either holed up in his room or comfortably tucked in the corner of the outdoor smoking deck, ferociously scribing away on one of the legal tablets he always had in hand between assemblies—politely removed from engaging with other patients, including Stuart.

The group therapy session was held in a spacious room, ironically named *Serenity*. It was peak elite rehab with soft, neutral tones that bathed the décor in creamy whites, warm beiges, and muted blues, complemented by rich wooden accents, fresh orchids, and rare bonsai trees. The walls were punctuated by framed abstract art—pieces chosen more for their "center-yourself" vibes than any actual artistic merit.

Seating—arranged in a purposeful circle, featuring oversized armchairs upholstered in plush Italian velvet, shades of muted sage, sandy beige, and dusky blue. Every chair was deep enough to allow the most guarded CEO or washed-up rockstar to sink in and pretend to think about their inner demons while actually contemplating their next facelift. Brass side tables with marble tops, weighted for stability during emotional breakthroughs, were perfectly set between the chairs— each adorned with a discreetly branded bottle of sparkling water and a box of artisanal tissues.

A low, live-edge mahogany coffee table was a grounding focal point at the circle's center. Its surface held a decorative ceramic bowl filled with smooth river stones—ideal for nervously fidgeting without betraying a complete breakdown. A handwoven wool rug anchored the space with abstract waves of cream and charcoal. The air, scented with a faint blend of lavender and sandalwood, enticed the peaceful atmosphere.

The late afternoon's deep, soul-searching discussion was ***Authenticity and self-worth beyond fame and fortune***. The patients, clad in designer loungewear, T-shirts, and jeans, clutched their wellness smoothies like emotional support pets—except for pop singer BeBe Lu, who had brought her own: a white teacup Bichon Frise named CeCe, perpetually nestled in the sanctuary of her ample cleavage.

One by one, the participants shared their struggles—balancing public image with personal pain, the loneliness of success, and the pressures of industries that never slept. A rock legend confessed that even after sold-out stadiums, he still felt empty. A tech mogul, worth enough to buy a small country, admitted he had no real self-value. A twenty-two-year-old social media influencer, hidden behind sunglasses bigger than her problems, whispered that she was terrified of becoming irrelevant.

Then, it was Win's turn. He thoughtfully took a deep breath and chose to fully bear his greatest fear—that he was expected to take over his family's empire, but surprise, surprise, *he did not want to.*

As Win spoke, Stuart was mesmerized by how Winston's mouth moved, his body reacting to each syllable's slow, deliberate movement. Something lustfully yearned inside him like a forbidden Christmas gingersnap he *really* wanted to taste.

When Clarke finished, the group was invited to respond. It was feedback time.

Without missing a beat, Stuart leaned forward and, in his best *I'm-wise-and-hot* voice, asked, "Why don't you just take your Farmer Hicks fortune, give it all away, and set yourself free? Who really owns what here? You've been letting it own you for your entire life. Why not take control and do as you wish?"

Boom! The words hit Winston like a Monarch movie plot twist. His jaw dropped. His eyes widened. A million pounds magically lifted from his shoulders, and before he could stop himself, he let out a breathless chuckle.

"You're right," Win sighed as if Santa Baby had just handed him the meaning of life in a gift-wrapped box. A tear rolled down his cheek, and he practically glowed with enlightenment. "You're *absolutely* right, Stuart. I *can* just give it all away."

Win's gaze swept around the circle. The room vibrated with warm, unconditional, loving energy. The influencer, the billionaire, and the tortured artists beamed at Win, wearing expressions of quiet encouragement.

And just like that, Winston Clarke was free. *Poof!* His work here was done, he decided. He would check out in the morning.

The therapy session ended in a swirl of teary hugs and overly intense eye contact. Everyone was busy congratulating each other for being vulnerable as if they'd just won a Hollywood award for Best Cry.

Love was in the air—or maybe that was just the essential oils diffuser. Either way, it was a whole *moment.*

But lurking in the corner was Stuart Michaels, the opportunist and predator. He waited patiently as Winston worked the room with his charming send-offs until all the participants, including the therapist, finally left. Then Stuart moved in for his hug.

Of course, Winston obliged. Because who denies the man who presented the solution to ending a lifetime of fretting?

Stuart leaned in, wrapped his strong arms around Win's backside, and pulled him in tight, pressing his manhood against Winston's. In a low voice and breath suspiciously minty, he purred, "You remind me of my stepdad."

Winston smiled politely and backed out of the embrace. Stuart followed up by saying, "He touched me in special places and did things to me that felt good. And I'd like to do the same to you."

Win felt like his soul had left his body for a split second. His eyes briefly shifted to a large bonsai tree across the room, and he flitted his head in disbelief that Santa had just popped his euphoric bubble.

But then, because he was Winston Clarke and *had* survived a Marc Monarch party, he snapped back with a smirk, gave Stuart's right beard two strong pat-smacks, and said, "Santa Baby, I've seen roughly fifteen minutes of your show, and that was about all I could take. So, before you continue with another inappropriate analogy like the episode I cringed through when you seduced the shirtless blind lumberjack who only had one arm in a tent in the middle of the night, by sharing the time you went to band camp and described in *waaay* too much detail the instrument you wrapped your lips around … stop. Save your pickup lines for your campground syphilis show."

Winston purposely lifted his chin at the Kringle wannabe. "I'm not shopping. And even if I were, you are *sooo* not on my Christmas wish list."

Win sprung for the door and said aloud as he made his exit, "*What the fuck!*" and promised to himself to never, *ever* come back to rehab.

Monday

"This *is* a surprise," trilled Lucille Beedy, the petite admissions director, in a high-pitched voice that could etch glass. Her aesthetic was a full-frontal assault on minimalism—a lemon-yellow dress with white tulips and green stems dancing across it, silver cat-eye glasses with rhinestone embellishments, and a white beehive so towering it looked like it required FAA clearance. It wasn't just a hairstyle; it was a *statement*.

Tilting her head at an angle reminiscent of a slightly askew painting, she reviewed her computer monitor. "We customized your recovery treatment plan for twenty-one days when you arrived. You have completed fourteen."

Her eyes darted back to Winston without moving her head, blinking with an expression somewhere between suspicion and mild amusement. "What prompted you to terminate your plan early?"

Win's gaze flitted from the architectural marvel atop her head to the bronze nameplate on her desk that read *LUCILLE BEEDY* before finally landing on her unnervingly cheerful cheeks. He met her beady green eyes, matching her energy with a dazzling grin.

"I'm clean and quite clear. I know what I need to get to the bottom of."

"Do you feel you're ready?"

Winston continued to smile, feeling no need to explain further.

"I do. My bags are packed. I'd like to process the discharge and be on my way."

Lucille, unmoved, remained locked in her dramatic tilt, studying him as though she were recording a Rorschach test with her beehive as the inkblot. Win suddenly had his eyes captured as though he were hypnotized by a Hypno Spinner toy, warping his mind with things he didn't want to see.

"You're sure?" she asked, eyes narrowing.

Still under the spell of her hair, Win forced his attention back to her face. "Yes."

"Because you *are* free to leave any time you like."

"I'm ready to go."

With the flourish of a woman accustomed to making even the slightest movement a performance, Lucille slowly righted her head. The room's equilibrium corrected itself as if restoring balance to the universe.

"Very well," she said, her voice carrying the same energy as a flight attendant who *knows* you're about to struggle with the overhead bin but will enjoy watching it happen. She returned her attention to the computer, her long, lime-green painted nails clicking across the keyboard with the precision of a seasoned hacker.

Then, with the grace of someone who had *perfected* the maneuver from years of practice, Lucille pushed off her desk with her tiny, well-manicured hands. Her chair *glided*—not rolled but *glided*—across the floor in a perfectly executed spin, landing her directly in front of a hutch a few feet away. Without breaking stride, she slipped a purple spiral wrist coil from her arm, used the attached key to unlock a cabinet, and retrieved a sleek black box. After relocking the doors and an unnecessary but highly dramatic snap of the wrist coil back onto her wrist, Ms. Beedy executed a *second* effortless push-off and spun back to her original position.

She placed the black box in front of Win with the gravitas of someone delivering the nuclear codes.

"Here are your personal effects. I'll retrieve your phone from the vault. Excuse me," Ms. Beedy said solemnly. Then, without missing a beat, she rose and disappeared.

Win exhaled at the little embossed gold "3" on the lid. He sat comfortably relaxed, looking around Lucille's office, realizing the administration offices were eerily quiet. Then, faintly, from beyond the door, he heard *her*.

"Yes, he's discharging himself …"

"I'd say three to five minutes …"

"Yes, he's already packed …"

"Very well …"

"It's my pleasure …"

"Goodbye."

A chill pricked Win's spine.

Lucille reappeared, her expression unreadable, carrying his iPhone. She set it gently on the black box. "Fully charged," she said.

Win eyed the device. "Why was it in a vault?"

Lucille's lips curled into a smirk. "It's actually a containment room. But we call it a vault because it sounds less *ominous*."

His brow arched.

She sighed as if explaining something to a particularly slow houseplant. "All patient phones are stored in a fire containment room. If a battery ignites, the suppression system handles it—no risk to the building."

That explanation made sense. *Her phone call*, however, did not.

Lucille turned to the monitor, and her nails resumed tap-dancing on the keyboard. "Mr. Clarke, while I print your waiver and discharge papers, please turn your phone on to ensure it's working properly."

Win hesitated. The last time he powered on his previous iPhone after an extended digital detox in 1997, it had *exploded* with notifications like a jackpot slot machine in Vegas.

"How about I do that later?" he suggested.

Lucille gave him a look.

Win *looked back.*

She *did not blink, her eyes penetrating.*

Win relented and turned the phone on.

As the device booted, Lucille slid three sheets of paper toward him, tapping line by line with the aggressive precision of someone who *lived* for administrative dominance.

"Not all optional expenses were covered by insurance. This is the balance. Your credit card on file will be charged. An itemized receipt will be emailed to you."

Win nodded, barely glancing at the amount. He focused on his phone as it finished booting, waiting for the passcode screen to pop up. When it did, he entered it.

Lucille continued, shifting to the following sheet. "This is your dis-charge paperwork. Initial here, here, and here. Sign here."

Win scribbled.

Then, it happened.

A single vibration.

Then another.

Then, an unrelenting, *earthquake-level* surge of buzzing.

The numbers on his Messages, Phone, Voicemail, and Mail apps skyrocketed into the hundreds.

Before he could react, the screen switched—

AUNT D! Calling.

Win froze.

His eyes darted to Lucille.

She tilted her beehive ever so slightly. "Well, *look at that*," she said in a voice with a delicate blend of smugness and faux innocence. "Your first caller of the day. Please, feel free to answer it."

Win's grip tightened around the pen.

How would my aunt know to call precisely when I turned my phone on? He pondered with trepidation.

Lucille sat nonreactive, staring wide-eyed without a single blink.

The phone vibrated. And vibrated. And vibrated.

Ignoring her directive, Winston asked, "Who did you just speak with in the other room after you stepped out?"

Ms. Beedy pursed her lips, disapproving of his boldness.

Winston set the pen atop the signed documents, leaned back in his chair, and crossed his legs. Ignoring the vibrating phone, he locked eyes with her, his expression composed. He smiled—a patient, knowing smile that suggested he had all the time in the world.

But Ms. Beedy did not. Mr. Clarke's unexpected discharge had up-ended her morning schedule, and she had a new patient arriving within the hour.

Lifting her chin, she gave a slight bob of her voluminous hair. "Your mother is listed as your primary contact. Per our policy, she's notified upon your arrival, so she knows you're safe." Her voice was clipped and efficient. "I called Mrs. Clarke a few minutes ago to inform her you were being discharged and would no longer be in our care."

Win recalled something like that from his last stay. He had forgotten.

The phone stopped buzzing—only to start again almost instantly. Aunt D was calling back.

Lucille shot him a look: *Answer it!*

Slowly, he picked up and swiped the phone.

"Hello, Aunt Darceline."

"Have you finished checking out yet?" Her voice was deep and husky, like the '70s movie queen Brenda Vaccaro in her prime.

"Almost."

"My jet is waiting for you. A driver is on his way to pick you up."

Struck, Win blinked. "*What?*"

"I'll see you when you land."

Before he could ask what that meant, she *hung up*.

He stared at his phone.

Why was her jet in California?

And why was it waiting on him?

Lucille smiled knowingly as she lifted the lid from the black box. "So, *all is good?*"

Win exhaled, dazed. "I'm going home."

"Well, that is good," she chirped, her voice laced with a patronizing tone. Her gaze flicked to the box—a silent signal.

Win slipped his phone into his navy blazer, then reached into the box, retrieving his keys and wallet.

Lucille carefully replaced the lid, picked up a telephone receiver, and pressed a button.

"Mr. Clarke is officially discharged. Please have his luggage brought to the front entrance. Thank you."

She hung up and said with unexpected sincerity, "I wish you the best, Winston."

Then, she stood.

Win got up, and Lucille escorted him from her office to the lobby, where a black Escalade approached the entrance.

"Have a wonderful, healthy life," she said as he stood motionless, like a man caught between past and future.

He exhaled a deep sigh, completely stunned. "Thank you."

Once he thought of saying, "You as well," Lucille was gone. He turned to see the door to Administration closing shut.

He looked at the Cadillac, swapped his eyeglasses for his prescription sunglasses, and stepped through the large entrance doors, pulling a cigarette case from another blazer pocket.

A tall, polished man stepped out. "Mr. Clarke?"

Win lit up and exhaled a puff of smoke. "Yes?"

"I'm Gerard, your driver to the airport today."

Win smirked faintly. "Bags are on the way."

"Very well." Gerard assumed a classic chauffeur stance, facing the entrance.

Winston slowly paced the parking lot, dragging on his cigarette, his mind racing. This wasn't a casual pick-up. It was a calculated move by the family boss, who wasn't about to let him slip away from her grip like he had when he impetuously darted off to rehab two weeks ago. But he realized it didn't matter. He was going back to Hicksville anyway.

Gerard's voice cut through his thoughts as Win finished his cigarette.

"Your luggage is all in, sir," he announced, politely holding open the car door.

Win took one last drag, then stubbed his cigarette in the outdoor ashtray far from the entrance. Facing the morning sun, he closed his eyes. The heat pressed against his skin—intense but oddly comforting. He smiled, reassured there was nothing to fear.

Without a word, he climbed into the Escalade. But as the A/C vents above him blew refreshingly cool air across the back seat, one lingering thought refused to let go: Lucille's beehive.

Why am I thinking about this?

Clear Skies

"Welcome aboard Hicks America One, Mr. Clarke. I'm Trish," the flight attendant greeted, her voice smooth and warm, her wide brown eyes like a doe's.

Stepping into what was clearly a brand-new jet, Win took a moment to admire Darceline's aircraft selection. The space had a factory-fresh smell, futuristic cabinetry with rich wood veneer accents, space-age panoramic windows that lined the cabin, and toffee-colored leather seats. It was decadence on wings.

Peeking into the cockpit, he spotted two pilots seated before a sleek, cutting-edge avionics panel that looked like something out of NASA.

"This is Captain Gibson and Captain Roth," Trish introduced.

"Hello, Mr. Clarke," they greeted with chiseled jaws practically out of a men's cologne ad.

"Good morning, gentlemen. Thank you for flying," Winston said, adding with a grin, "Looks like you've got yourselves a new toy."

Captain Gibson boasted like a proud dad at a little league game. "This is a Cessna Citation CJ4 Gen2."

"She's a beauty," Winston marveled.

"She sure is," Captain Roth replied with pride.

"When was her maiden flight?" Win asked.

"Last Wednesday, when we flew in from Hicksville," Captain Roth said with a grin.

Captain Gibson got down to business. "Our flight time today will be five hours and twenty minutes."

"If you need anything, just ask Trish," Captain Roth added warmly.

"Thank you," Win replied, selecting a seat in the cabin's center. He placed his folio on the seat across the aisle, removed his vape, tin of Altoids, and phone from pockets inside his blazer, and draped it neatly over it. With the graceful pose of a Victoria's Secret model, Trish patiently waited for him to sit and plop his gadgets in a cupholder, then pulled out a side table from the fuselage beside his seat.

"Your beverage," she announced, carefully placing a napkin and glass of whiskey with a single large ice sphere.

Winston cocked his head. "What's this?"

"Miss Hicks thought you may like a Gentleman Jack before takeoff."

The sheer absurdity of being served a cocktail struck him as comedic. Obviously, the flight crew had no idea he had been locked up in detox, let alone fending off a stalking Santa.

"How thoughtful," he chuckled. "But since it's nine-thirty in the morning, may I swap this for an espresso and some water?"

"Of course," Trish replied, whisking the glass away like a magician performing a disappearing act. "Would you like me to hang your jacket in the galley closet?"

"Please," Win said, grabbing his phone. He sat back.

Trish explained the Wi-Fi with an amused glint.

"The connection is HicksIN and the password is DDDDcup."

Winston nearly spat out the espresso he didn't yet have. Darceline's infamous chest jokes were alive and well. The memory of DDD&D's acquisition flashed through his mind, a sharp reminder of what triggered his relapse.

"Catchy, isn't it?" Trish grinned.

"Unforgettable," Winston deadpanned, mentally preparing to make D answer for this later.

"Trish, may I ask you something?" He asked.

"Of course," she paused with a mysterious smile before returning to the galley.

"Have you and the pilots been on standby since you flew to California last week … waiting on me?"

She smiled just enough to be coy. "Yes."

"Where did you stay?"

"The Holiday Inn Express, down the road."

Win smirked.

"When did you get the call to prep the jet this morning?"

"We have been here every morning at 8 a.m., fully prepared for your ETA." Trish grinned. "I will bring your beverages straightaway."

Win gave her a nod and sank into his seat, glancing out the window. Thinking of his assistant Ginger Brooks, he dialed. The moment she answered, her voice was full of relieved elation.

"Well, there you are! When did you get home?"

Win chuckled. "A funny thing happened on my way out of the forum."

"Oh, crap. Your aunt found you."

"First, let me say I'm spic-and-span clean. All is good in that department. No, I'm not home. And yes, she did."

"Did you check out of the cuckoo's nest, or were you broken out?"

Winston laughed. "I'm not entirely sure. One minute, I'm signing discharge papers about to escape on my own, and the next, I'm sitting on my aunt's jet about to fly out of California with a Wi-Fi password straight out of a burlesque show."

Ginger cackled.

Trish returned with an espresso, sugar box, and water bottle on a silver tray. "We're cleared for takeoff," she whispered.

"Thank you," Winston whispered back. Then, speaking into the phone, he said, "And now we are clear for takeoff."

"She got you."

"She got me."

As Win sipped the espresso, Ginger's voice softened.

"Next stop, Hicksville?"

"Apparently."

"It's October cold in Indiana. Do you have any warm clothes packed?"

Winston smiled, touched by her concern. "Only a few layers. I'll be okay."

As the jet began to taxi, Winston watched the runway crawl by, binge-sipping quickly to finish the coffee.

"Anything I can do?" Ginger asked.

"I'll check in tomorrow."

"Okay." Ginger agreed, then asked, "Win?"

"Yes?"

"I'm happy you … you took care of yourself."

"Me, too," he said, meaning it.

"Okay."

"Okay."

After they hung up, he dialed Steph Denino and took another last sip to finish the joe. Trish returned, checking Winston's seatbelt, which was fastened, graciously removing the silver tray holding the emptied cup and accoutrements.

"Win! How was Betty's?" he answered, already in the loop.

"Good. I'm clean. And clear."

"Good. Where are you?"

"In the middle of a snatching back to Hicksville."

"Oh, shit."

"Yep."

Steph laughed. "So, they gotcha."

"I'm on my aunt's jet. I'm quite sure my mother has her mitts in this somewhere."

"The twins are up to their shenanigans?"

"Yes. But that's not why I'm calling …

"How are you?"

Steph hesitated. "A wellness check?"

"Yes."

His voice relaxed. "I've realized something, Win.

"I have this incredible collection that was taken.

"And a few days after it was returned after you left for rehab, I stood looking at all the stacks of tubs filled with so many beautiful pieces and wondered, if I value this so much, why am I stashing everything away in plastic containers in my garage?

"Why am I not placing them on display—for all to see and enjoy?

"So, I've decided to open a museum and show the girls off."

Win broke into a full smile. "That is super cool! I love it!"

Humbly, Steph replied, "Thank you.

"And I have also decided to reclaim that person you met twenty years ago."

Winston cheered. "YES! That is fantastic, Steph! Bravo!"

"I shuttered the magazine. Didn't want the building. Bill and Gill listed it. Sold in a day."

"That was quick."

Steph grew serious. "*How are you?*"

Win chuckled.

"I met a peculiar man at Betty's who gave me clarity …

"I'm going to give it all away."

Steph laughed. "Why didn't I suggest that? That's brilliant!"

Win grinned, grateful for the reminder of why they were friends. "I'm happy you're back to being happy, Steph. You sound good."

"You do, too," Steph replied.

The aircraft slowly spun around on the tarmac and immediately accelerated along the runway.

"I'll call once the shackles have been released."

Steph chuckled. "Safe travels. And don't let your mother and Aunt Darceline beat you up."

Win laughed, hung up, and the Cessna lifted.

As the jet soared, Winston Clarke settled into the luxurious leather. The power-slammed espresso warmed his chest, and for the first time since Chris died, a genuine, honest-to-goodness smile crept across his face.

An hour into the flight, Win woke up from a deep nap, stretching and yawning like a cartoon bear emerging from hibernation. He grabbed his phone and slogged through emails, texts, and voicemail transcriptions. Ninety minutes later, he reached the elusive state of Inbox Zero.

With three hours of flight left, he popped in his AirPods and queued up some light jazz, hoping to drown out the Chatty Cathy marathon airing live in his brain about whatever fresh hell his mother and Aunt Darceline had planned for his homecoming. After a solid twelve rounds of Spider Solitaire on his iPad, Trish appeared with a cold roast beef sandwich on rye with horseradish and a fruit salad so aggressively fresh it looked like it had been picked mid-flight.

Win briefly considered texting some old Hicksville friends to announce his return but quickly thought better of it. He was in the middle of a surprise ambush—there was no need to call in extra witnesses just yet.

Determined to make productive use of the time, he pulled out a fresh writing tablet to work on his book. He stared intensely at the blank page. Then, out the window. Then, back at the page. This artistic tennis match went on for an hour. Maybe two.

Eventually, the jet began its descent into Indiana airspace. Bruce Springsteen's "I'm Goin' Down" queued up—an on-the-nose soundtrack to his inevitable demise. Then something hit him. A sneaky, stupid, emotional wave. Win slipped into a quiet, ugly cry. Somehow, in some way, he felt like he was going down, too.

Trish approached, her usual warm smile faltering slightly at the sight of Win's damp face. He paused the music.

"Would you like a cocktail or beverage before we land?" she asked gently, the unspoken 'Or perhaps a hug?' lingering in the air.

He sniffled and shook his head. She kindly reminded him to fasten his seatbelt and mentioned they'd land in about fifteen minutes. With that, she returned to the galley.

Win gave himself exactly one more play of Springsteen (okay, four) before pulling himself together. The lights of Hicksville twinkled below on the post-dusk horizon, no longer a town of dark four-way stops but a small city, glowing with a grid of streets and sprawling neighborhoods circling around cul-de-sacs.

"Oh, how much safer you are up here than down there," his inner monologue sneered, the world's least helpful co-pilot.

And that was it. The pity party is over. The Boss went silent. Win slapped on his best semblance of composure. Tucking away his gadgets and writing tablet, he glanced at the lone, underlined word across the top of the page: ENDGAME.

The jet decelerated across the tarmac and rolled into Darceline Hicks' vast hangar, where a burgundy 1973 Chrysler Imperial LeBaron with a cream hardtop gleamed under the overhead lights. It looked like it had spent the last fifty years on an untouched, unbothered, unapologetically luxurious yoga retreat.

Trish opened the clamshell-style door and lowered the airstairs. Captain Gibson emerged from the cockpit.

"Welcome to Hicksville, where it's a breezy fifty-three degrees. I hope you enjoyed your flight, Mr. Clarke."

"Yes, thank you," Win replied, reluctant to unbuckle his seatbelt, dreading what awaited.

Captain Roth, all square jaw and GQ stature, stepped forward. "It's been our pleasure to serve you today."

Trish returned with his blazer. "Enjoy your stay in Hicksville."

Win thanked them, lingering a moment. Out the window, the trunk lid of the Imperial popped open. Darceline's lifelong houseman, chauffeur, and all-around gatekeeper, Mr. Peters, emerged. The epitome of stately professionalism, he moved with crisp precision to the rear passenger side. He opened the door and extended his hand.

And there she was.

Darceline Hicks was swathed in a full-length black sable coat that likely weighed as much as she did. Her spiky white hair and oversized black square glasses screamed, *Don't fuck with me!* That was Win's cue to get moving.

Slipping on his blazer and grabbing his folio, Win stepped into the crisp air. Crossing the brightly lit hangar, he opened his arms to greet his aunt. Up close, the slight frailty in her once-imposing petite frame and face caught him off guard. The hug lingered, significant in a way he hadn't expected.

Darceline pulled back, adjusting her billboard-sized glasses to examine him like a jeweler inspecting a flawed diamond. Then she opened his blazer and gave his torso a quick once-over.

"Your pecs have softened," she declared. "I would have thought RehabLand would have included a workout regimen."

Win imagined Rafael from Marc's party chiming in: "Fuck off, you furry little Darth Vader munchkin!" He smiled tightly and kissed her cheek.

"I'm not saying you're fat," Darceline continued because she did. "But you may want to tighten your front end before it becomes a bumper the size of my Chrysler's."

And ... she's out of the gate! Win heard his mind scream.

"At any rate," she added, linking her arm with his for the four-step journey back to the car, "you're not here for me to talk about your tits. I have other matters to discuss that are in better shape."

Winston settled her into the car, closed the door gently, and walked around the Imperial as Mr. Peters retrieved his luggage from the jet's exterior cargo compartment. Win shook his head with a slight chuckle and couldn't help but glance down at his torso, wondering what Aunt D saw that he didn't.

Capo dei Capi

Life events had a stubborn way of sticking to Winston's brain like gum on a shoe—impossible to scrape off. Even his baby memories had timestamps. As an infant in his crib, he distinctly remembered Aunt Darceline peering down at him through her comically oversized glasses, studying him like a rare insect trapped in amber. She always had the air of someone conducting a complete medical exam using only her eyes.

By fourth grade, Win's thoughts had shifted from basic survival to life's more perplexing mysteries.

"Mom, what does it mean to have perfect bone structure?" he asked one evening as she prepared dinner.

His mother blinked. "Where did you hear that?"

"Aunt D said I had it."

She smiled, gently running her soft hand across his face, assuring him it was a nice compliment.

"But what is it?"

"It means you're a handsome boy."

"Mom! That tells me nothing. What *is* perfect bone structure?" Win pressed, frustrated.

It was Marci's mission to instill humility in her children. "Winston, nobody is perfect. Perfection is in the eye of the beholder. Aunt Darceline, in her own way, thinks you're handsome. Your father and I see it, too. But remember son, nobody is perfect—not even their bone structure."

Of course, that explained nothing. It wasn't until he asked his homeroom teacher that Win finally got a textbook definition.

At eleven, Winston turned to stress eating as his parents went pro in competitive arguing, evolving into the Bickersons. By twelve, he'd packed enough pounds that Marci resorted to driving to Fort Wayne to shop at Montgomery Ward in the euphemistically named Huskies section—*The Fat Boys' Department*. No one mentioned how plump he had become, not directly.

Except Aunt D.

Every family dinner at her house came with a side of emotional trauma. She'd sweep him into a smoky embrace upon arrival, her cigarette dangling perilously close to setting his hair ablaze. Then she'd launch her signature grenade of unsolicited commentary. Win arrived in his best navy Huskies and a red-and-white checkered shirt one evening. Aunt D clutched him tight, took a drag, and bellowed through a haze of smoke, "Who's my chubby checker?!"

His dad, Max, laughed. Marci gasped and scolded them both. And in that horrifying instant, young Win realized his body had become a punchline.

That summer, Winston made a series of lifestyle choices for his junior high debut. He bid farewell to Sandra Dee and became a smoking anorexic. Cigarettes made him feel cool and, more importantly, curbed his appetite. If he didn't eat, no one could call him a chubby checker again.

Fast forward to the summer before senior year. Winston was manning the fry station at Balls & Beers when Aunt D sauntered through the back door like a femme fatale in a low-budget noir film, cigarette clamped between her lips. She stopped and scanned him like a TSA agent, flagging a suspiciously large bottle of shampoo.

"How much do you weigh?"

"Uh ... one-sixteen."

"How tall are you?"

"Five-eight."

She took a long, smoky pause. "Winston, you need to beef up and put some muscle on. You're too handsome to be this skinny. You look like a malnourished Labrador Retriever in one of those SPCA commercials."

"I do?" Win blinked, deflated.

"Eat more meat. Swim more laps. Get on the lake and waterski three times a week."

Winston returned to slicing potatoes, his ego now diced to match.

She added, "That'll put some muscle on and make you manly. There's no reason to let yourself go at seventeen. Let's see how you've done by your next birthday, okay?"

"Okay." Win submitted, feeling like he'd just been castrated by her words.

Aunt D lowered her voice conspiratorially. "And let's keep this little pep talk just between us. There's no reason for anyone to tell you that you can't achieve perfection. And I'm speaking about your mother and her '*nobody's perfect*' bullshit. Agreed?"

"Okay." Win agreed.

She sealed the pact with a forehead kiss, like a mob boss blessing her favorite nephew before a heist, then promptly inquired about the sandwich options.

After Winston left for college, he felt liberated—finally escaping Aunt D's body audits and backhanded motivational speeches about his physique. He built a healthier relationship with his body and never again fixated on his appearance.

Until now.

Welcome to Hicksville!

H

Win climbed into the Imperial's expansive backseat beside Ms. Vader, sinking into the supple cream leather. The car felt smaller now than when he was a child, but its allure was intact. There was something deliciously nostalgic about being transported to a bygone era of glamour and sophistication—even if the ride would be less than ten minutes to her place.

As Darceline tapped her unfiltered Chesterfield dramatically on a gold cigarette case, Win reached inside his blazer pocket for his own, popped it open, and placed one between his lips. Igniting his lighter, he leaned over to offer her the flame first. She tapped the cigarette several times, relishing his prolonged patience as the butane flared. The flickering light caught the icy brilliance of her emerald-cut diamond ring—easily twelve or thirteen carats—perched regally on the fourth finger of her bony left hand. Then, his gaze shifted upward, where the fire shimmered upon an eight or nine-carat round diamond stud earring peeking just beyond the sable collar near her left ear.

Finally, the queen accepted his offering. She tucked the cigarette between her ruby-red lips, the same shade as her meticulously manicured nails, and inhaled with the satisfaction of someone savoring both nicotine and their own perceived superiority. Win lit his own, exhaled with practiced nonchalance, and lowered the window several inches for fresh air.

"It's chilly; put the window up," she ordered.

Win leveled her with a look of respectful defiance. "I've been in an airline cabin all day. I prefer the fresh air."

"It's chilly; put the window up," she repeated, this time with the certainty of someone who had never once entertained the concept of compromise.

He contemptuously closed the window one inch. "Shall we talk about the weather or cut to the chase? What. Is. Going. On?"

The sound of Mr. Peters shutting the trunk echoed through the crisp evening. Darceline smirked like a cat who had already knocked the vase off the table. Reaching for a cocktail from the fold-down table behind the front passenger seat, she gestured lazily toward the minibar between them, a gleaming treasure trove of decanters and cut crystal.

"Care for a bourbon?" she taunted. "There's a fresh lowball if you need to take the edge off."

Win forced a smile at her brazen pluck. Without answering, he smoked with steely determination. Mr. Peters slid into the driver's seat, backed the Imperial out of the bright white hangar, and drove into the darkening evening.

Taking her time, as she always did when someone else's patience was on the verge of collapse, Darceline sipped her drink and drew deeply on her cigarette before finally speaking.

"I must compliment you," she said, exhaling a plume of smoke.

Win arched an eyebrow, waiting for her to elaborate … *and explain.*

"I'm proud of your success. You built a business from scratch and never asked for my help. I respect that."

He smiled cautiously, sensing the setup.

"Congratulations on selling your publicity machine and little sky-scraper."

There it was.

Winston sat quietly, corralling his anxious pack of accusations like a circus tamer. He braced for the next act.

"Now that you're professionally homeless, what are your plans?"

And there it was again.

"No need to answer," Darceline dismissed him with a wave of her bejeweled hand, the grandiosity of a monarch sending away a court jester. "You're here now."

Win inhaled deeply, releasing the breath in slow, deliberate control. He was determined to keep his inner Moment of Zen from losing its shit.

Suddenly, Darceline broke into a wet, slurpy smoker's cough. She produced a handkerchief from her sable pocket, covering her mouth as she hacked without self-consciousness. Years of experience had taught Winston to let these episodes pass unacknowledged. As the Imperial approached the tall wrought-iron gates of her estate, he gazed out at the dark woods ahead, unphased.

Mr. Peters pressed a button clipped beneath the visor. The massive gates creaked open, revealing the winding quarter-mile driveway. The car glided upward through the forest, its pathway lights casting a golden glow on the fallen leaves. Graceful curves and bends carried them higher until they emerged onto a vast clearing. The mansion—a contemporary 20,000-square-foot masterpiece—was illuminated in its grandeur, surrounded by immaculate landscaping and further lined with glowing pathways.

As her coughing fit subsided, Darceline straightened herself, casually took another long drag, and regarded Winston with an unexpectedly soft gaze. For a fleeting moment, she resembled a sweet, eccentric grandmotherly figure—a mirage Winston wasn't foolish enough to believe.

"This visit," she declared, the weight of her words hanging heavy, "is to bring you up to speed—and prepare you for what's to come."

Win's stomach executed an Olympic-level somersault. He locked eyes with his aunt, her enormous glasses reflecting the glint of her diamonds. He felt himself losing his grip, falling into the depths of her calculating gaze. Then, a sudden sense of foreboding settled over him.

Oh shit ...

I have just landed inside my worst-case scenario ...

Bucks Peak

In the year 1799, two brothers, Matthew and Josiah Hicks, set their sights on the vast, untamed landscapes of what would become northern Indiana. Seeking opportunity and solitude, they journeyed westward from the crowded settlements of the east, guided only by whispers of fertile lands and boundless promise. A year before the Indiana Territory was formally established, the brothers arrived upon a stretch of wilderness just south of what would become the Michigan border. Before them lay a pristine, glacial lake—a gleaming expanse of water stretching two miles wide and half a mile across. Its surface mirrored the sky, a serene pane of blue that shifted with the breeze.

It was along the eastern shore of that lake that Josiah Hicks resolved to build a town—a welcoming outpost for pioneers traveling in all directions. He named it Hicksville, and in its earliest days, it thrived as a modest fur trading post. Traders and trappers navigated the dense woodlands, bringing beaver, mink, and fox pelts to barter. Soon, the town drew settlers eager to claim their share of the wild frontier.

Matthew and Josiah constructed a hotel and saloon to accommodate the travelers, transforming Hicksville into a bustling young community. Families picnicked along the lake's edge behind the Hicksville Hotel, delighting in the sparkling waters and tranquil views. Many decided to stay, working alongside the brothers and contributing to the town's steady growth.

But it was not only the town that left its mark upon the land. Rising from the northern shoreline of Hicksville Lake was a lone and formidable hill, standing 252 feet high. Isolated from any neighboring range, it loomed like a silent guardian, its broad shoulders commanding the landscape. Towering walnuts, oaks, and hickories crowned its slopes, their leaves igniting in a blaze of gold and crimson every autumn. On still mornings, the lake below reflected the sky and the hill in perfect symmetry, as though the world had doubled.

Matthew and Josiah, ever drawn to the land's quiet grandeur, were captivated by the hill's presence. One morning, while exploring the dense woods atop its rise, they startled a white-tailed buck—a magnificent creature with a proud rack of antlers and a muscular, graceful stride. The animal paused, locking eyes with the brothers in an ancient, knowing gaze. For a fleeting moment, man and beast shared a silent understanding before the buck disappeared into the trees. Taking it as a symbol of the land's untamed spirit, Josiah named the hill Bucks Peak, a name that met his brother's hearty approval.

Determined to make the summit their own, the brothers cleared the hill's crown, opening it to the endless sky. From the surrounding forests, they felled timber. With the sweat of their brows and the help of a small crew of settlers, they built their two modest homes of rugged elegance. Wide porches wrapped around each house, inviting the breeze, while tall windows captured sweeping views of the shimmering lake, the verdant fields, and the growing town below. From their high perch, the Hicks brothers watched over the world they had carved from the wild.

Bucks Peak became more than a residence; it symbolized resilience and vision. As Hicksville flourished, the brothers expanded their holdings, cultivating the surrounding land into thriving farming enter-prises across five thousand acres. Like the peak, their legacy stood tall against the horizon—a testament to the bold spirit of those who dared to build a life from the untamed frontier.

H

In July of 1915, Theodore Hicks was born, becoming the seventh gen-eration in the Hoosier clan. To celebrate the arrival of another son to lead the family dynasty, his father, Patrick, or Patty as the locals called him, rewarded his mother with a new house atop Bucks Peak. This grand home would boast the latest modern technologies: plumbing and electricity. The two old homesteads were cleared, making way for con-structing a three-thousand-square-foot mansion that stood proudly over the landscape.

But in 1961, the estate—where Darceline, Marci, Phil, and Bill grew up—was reduced to ash after a devastating kitchen fire. Unde-terred, Darceline resolved to rebuild. With her twin sister's architect husband, Max Clarke, she launched into action. The two worked tire-lessly, like ants in a frenzy, racing to complete blueprints and begin construction on the new Bucks Peak.

Three years later, Northern Indiana had a new landmark: Darcel-ine's estate, or as the kids called it growing up, *Camp D.* The *new* Bucks Peak was paradise. Playing hide and seek, indoors or out, often escalated into a full-blown search party led by the staff for the best hiders.

The mansion itself was a marvel of 1960s modernism—entirely *"Look. At. Me."* It had two stories of floor-to-ceiling windows and a flat roof that boldly proclaimed, *"We don't need no stinkin' shingles!"* Endless limestone accents added to its grandeur.

The entrance was so magnificent it practically deserved its own red carpet. Double mahogany doors stood flanked by hanging tri-cluster outdoor lamps, their frosted white glass orbs suspended at varying heights. Two three-foot black orb planters, overflowing with royal blue mist shrubs, elegantly anchored each side of the entranceway. It was a dramatic statement that warmly invited guests in.

Approaching the manor, the driveway split like a dramatic scene from *The Bachelor*—the left led to the main entrance, circling around a glowing limestone fountain, while the right guided visitors to the six-car garage, guest house, tennis court, oversized pool, and secondary circular drive looping beneath the west-side portico. And naturally, to the east, there was the helipad—because no grand estate would be complete without one—nestled between the master's house and the servants' quarters.

Out back, the southern view of Hicksville Lake was pure postcard perfection—accessible by 125 steep limestone steps that zigzagged down the hillside, threading through tiered flower beds to reach Darceline's private beach. Adirondack chairs, picnic tables, a fire pit, and docks tethered with a pontoon and a power ski boat welcomed lakeside leisure. For less pedestrian journeys, a narrow paved road branched from the garage, winding through the woods down to the water's edge, where golf carts frequently hauled coolers and watersports gear.

Bucks Peak was no longer just a home but a kingdom—a monument to reinvention and a testament to Darceline's audacious spirit.

As Mr. Peters slowed the Chrysler beneath the portico, Win extinguished his cigarette in the Imperial's door ashtray. He saw the side house door opening through the car window. One of the household staff swiftly emerged, ready to greet Ms. Hicks.

His gaze flicked to his aunt. With casual stateliness, Darceline shot Winston a wink. The silent message was clear: Checkmate, kid.

Mr. Peters opened Win's door. He grabbed his folio, stepped out, and took a long look over the top of the Imperial at the house that could easily double as an art museum. He sighed.

"Would you prefer your usual second-floor room or the guest house?" Mr. Peters inquired as if either was less than a four-star experience.

"I'll take a cell in the hive upstairs," Win replied, smirking at his bad joke. "If I'm here to be stung, there's no reason for the queen bee to travel far."

Peters blinked, half amused, half indifferent.

"Upstairs will be fine. Thank you," Win added, forcing a polite smile.

"May I take your folio with your luggage?" Peters gestured.

"Please," Win said, handing it over. He immediately second-guessed the decision. Should he have grabbed his phone? Probably. But what was the point? Fourteen days without it had been surprisingly liberating. Besides, there would be no shortage of full-sensory overload soon enough. Let the phone go.

Inside, the hallway stretched eight feet wide, floored with polished ivory limestone and softened by a silver tufted carpet runner. Spotlit artwork practically lunged from their frames as if this were another one of Bill and Gill's art gallery soirées featuring the latest, hottest, most talented ever artist with a name no one could pronounce. Mahogany doors lined the hall every ten feet because why have one door when you could have twelve?

Two of Darceline's staff greeted him—white blouses, black skirts, tasteful pearl earrings, and traditional pearl chokers. A curated aesthetic. Win grinned, recalling how the domestic staff always looked like they'd stepped straight out of a 1940s black-and-white movie: immaculate, poised, and perpetually unmarried.

The manor's temperature, conservatively, was set to "bake at 350°." Win pulled out his cigarette case and lighter, then ditched his blazer over his arm before it fused to his back. One of the staff stepped forward.

"May I take your jacket to your room, sir?"

"Thank you. I'll hold onto it in case I need to step outside for air to avoid spontaneous combustion," he replied with a crass smile.

And then, there was Aunt Darceline herself. Regal in a classic Chanel red tweed dress that perfectly fit her petite frame, she wore a Plume de Chanel white gold necklace encrusted with hundreds of brilliant-cut diamonds. The necklace's 1-carat pear-cut stone centered one's eyes from her earlobes, sagging under the weight of diamond boulders. Completing the ensemble: practical black flats.

Win had to admit, she was powerfully stunning, particularly in those blockbuster eyeglasses—appearing like a fashion editor and someone who could order a hit without breaking eye contact. She elegantly tamped out her cigarette in a crystal ashtray held by one of the staff, her expression both warm and ominous.

Winston braced himself.

"Welcome home, darling," she purred.

Win approached her, and Darceline took his arm. He quietly followed her lead without another choice or anything more to say.

They strolled until they reached what Darceline called the shotgun foyer. This expansive indoor runway sliced the mansion in half, from the grand front doors to the tall double glass doors that opened onto a wrap-around deck overlooking Hicksville, including the lake. On either side were intimate seating clusters for two, flanked by two half baths near the front and two more near the back. Midway along the west wall, tucked between two enormous abstract paintings, was a small open elevator with tufted black leather benches to the left and right, open at the rear for the second-floor exit.

The mansion's first floor resembled a luxury theme park—the kind that required a map:

To the right on the right: The Grand Room. Not a dining room. A *Grand* Room.

To the left on the left was a library extensive enough to host the UN.

Ahead and left: Endless surprises—a tearoom, walk-in pantries the size of bodegas, an exercise room and spa, a commercial-grade laundry room, Mr. Peters' office, and, naturally, an in-house clinic. Because even the Band-Aids needed their own safe space.

To the right on the left is the Business Suite, affectionately abbreviated to the BS Room, or simply, BS. Darceline's personal headquarters. Pure 1950s Hollywood glam with a splash of corporate menace. The room exudes warmth and elegance with its dark wood paneling, ornate crown molding, and plush frieze carpeting in regal blue. Vintage Hollywood memorabilia graced the walls, including framed, signed movie posters and black-and-white photographs of iconic film legends.

At the room's center loomed a massive oval conference table flanked by eighteen leather club chairs. Upholstered in supple brown leather with chrome nailhead trim, each chair stood atop ornately carved wooden legs. Vintage sconces lined the walls, while four matching table lamps were spaced evenly across the table's center. Small, solid black marble ashtrays sat two feet before every chair.

Adjacent to the table was a cozy seating area along the tall, narrow windows that commanded views of all Darceline owned, including the sky and clouds. Eighteen more leather club chairs faced each other in two neat rows of nine, with black and chrome vintage deco ashtray stands sparkling between each seat. Three low coffee tables were strategically positioned for every six chairs. The space invited conversation and contemplation, ideal for informal meetings or casual lounging.

A vintage bar exuded old-school glamour on the back wall, seemingly mandated to serve only Manhattans. Towering wood cabinets with frosted ribbed glass doors loomed over the black marble countertop, which housed a black wine cooler and ice maker. The watering hole was always open, ready for pre- or post-business cocktail hours.

Anchoring the room's rear, a sleek limestone fireplace blazed like the gates of hell—because what better way to say "welcome" than with twelve feet of roaring fire?

In the back left corner was Darceline's command center. Mounted high upon the fifteen-foot paneled wall, a single, monstrous 110-inch flat-screen TV displayed a live satellite feed of her estate, every seat in the room could see. Just below, at eye-level, were three side-by-side smaller 30-inch monitors cycling through Hicks America agricultural screensavers on a wall workstation with keyboards, mice, and a crystal ashtray. Facing the room was a massive wooden desk topped with just a small crystal box of cigarettes, a matching crystal table lighter, and a crystal ashtray. A high-back leather chair was sitting between, ready and waiting. And before the throne from which she ruled, two additional club chairs flanked a single deco ashtray stand, reserved for her visitors, or perhaps, victims.

They entered together, Win pausing at the conference table to drape his blazer over one of the chairs. Darceline made her way to the bar, pouring two fingers of bourbon into Baccarat crystal tumblers. She turned to him with a wry smile, then crossed to her desk, placing one glass on its edge before the chair now designated as his. The grandfather clock in the shotgun foyer began its slow chime.

Win stood unmoved, giving no energy to her continued dominance. He watched as she moved with an elderly elegance, her posture upright despite the years. The glass in her hand sparkled. She stepped behind her desk. Waiting.

And there he was—back to face the legacy he had spent decades running from. A strange electrical current surged from the base of his neck, down his spine, and through his limbs. The hairs on his arms stood on end as the clock struck seven and fell silent.

The heat, lingering cigarette smoke, and seeing D's enormous executive chair swirled around him. The bourbon glinted like a reward for good behavior. Show up on demand and receive your prize. Just like chores as a teenager.

He stared at the bourbon, calling his name. He glanced at his aunt. Then Win's eyes lifted from the dainty wizard to the enormous satellite feed of her estate above.

If I click my heels three times, can I just go home?

H

On a late summer afternoon in 1994, Darceline Hicks stood at the edge of Bucks Peak's deck, the golden light casting a warm glow over her farmland that stretched beyond the horizon in every direction—five hundred thousand acres of corn, wheat, soybeans, and oats swaying gently in the breezes across fourteen states—a living testament to generations of Hicks family stewardship. But Darceline wasn't one to merely uphold tradition; she was determined to innovate.

For decades, she had witnessed the unpredictable swings of weather and the subtle shifts in soil moisture that plagued even the most experienced farmers. No matter how skilled her field managers were, they could never outmatch the sheer force of nature. But Darceline believed in a different force: technology.

She spent the better part of the previous year engrossed in research, attending conferences, and meeting with the brightest minds in agricultural science. The answer became clear: satellites. With a customized satellite in geostationary orbit, Darceline could harness real-time data to monitor soil conditions, measure water evaporation, and predict the perfect planting and harvest windows. It wasn't just about efficiency; it was about control.

But she needed a partner. She reached out to the frontier of innovation—California. There, she met with the engineers and developers of Agri-Aero Space Technologies, a boutique satellite design firm with a reputation for turning ambitious visions into orbital realities.

"You want a dedicated geostationary satellite," one of the engineers, a wiry man named Nolan Dodd, mused during their first meeting. "Positioned over North America, with exclusive control. That's not small potatoes."

"Nolan," Darceline replied smoothly, tapping the rim of her coffee cup, "at Hicks America, we grow a lot more than potatoes."

The collaboration was set into motion. Agri-Aero would design, build, and launch a custom satellite: HicksSat-1. It would feature hyperspectral imaging sensors to detect soil moisture variations and monitor crop health alongside advanced radar technology to create hyper-accurate terrain maps. Darceline envisioned the future: GPS-integrated auto-steer systems would ensure Hicks America's massive fleet of tractors and combines could navigate even the most uneven fields in any weather condition—with or without an operator behind the steering wheel.

The satellite would also provide predictive analytics. Historical data and real-time atmospheric readings would report the best times to plant, irrigate, and harvest. Every square inch of farmland would be accounted for—no wasted resources, no unnecessary guesswork.

When launch day arrived—April 16, 2000, in the Mojave Desert—Darceline stood in the VIP observation area of the aerospace test center, flanked by her family and Hicks America executives. The weather was flawless: cloudless, windless, seventy degrees. It was a perfect day not only to watch a rocket pierce the sky but to kick off the bicentennial of Hicks America officially.

As the countdown echoed from the speakers, Darceline considered what this moment represented. No longer would Hicks America depend on external data or generalized weather forecasts. From now on, they would own the sky.

Three. Two. One.

The rocket roared to life, propelling HicksSat-1 toward its orbital home.

Within weeks, the satellite was fully operational, streaming a wealth of data to the newly constructed, state-of-the-art operations center on the outskirts of Hicksville, just west of the old drive-in movie theater. Darceline watched the display monitors as vibrant, high-resolution images of her fields flashed across the screens. Sensors reported ideal soil moisture levels in the eastern corn plots, and a rainfall projection suggested reducing irrigation for the week.

But Darceline's vision didn't end there. She signed exclusive contracts with major agricultural corporations, leasing access to HicksSat-1's data and services. What had begun as a bold private investment had become a thriving revenue stream.

In the first morning light of Independence Day 2000, Darceline stood on her deck at Bucks Peak gazing at the sky. The next century of Hicks America was secured—not just in the soil beneath her feet, but in the silent orbit above.

Penny for Your Thoughts

"Come and sit, Winston," Darceline beckoned with a honeyed charm, gesturing to the chair across from her. Gone was the cranky airport gremlin; in her place was a glamorous villainess, one monologue away from revealing her evil plan. Winston, however, was determined to meet her on level ground, after a pitstop.

He detoured to the bar, plucked a bottle of water from the fridge, and chugged half like a man trying to drink away family dysfunction. Finally, he took his seat, the air thick with unsaid plots and whatever perfume Darceline bathed in—probably called something like "Succession No. 5."

Darceline sank into her black leather throne, pressed a button on the armrest, and slowly elevated herself to eye level.

Silent in their synchronized chain-smoking, D and Win lit cigarettes.

"My God," Darceline cooed, locking eyes with him. "Your eyes are still that bright sky blue. Like a baby angel."

She lifted her cocktail as if to toast his cherubic irises. Winston raised his water bottle like the proud designated driver of this family reunion. Hydration never looked so sarcastic.

They sipped.

"I like your new hairstyle," she wheedled. "Much better than that Chuck Woolery coif you've had since puberty."

Winston exhaled a plume of smoke, crossed his legs, shaking off yet another tongue-in-cheek jibe about his fucking hair, and made himself comfortable in her BS for more of her BS.

"I know what you did, Aunt D," he said, deadpan. "Why the cloak and dagger?"

Darceline pivoted from affectionate to the assassin. "Because you left and didn't crawl back. And I thought you would. And you didn't. And I need you here."

"Buying my company *and building* to lure me back—that was your plan?" Winston asked, eyebrows climbing.

"You put them up for sale. Those were the moves I've waited years for you to make."

He scoffed. "So, you've been keeping tabs?"

"A watchful eye," she corrected.

"Why not let someone else buy it? Why pounce?" he pontificated with a hint of irritation.

She sipped her drink with the gravitas of a woman who considered patience inconvenient. "Because I didn't … *I don't* have time for buyers to piddle-paddle around with inspections and due diligence."

Winston narrowed his eyes. "Why is my business suddenly all about you?"

Darceline grinned, the smile that usually preceded someone revealing they control the moon's tides.

"Well, I don't want them back," Win said, his expression adamant. "My decision was final. My slate is now clean."

"That is exactly what I want you to have, *a fresh start.*"

Suspiciously annoyed, Winston took a long drag and spoke in smoke, "For what?"

She deflected, looking at a gold watch around her bony wrist. "Your mother said she would be here for dinner in half an hour. Or, you know, whenever the voices in her head agree on an arrival time.”

“I am not moving back to Hicksville, Aunt D.”

She grinned like a tell in poker, holding far more than the winning direction of their conversation in her hand, and was ready for the showdown.

Winston pointed to her desk. “I’m telling you right now: I will never sit behind that desk. And I’m never sitting in the chair you’re in now. So, we can call it a day, and I’ll fly home in the morning.”

Like she didn’t hear a word he said, Darceline continued. “Before your mother arrives, I will share a few things you may or may not know about her.

“First, you have no idea what it’s like to carry a child for eight months in utero, then have it die inside you … and then to have to carry it another two weeks for labor to begin naturally. Doctors didn’t induce something like that back then.”

Win was completely thrown as she dove right into the loss of his older brother, Wells.

Darceline continued. “It was horrific. We all watched your mother go through two weeks carrying death.

“It broke her. As it would anyone.

“But your mother? Shattered. The pieces never quite fit back together.

“And then there was everything that came after … the depression, the mania.”

Win sat stunned, stiff in the chair, like a fainted goat, his throat tightening. He took a swig of water and smoked.

Darceline picked up her bourbon and briefly stared at the Baccarat glass before taking a long sip. “I’ll never know the agony my sister went through. You will never know the agony your mother went through. No one shall.”

Winston could hardly breathe. His eyes became teary as he continued to listen to this heart-wrenching narrative.

Another drag, then D said, her voice softening, "And when Marci and Max brought you home from the adoption agency, you were this family's redemption arc.

"With bright eyes and a perfect little face, you healed a wound none of us thought possible. Your arrival was what we all desperately needed.

"And once you became a man, you couldn't escape us fast enough."

Winston felt his face collapse into an existential crisis.

What. The. Hell.

Reading his expression like a well-worn book, Darceline leaned back, blowing smoke to the ceiling.

Win closed his eyes, removed his glasses, and gently rubbed each lid. He was tired from the day of travel and feeling overwhelmed. His mind returned to the day he met Chris—feeling the spark, energy, and undeniable love ... and immediately felt calm, centered, and happy. His breathing slowed. Then ... he smelled Chris—his familiar, comforting scent ... prompting a mental smile.

Winston put his glasses on and opened his eyes with a grounded sigh, saying nothing.

The two took long drags from their cigarettes.

Darceline's gaze shifted to a bare area on her desk, seeing something more than polished wood. Following a deep breath, she spoke profoundly but softly, "The Irrevocable Trust Daddy established a century ago may as well have been carved in stone. It was unbreakable and quite clear: the firstborn in every generation would be named as beneficiary and principal trustee of said Trust upon the expiration of their predecessor."

Her eyes shot to Win.

"Daddy was a progressive man who intentionally did not designate that for the firstborn male, as the norm of the time would have it. No. It was the first*born*.

"He was a forward-thinking man—ahead of his time. Possibly, it was because of Mother.

"But his younger brothers and sister were of the previous century and backward in thought and scorned his decision.

"Possibly out of greed or old school expectations or just plain ignorance.

"Which may be why Daddy felt compelled to establish a trust."

Darceline paused for another sip and drag of smoke.

"But I was the firstborn of the next generation," she continued, "eight minutes before your mother.

"You are the second born of your generation—eleven months after your brother's death. Therefore, the next in line."

"Well, I don't want it," Winston came out and said it.

Darceline's eyes popped. "I didn't want *this*!" She reacted defensively, her hands fluttering dramatically, sounding like someone Win had never met.

"But Daddy designated me. So, I had no choice and did what I had to do."

D paused for another sip of bourbon. Win smoked.

Then she continued, "Daddy began teaching me everything about the family businesses when I could add two plus two. *Everything*. From how our land was more precious than gold and to give more in value than the prices we charged.

"To me," Darceline said, dropping air quotes, "it didn't matter about 'everything.' I wanted my own life."

She paused, then said with a parallel sensibility, *"Sound familiar?"*

Winston was taken by her sudden empathy.

Taking a drag and speaking smoke, she calmly asked, "Did you know I wanted to be an artist—a painter?"

Win didn't, shaking his head.

D continued her deep reflections. "One of the happiest days of my life was when Marci and I left for the University of Chicago. I felt the freedom to be *me* for the first time.

"And then … when Daddy died so unexpectedly … my new world literally came to an end.

"As you know, Mother died giving birth to your Uncle Tilly."

That, Winston did know. He nodded slightly.

"So, there I was. The designated one. I had no choice but to drop out and tend to business while raising my youngest brother. Tilly was ten."

Darceline snapped her fingers. "Like that. Not only had I become the matriarch, *but also had a child*, who was now my responsibility."

D and Winston's eyes locked. In unison, they took a last drag and extinguished their cigarettes.

She continued. "Your mother graduated and went on to get her master's. And bless her heart, she fell in love and married."

Darceline paused, her eyes returning to her desktop.

"Me? I was forced to give up my first love because our elders disapproved of my affection for a woman.

"They were ignorant, prejudice bigots.

"And their hate for me grew—being a woman with more power and wealth than all of them combined."

Darceline shifted her gaze to her cocktail for a sip and lit another smoke. Winston patiently became interested, hearing a side of her he never knew about, and lit a cigarette, too.

Her eyes returned to Win. "Violet was her name," she said with adoration and painful regret.

"We met in my first class on my very first day of college."

Winston relaxed into the chair ... awash in déjà vu, again thinking of Chris.

"I brought her home with me from Chicago over Christmas vacation before Daddy died. Her family was in Europe, and my consideration was for her ... for us ... not to be separated and alone over the holiday break."

Darceline's tone shifted. "It was *wrenching*.

"Not from Daddy. He adored Violet's personality and spunk and wit."

She dropped Win a sly smirk. "He knew."

Darceline took a long drag.

"He knew we were more than friends. He knew we were lovers.

"All that mattered to Daddy was that we were happy.

"But not his siblings. Because over that Christmas dinner, my aunt and uncles took less than one hour to push me and Violet out the door with their indigent, cruel insults cloaked in clever words. One snipe after another … with their wicked tongues."

Darceline shook her head in dismay. "Daddy was beside himself when Violet and I left. We returned to Chicago that Christmas night. And on that tearful drive, I promised Vi she would never have to experience that with my family again.

"And then Daddy died.

"And obligations beckoned.

"And the elders quickly stepped in with threats of placing me in a mental institution if I saw '*that woman*' ever again."

Consumed with another round of sadness *from this story*, Win gulped and then pressed two fingers against his lips.

D continued with a mix of sorrow and anger. "It was heartbreaking to be forbidden to ever see Violet again."

A spiteful tone filled her voice, "Once I had let her go … according to *them* … the elders … *our elders* … *they* declared my phase with blasphemy was over.

"And that was that."

Winston's entire body was numb.

"I *sooo* loved that woman," Darceline sorrowfully said, returning to her cocktail for another sip.

"And so, I did my best with everything I had to do. Your Uncle Tilly was a handful, but that's another story."

"Where were Uncle Phil and Uncle Bill during all of this?" Win asked.

D grinned. "You Uncle Phil was in his senior year of high school when Daddy died. I pushed him to go to any college he wanted since I no longer could, but he continued his job at the marina, where he built that side of the business.

"Your Uncle Bill was a high school junior and quite self-sufficient. He graduated early and went to Purdue University."

Win smoked, soberly taking it all in.

"When did you meet Aunt Penny?" He asked.

Darceline's tense strain of reflective pain fell away to an adoring smile. "I met her on a business trip a year after your Great Aunt Edna died—the last of the bitter elders to return to their Maker."

It was no secret Darceline Hicks was a lesbian. Marci thoughtfully explained to little Win that "Aunt" Penny was a *beloved friend* after five-year-old Winston witnessed his aunt and Penny kissing under the mistletoe at Max and Marci's Christmas party. Though his mother never actually used the word *lesbian*, even at five, Win decoded that "beloved friend" meant something special.

"The year was 1964," D resumed, settling into the start of another sweeping love story. "Bucks Peak was finally built, and I had just moved in.

"At the time, I was buying a dairy farm in Madison, Wisconsin. Penny was the owner's executive secretary. We'd spoken on the phone a few times, and when I flew out to close the deal, she picked me up from the airport and ..."

Here, D paused, smiling as though she was about to tell him of a forbidden romance straight out of a paperback.

"Sparks flew ..." Darceline continued dreamily. "We became inseparable. After the deal closed, Penny came with me, and we made a new home *together*."

Win smiled tenderly, remembering Penny. It had been brutal returning to Hicksville in 2012 for her funeral after her battle with breast cancer.

Darceline nodded, clearly missing her, too. Then, as if hitting the emotional brakes, she cleared her throat and checked her watch.

Winston immediately thought of Marc Monarch.

Was this the dairy farm D bought from his family?
Is that how he knew Aunt Darceline?

Should I ask?

Maybe later.

"Win," Darceline said, shifting directions again, "me, your mother, and your uncles are vintage cars with no spare parts. Our warranties are long expired. Every morning is a gamble. Planning anything more than twelve hours out is optimistic at best. We're all just running on fumes. And let me tell you, kid, there are only so many seconds left."

Win blinked in thought. *Okay, that got dark again quickly.*

D leaned forward on the desk and gave him the full weight of her stare. "So! Why don't I just die and leave you to figure it out?" she asked as if pitching a place to have brunch on Saturday.

Win wasn't sure why his mouth opened to say something; there was no response.

"Because that's exactly what happened to me," Darceline chirped. "One minute, I was living my life. And the next? Daddy is dead, and I'm the boss who was forced into the closet. For me, there were no choices on either matter."

D paused to stub out her cigarette, giving him a look that was somehow maternal. "I wouldn't wish that on anyone.

"So, once I'm dead, keep it all or don't.

"The choice will be yours.

"In the meanwhile, tomorrow I'll give you a tour of the Hicks America corporate campus and show you the books."

Darceline leaned back into her seat with a calculated grin.

Win sat reeling. *She just gave him an out*—permission to have a choice!

Suddenly, something inside him short-circuited and turned on the waterworks. His eyes filled with tears, and he felt he was about to cry. Win swallowed hard before wrestling the emotions into a box, saving them for later—possibly in his room upstairs after turning in.

Winston removed his glasses to wipe away the tears, put them back on, pressed his palms together, and bowed his head slightly to his aunt, whispering, "Thank you."

When Winston's gaze returned to hers, D gave him a knowing nod, studying him as always. She watched Winston's eyes drift to the untouched cocktail before him and then decidedly sat up to open a desk drawer.

"I have a gift for you," she said, retrieving a small box the size of a fountain pen case wrapped in fine beige paper and tied with a thin navy ribbon.

And without warning, the skinny little lady detonated into another smoker's jag. This wasn't just a cough—it was a full-body exorcism. She hacked. She wheezed. She convulsed like a possessed Linda Blair. Win watched respectfully and with silent concern as she set the gift down to ride out the storm. D thrashed until she finally horked up a series of golden-brown projectiles splattering across the desk like abstract art no one asked for.

Darceline clutched her chest, gasped for air, and, after a brief existential reboot, spotted the damage.

"Son of a *bitch!*" she barked, glaring at a glob of chocolate butterscotch pudding now oozing down the side of the delicate little gift.

Without missing a beat, she yanked another desk drawer open to produce a handkerchief, delicately wiping the phlegm off the present like this was a regular part of gift-giving. She gave the corners of her mouth a dainty dab, then slid the box across the desk toward Win.

He stared at it, briefly thought, "*Ew!*" and then made eye contact with her before reaching for the gift. With the enthusiasm of someone opening a box labeled "*SURPRISE: SNAKES!*" Win tugged the ribbon. It fell away and landed in his lap. He peeled back the paper and lifted the lid, revealing folded gold tissue sealed with a tiny black sticker stamped *DH*, as if this was a high-end boutique and not a mucus crime scene.

"Your labels are nice," he offered, because what else does one say after all that?

She winked.

Inside was a thin metal cylinder-shaped pendant three inches long and less than a quarter inch thick, attached to a round box chain necklace of exquisitely handcrafted gray fine links. Gently, he removed it and dangled what looked like a small lead pipe. A tiny diamond sparkled near the top, and at the bottom were three micro shapes—triangle, square, and circle. It looked like a fancy weapon from a spy movie.

"Is this titanium?" Win asked, turning it over in his hands.

"It is. Put it on."

He did.

"It's a key," she said.

Now, she had his attention. He held the pendant up from his chest for closer inspection.

D pointed toward a door between her desk and the conference table. "See the light switch to the left with a chrome plate with three switches?"

Win nodded.

"See the round hole an inch above the bottom in the center?"

"Yes."

"When I'm dead, stick it in," she instructed.

"*What?*"

"It's to the vault downstairs. Bet you didn't know there was a vault downstairs."

Correct. He did not.

"That is your copy. I have one upstairs behind the Monet—but that's between us," she added.

"What's in the vault *downstairs?*" Winston pried.

She licked her top lip and said cryptically, "Family history."

"Daddy had an old war bunker off County Road 800 to store the essential things he treasured, like his collection of gold coins and family heirlooms.

"When the homestead burned, I thought having your father add a new bunker to the plans below the basement was best. I've been using it as a vault to store Daddy's compendiums and a few things I've collected over the years.

"The main entrance is through that door."

Winston hummed a curious "Hmm" and nodded.

"And there's one more place you'll need the key," she added.

He tilted his head.

"Remember when your parents went to Hawaii, and you stayed with me for a week?"

Win nodded slowly. Somewhere in the back of his mind, the words *800* and *Disc* started bouncing around like rogue pinballs.

She smirked. "Remember our little drive to the farm on County Road 800?"

He did ... but ... for some strange reason ... he could not remember ... what happened after they arrived. "I ... yes ..." Win replied, baffled.

"There's a gate there now. You'll need that key."

Darceline checked her watch, moving on. "Your mother should be here any minute ... or will be late as usual. Either way, it's dinner time," she said, with the thinly veiled disappointment of someone perpetually let down by her sister's concept of punctuality.

D lowered her chair, stood, and shuffled around the desk. Winston rose, and she looped her arm through his as they started toward the Grand Room. His brain gyrated over why the hell County Road 800 suddenly felt relevant. Then Lucille's beehive popped into his mind.

Winston glanced back at the chrome plate, to the hole beneath the switches, and then down at his shirt, where the pendant key rested. Moving with D's slow stride, he was saturated with gratitude and relief ... yet strangely flabbergasted, not one of his fantastical scenarios of family doom came true.

His thoughts suddenly broke off:

The barn!

Why can't I remember what was in that barn?!

Bon Appétit

While visiting Ireland in 1959, Darceline fell madly in love—with a half-moon bar in a Dublin pub built just after the Great War. Naturally, as she and Max set about raising their own personal Phoenix from the homestead's ashes, she decided the best way to commemorate the tragedy was to recreate that bar in her brand-new home.

She promptly dispatched her trusted Chicago-based interior designer across the Atlantic to photograph the Irish pub from every conceivable angle, down to the coasters' shape and the ricketiest barstool's precise wobble. It was a critical mission. But there was a slight hiccup: upon arrival, the designer discovered the owner had kicked the bucket, the pub had closed, and not a single inheriting soul wanted it. The whole bar was for sale.

Darceline's solution? Buy it all.

She scooped up the entire pub like it was a slightly haunted estate sale find. The walls, the floors, and the beer taps were still sticky with decades of Guinness residue. Local carpenters were hired to dismantle it plank by plank, pausing only to fend off the occasional rat who was, frankly, part of the establishment's charm. The pieces were shipped back to Indiana for reconstruction after being packed like a boozy jigsaw puzzle.

By the time the new Bucks Peak interior hit the drywall stage, Darceline's prized bar had arrived, ready to be resurrected piece by piece. However, a minor oversight became apparent: the stools, bar top, and most of the once-lovely wooden trim reeked like an old fisherman's boot and were, unfortunately, halfway to mulch. Time and thousands of spilled pints had reduced much of the pub to what could only be described as 'soggy splinters.'

Disappointed but not deterred, and with a forest of mature black walnut trees on the western edge of her estate, she had what she needed. Darceline hired five local Amish carpenters who, despite never having tasted whiskey, were happy to masterfully duplicate each piece of dismantled wood from the original bar to recreate her vision. After a three-month delay, the half-moon bar was reconstructed, and the Grand Room was finally complete.

It was precisely what Darceline envisioned—a cozy embrace of that Irish pub that evoked a sense of old-world charm. Massive brass chandeliers with vast arms, decorated in scrollwork inspired by Celtic motifs, dripping in crystals, bathed the room in a golden glow. Emerald green carpeting conjured the feeling of the countryside, grounding the space. At the heart of the dining room sat a long, hand-carved walnut table, polished to a glossy sheen that reflected the chandelier light from above and stretched nearly the entire room's length. Three flickering brass candelabras stood evenly spaced, flames swaying like gossiping tongues. Eighteen tall-backed walnut chairs with velvet-padded seats in a deep shade of orange projected an air of refined elegance.

Parallel to the table, low built-in walnut cabinets lined the wall, their tops buffed to a mirror shine, perfect for serving. Three massive vases stood proudly, displaying enormous arrangements of long-stemmed flowers. In the front and the back of the room, swinging service doors to the kitchen bookended the buffet.

On the opposite side, along the wall of windows, a lounge space was appointed with classic black leather armchairs and sofas arranged around low walnut tables—an inviting sanctuary for after-dinner drinks and conversations.

But the true showstopper was the magnificent half-moon bar along the back wall. The Amish artisans had painstakingly carved ornate Celtic symbols and mythological creatures, capturing the whimsy and enchantment of the original. A polished brass foot rail ran along the base, inviting guests to linger, while backlit stained-glass panels featured intricate scenes from folklore. A gleaming ivory limestone countertop provided a striking contrast against the dark walnut. Surrounding the bar were eighteen plush, black leather bar-height chairs with arms, ready for libations and celebration.

The opulence was undeniable when Winston escorted Aunt Darceline into the room for dinner. He pulled out her chair—a throne-like monstrosity requiring Herculean strength—grunting it into position. With a satisfied smirk, she motioned for him to take the opposite end of the table, a distance so vast it practically required binoculars.

Once seated, a brunette housemaid swiftly served Darceline a fresh bourbon. D retrieved a Chesterfield from a small cigarette box and struck a flame with the flick of her lighter. Another domestic approached Winston with tightly combed gray hair and a face devoid of expression.

"What is your name?" He asked with a smile that joyously reeled *he had an out*.

"It's Judy, sir."

"Water, please, Judy," Win said. "Thank you."

She returned with a tall pewter pitcher and filled his crystal goblet. But as Win peered through the absurd number of candelabras blocking his line of sight, he realized the impracticality of their seating arrangement.

"I'm moving down there," he declared, with all the defiance of a teenager rejecting the kids' table. Darceline smirked approvingly as

Win abandoned etiquette, goblet in hand, and strode down the length of the table—thirteen long strides, to be exact.

After he settled by her side, a pleased smile crossed D's face, and she reached over to gently pat his arm. The staff promptly relocated his place setting, and Darceline ordered Marci's setting to be moved opposite Win.

D glanced at her watch again and sighed with irritation. "It's seven-forty-one. For once in her life, of all days, I expected my sister to be early since her precious baby was home." She looked at Win with a smirky wink before deciding. "Well, we are not having dinner at midnight waiting on her."

She addressed the brunette domestic, "Susan, let's begin. My sister will join us whenever she's up to it."

"Yes, ma'am," Susan confirmed and scurried through the swing door to the kitchen before promptly returning with a small plate in each hand.

Caprese salads looked delicious on the china plates before D and Win. Hungry, he reached for the cloth napkin, shook it open, and rested it on his lap. Pausing politely to wait for his aunt to finish her cigarette, Darceline directed, "Eat!"

Cutting into one of the beautifully sliced tomatoes topped with a wedge of mozzarella, a basil leaf, and balsamic glaze, Winston asked before taking his first bite, "If I were to resign as trustee, who's next in line? Kaitlyn?"

Aunt D delivered a savory squint. "Yes."

Win finished the first chew and swallowed. Slicing again, he asked, "How is Katie … I mean Kate? The last time I saw her, she was going by Kate. I think."

Darceline arched her brow. "She's been going by Kate ever since she commandeered her way to the presidency of the Hicksville Chamber of Commerce."

"How old is she now?"

"That's the *wrong* question," Darceline teased.

"How is she?" Win tried again.

"Try: *Is she worthy?*" D taunted, hinting at a backstory.

"Is Kaitlyn worthy?" Win played along before taking another mouthful.

"That's for you to discover."

He then asked, "Do you feel she's worthy?"

Darceline broke into laughter with such gusto that she threw her head back. Winston knew he'd missed some inside joke, but he smiled as he sliced again, enjoying the sound of her amusement and patiently curious for her to share what it was.

Then, she began to cough. Another smoker's jag. It sounded rough, like a cheap blender on its last legs, kick-starting a muffled glug of syrup and ice. A low, stuttering gurgle deepened into a fight of raspy slushy resistance. She coughed hard like her lungs were filled with buckets of sludgy mud. Then she coughed harder.

Win froze mid-bite, his fork suspended in the air.

"You …" she sputtered, coughing harder still.

Winston mentally winced, shifting his eyes to focus on her bourbon to avoid watching her convulse.

D took a slurpy breath, attempting to finish her thought. "You …"

But the hack had its grip. Barely able to drop her cigarette into the crystal ashtray, Darceline hawked and croaked and struggled for breath. Her bony hands gripped the table as though it were the only thing tethering her to the mortal plane. The coughing persisted.

Win returned the fork to his plate and watched her with growing concern. An alarming unease settled heavily over the table. He sat upright, shifting to face her.

Darceline's worn eyes met his. "You … Win …" she choked out before her frail body slumped back into the chair. Her hands clutched their arms. Then, silence. The violent spasms stopped as quickly as they had begun.

She gasped, released a final squeaky wheeze, and went still. Her eyes magnified behind her oversized glasses, and she stared blankly across the room toward the bar.

"Aunt D?" Winston's voice cracked, panic rising.

"Aunt Darceline?!" he yelled, looking wildly at the stewards. They stood stoically, like statues bearing witness to a mildly inconvenient but otherwise routine dinner interruption.

"Call 911!" Win barked.

They exchanged glances but didn't move.

Win pushed his chair back and stood, rushing to Darceline's side. He reached to take her pulse.

"Sir!" yelled Judy.

"Don't touch!" Susan rapidly added.

"*What?*" Win gasped, pulling back quickly. "Why not?"

"It's protocol. You cannot touch Madam."

"This is my aunt! I'll touch her if I want to!" Win defiantly shouted.

"*It is strict protocol* should Madam Hicks transition that she is not to be touched for three hours."

"What does that mean?" Winston frantically asked. "Who came up with that bullshit?!"

"Madam."

"So, I can't touch her?" He confirmed in dismay.

"No," the two said in unison.

"Then call 911!"

"We can't do that," Susan replied calmly, prepared for this scenario.

"What do you mean you can't?!"

"Madam has a living declaration. A DNR. No touching for three hours. These are her rules."

"*Three hours?!*" Win yelped, not believing his ears. "What the fuck is *that?!*"

Ignoring them, he leaned closer to check Darceline's breathing. Nothing. Instinctively, he reached for her neck to check for a pulse.

"Sir!" Susan warned, but he ignored her.

His fingers grazed the pale, fragile skin along her neck, just above the necklace of diamonds. No pulse. Nothing. He stumbled back, frozen.

"Oh, shit," Winston whispered, choking up.

Susan calmly walked to a phone on the buffet beside Darceline. She dialed a number. "It's happened. One of her jags did her in."

Win watched, tears brimming. Susan glanced at him and added, "A minute ago."

She nodded and hung up, and moments later, Mr. Peters entered from the foyer, cell phone in hand. His gaze fell on Darceline, and with one glance, the confirmation was evident. He dialed a number.

"It's happened …" Peters said solemnly into his phone. "Just now …"

Mr. Peters's eyes met Susan's. "She coughed to death," he relayed before looking at Win, then back to her. Ending the call, he tucked the phone into his jacket and instructed, "Mr. de Beaumont is on his way. Open the front gate and lock it open."

Susan nodded and swiftly left for the kitchen.

"What about 911?" Win pleaded, tears now dripping.

Mr. Peters gently patted his shoulder, then gave a tender squeeze. "I'm sorry, Winston. But there will be no emergency calls."

Shocked and bewildered, Win's gaze shifted from his unfinished salad to Judy. The weight of it all crushed him.

"There are protocols and a plan of action for this moment," Peters explained calmly. "Mr. de Beaumont is Madam's personal attorney and will arrive shortly to make two tiers of calls—the first to your mother and uncles. Once they have all arrived and had their time, a second tier of calls will be made to your sister and cousins."

Win wanted to object, but words failed him. Mr. Peters added softly, "I'm sorry, Winston. I know this is a shock."

Win numbly nodded.

"Protocols and a plan of action," he muttered.

"Yes," Peters confirmed.

Still nodding, Win yielded. This was not his universe, and he needed to comply. He removed his glasses, wiping each eye with the back of each hand. "Okay."

He slowly walked to the lounge, found a chair facing Darceline's still body, and collapsed, not bothering to put his glasses back on.

Mr. Peters motioned to Judy, and the two exited through the swinging kitchen door. Winston instinctively pulled a cigarette case from his trousers pocket for a smoke. He couldn't believe his aunt had died upon his arrival. He just couldn't …

"Oh, shit," he whispered once more, burying his face in his hands, his sobs silent yet immeasurable.

After soaking himself with tears for some time, Winston pulled his hands away from his face and sat up when he heard Mr. Peters quietly address him, sitting in a chair by his side.

"Yes?" Win replied, wiping his face.

The house gentleman spoke kindly. "Your uncles are en route. I called your mother and offered to pick her up, but she insisted on driving herself. She'll be here shortly."

Win wiped his eyes again, sniffling.

"I've also called the sheriff to apprise him of the situation and requested discretion—no sirens, no flashing lights."

Nodding, Winston asked, "Is there anything I need to do?"

Mr. Peters offered a somber smile and shook his head. "Not at this time."

Win gave his eyes one final rub, put on his glasses, and took a steadying breath. "I'll freshen up."

"I'll be in the kitchen if you need me," Mr. Peters replied calmly before standing.

Winston thanked him, and he exited with his usual politeness.

With family on their way, Win pulled himself together. He retrieved his blazer from the office and stepped onto the back deck for a cigarette. The crisp air was refreshingly cool as he gazed at the oval, olive-shaped moon hovering at ten o'clock in the east. Clusters of shimmering stars filled the sky—a spectacular offering from the rural Indiana countryside on a clear night. The black lake below was tranquil, mirroring the celestial display above.

He stared across the horizon in disbelief, shaking his head. And yet, he was still. An unexpected peace had wrapped around him like a soft blanket. D was gone, but it felt like she had taken with her the countless scenarios he'd spent a lifetime churning and burning in his mind. Win felt free for the first time—for the first time in his life. Mentally, emotionally, and spiritually free.

And then he wondered where his mother was. She had always insisted on being the first one he saw whenever he returned home. Had Mr. Peters not just spoken to her, Win's concern for her whereabouts would have been a trigger. But she was late, as usual. With a resigned sigh, he flicked his cigarette butt into the ashtray by the door and headed upstairs.

The oversized guest room was a retreat designed for comfort, privacy, and indulgence. White paneled walls, high ceilings, and expansive floor-to-ceiling windows made the space airy and serene. A plush white velvet carpet blanketed the floor. Pastel landscape paintings hung in perfect arrangement. At the entry, a cozy seating area featured two armchairs upholstered in soft yellow fabric, a sleek white coffee table, and a chrome floor lamp. On the table sat his folio, and nearby, a crystal vase brimming with fresh-cut white roses added a touch of elegance.

To the right of the desk, a chrome Keurig coffee maker stood on a polished drawer stand. Beneath it, open shelves were neatly stocked with white porcelain java cups and packets of Lotus Biscoff cookies.

The bedroom area was equally lavish, with a king-sized bed dressed in a soft yellow duvet and light green decorative pillows. Matching white 1960s Deco nightstands and a dresser completed the space. A box of Frango Mint Chocolates sat at the center of the dresser, below a large, round, white-framed mirror. His suitcases rested on two white wooden luggage racks, waiting to be unpacked.

Win unzipped one and stared at the stack of thirty-two legal tablets—nestled between folded clean socks and underwear—he had filled with his novel, every sheet written on the front and back. Pursing his lips sideways, the book no longer seemed relevant.

He retrieved his toiletry bag and made his way to the en-suite bathroom. White pebble tiles lined the floor, complementing the sleek 1960s vanity with a white marble countertop and sink. A separate walled-in space housed the toilet, while a large walk-in shower stood to its right. Fluffy, soft yellow towels perfectly matched the armchairs and were hung on chrome towel bars. Behind the bathroom door, two luxurious white bathrobes draped over chrome hooks.

He unpacked his toiletries and, deciding a shower would wash away the travel fatigue, removed the necklace D had given him. Stripping down before the vanity mirror, Win regarded his reflection—the broad chest, the softened stomach. Darceline was correct; he needed to return to the gym. He smiled, mentally moving that goal to his to-do list.

Stepping into the shower, warm water cascaded over him. But as the steam rose, so did the tears. Giant, unstoppable tears. An ugly cry burst free, raw and unrelenting. He hadn't yet turned in for the night, but this would do.

Reunited

With his blazer and cell phone in hand, Winston moseyed downstairs into the majestic foyer, pausing to glance toward the Grand Room where Aunt Darceline sat in peace. He gazed across the endless stretch of polished limestone before breaking for the front doors, desperate to escape the house's stifling heat.

Stepping outside, the brisk October air was a refreshing balm, cooling his body after the hot shower. The subtle scent of burning leaves wafted across Bucks Peak. He reached for his cigarette case, lit one, and admired the star-speckled sky.

Headlights peeked through the trees, illuminating the circle drive. A pristine white Lincoln SUV rolled past him, pulling around the bend to make room for other arriving vehicles. A tall man emerged, sleek leather briefcase in hand. Dimly lit by the pathway lights, he moved into the brighter glow of the front porch. The stately gentleman approached, dressed in a brown tailored topcoat impeccably crafted from the finest wool.

"Leland de Beaumont," he introduced himself, extending a hand.

"Please, call me Leland."

"Winston," Win replied, studying the man's distinguished presence. His neatly groomed brown hair, streaked with silver at the temples, hinted at wisdom and authority. They seemed close in age, and Winston couldn't help but wonder if this was how he might have appeared had he pursued law instead of … whatever this was now. "Call me, Win."

"I feel I know a great deal about you," Leland said, his face exuding an affable charm.

Win smiled, curiosity piqued. They stood silently for a beat as Winston took another drag from his cigarette.

"Were you with her when she …" Leland began cautiously.

"We had just started dinner."

Leland shook his head, staring down at the concrete steps. "That must have been terrible."

"It was."

Then, the question came out of nowhere. "You didn't touch her, did you?"

"I did."

"Ohhh …" Leland exhaled, his dread palpable.

Winston suddenly felt like a guest star in *The Twilight Zone*. "I checked for a pulse like anyone would."

"Uh … uh … okay," Leland stammered.

Win's patience thinned. "What's with the no-touching thing?"

Leland drew a deep breath, wiping his mouth as if recalibrating. "Excuse me, I need to make several calls."

Win darted before him to break his stride. "What's going on here, Leland? Why can't my aunt be touched? Because Aunt Darceline was always physically affectionate. She just patted my arm at the dinner table!"

Understanding Winston's concern, Leland explained, "Miss Darceline had me prepare a post-mortem directive—a PMD. Upon her death, she was not to be touched, receive medical attention, or be moved for three hours."

"What?"

"It was her decision. She was adamant."

Win couldn't believe what he was hearing. "A *post-mortem directive?* I thought a post-mortem directive is a food safety inspection that ensures slaughtered livestock and poultry products are suitable for consumption."

Leland nodded. "Technically, yes. But with your family's farming background, perhaps the terminology appealed to her."

"Why would she do that?"

Leland shrugged. "Why was baseball legend Ted Williams cryogenically preserved? People make all kinds of choices about their remains. Darceline Hicks didn't want to be touched for three hours. She also specified cremation, and we'll discuss those arrangements later."

Winston shook his head, pointing toward the door. "But why the panic that I touched her?"

Leland pursed his lips. "She had her staff sign agreements stating that any violation of the directive would forfeit their pensions."

Win gaped. "That sounds illegal." The breeze suddenly pricked him with a chill, and he slid on his jacket.

"Oh, it's legally binding," Leland assured him. "We'll pretend you never touched her. But from this moment on, please don't."

"What?" Win sputtered, exasperated.

"Excuse me," Leland said politely, brushing past him into the house.

The foyer was now abuzz with staff, their eyes fixed on the attorney's arrival.

"Mr. Clarke touched her," Susan, the one who had sternly warned him, anxiously declared.

"Yes, I'm aware," Leland replied with practiced calm. "It doesn't matter. None of you did. Your pensions are intact."

Every pair of eyes burned into Winston.

Leland glanced at his watch. He said he had calls to make and stepped away.

Just as the tension peaked, Judy, the server with her tightly pulled gray hair, suddenly erupted into sobs. The room stilled, watching as she wailed for a full fifteen seconds. Then, with whiplash-worthy precision, she wiped her face, beamed with glee, and proclaimed, "This is the happiest day of my life!"

Judy pivoted sharply, sobbing once more as she fled to the kitchen.

All gazes returned to Winston, who stood wide-eyed and bewildered.

Mr. Peters, ever composed, suggested, "Everyone, back to work. The house will soon be filled with family, and we must be ready."

The staff dispersed, and Win slipped out to the front porch. Lighting another cigarette, he mulled over the absurdity of it all. The crisp air did little to cool his mounting frustration. He shook it off, mentally noting to have Mr. Peters turn the furnace off.

However, one question burned bright: why had Aunt Darceline's death become the happiest day of Judy's life?

Win couldn't help but picture her gleefully skipping through the kitchen, belting, *"Ding Dong! The Wicked Witch Is Dead."*

Another set of headlights emerged from the trees, creeping up the drive as if the car were running on fumes. Win guessed it couldn't have been going more than five miles per hour until his Uncle Bill's classic white 1976 Cadillac finally emerged. With a sudden roar, the engine floored—launching the Fleetwood forward like it had been given the green light at a drag race. The car zoomed towards the portico before a thunderous crash shattered the quiet night.

Frantic, Winston bolted toward the commotion. Bill's Cadillac had obliterated the portico's two support columns. The car's rear teetered on a limestone footer while the front end perched precariously on another. The enormous flat roof of the portico hung at a drooping tilt, creaking ominously. As Win took in the whole sight, the roof's outer end plunged downward to smash onto the roof of Bill's car when it suddenly stopped a few feet from impact. All was quiet for two seconds before a loud moan was chorused by snapping wood, followed by a thunderous crack, and the structure broke from the house, plummeting, only to halt again with the outer edge of the flat slab bobbing up and down, tapping the roof of the Fleetwood. Held by two strained black electrical wires, like marionette strings dangling a puppet for one last dramatic scene, the mammoth edifice dangled until they snapped. The entire structure collapsed, pancaking the Chrysler Imperial and Cadillac in a deafening smash.

Win's cigarette slipped from his fingers as he sprinted forward. The passenger side of Uncle Bill's car was the only part without shattered glass or crushed metal. Inside, his Aunt Betsy was visibly hysterical in the front seat.

Her muffled shrieks echoed from within. She dramatically screamed at Bill. "THAT'S IT! THAT'S IT! THAT'S IT!"

"Is everyone okay?" Winston shouted, careful not to stumble over random chunks of broken limestone and roofing debris as he yanked open Betsy's door. The engine sputtered one last time before dying with a gurgle.

"Get me out of this car before it explodes!" she shrieked as she quickly unfastened her seatbelt.

"Aunt Betsy, it's Winston. Are you okay?" he asked, trying to calm her down.

"I think so," she yelped with solid hints of distress etched into her brow. She focused on Win's face and cooed, "Oh Winston … it's so good to see you. Please get me out of this car."

Win looked into her blue eyes, which were slightly clouded with a haze of being eighty. Betsy's long white hair was pulled back into a bun, held into place by gold hair pins with diamonds. Her heavy face was clearly displayed, etched with lines and wrinkles of age—each crease telling a story of a life well-lived.

"Let's be sure you don't have any injuries before you move," Win gently insisted.

"I don't have time for that!" she howled, wriggling to exit. "It's going to blow up!" She thrust her hand toward him. "Here! Help me out!"

Win carefully assisted her, guiding her over and through the wreckage. "Careful. Watch your step."

"Oh my God! Oh my God! Oh my God!" Betsy wailed in her camel hair coat as they reached a clear driveway patch.

Behind them, the mansion's side door burst open. Through a billowing cloud of dust, Mr. de Beaumont and Mr. Peters appeared with several staff members, their expressions a mixture of horror and disbelief.

"Is everyone all right?" Mr. Peters called out.

"I think so!" Win shouted back, already turning toward the car for Uncle Bill.

"Winston!" Betsy hollered. "Grab my purse! Black Coach bag! You can't miss it!"

Win slid onto the front seat.

Still gripping the steering wheel, Bill shook his head, appearing confused.

"Are you okay, Uncle Bill?"

"I thought I had my foot on the brake. I kept pushing harder to stop. I don't know what happened," the little old man with a healthy head of white hair in a navy cardigan said, shaken up.

"It's okay," Win assured him. "Are you hurt?"

Bill examined his arms, patted his chest, and then looked at his nephew. "I don't think so."

Like Marc Monarch's Miss DeVille, this classic Cadillac was equally broad. Winston scooted across the navy passenger lounge seat close to his uncle. Spotting the black purse near Bill's feet, Win grabbed it and placed it on the dashboard. He then patted Bill's forearm.

"How about we start by letting go of the steering wheel?" Win suggested.

Bill exhaled sharply, finally releasing the wheel. "I thought I had my foot on the brake," he repeated.

"Hey," Win leaned in, smelling alcohol on his breath. Offering a warm smile, he said. "It's good to see you, Uncle Bill."

Bill's glassy eyes focused on him, momentarily grounding him.

"Winston?"

"Hi."

With a shaky hand, Bill reached over and patted Win's cheek. "I'm glad to see you."

Winston noticed the red engine light. "Now let's shift to park, turn off the car, and kill the headlights."

Bill nodded and complied.

"Shall we go?" Win coaxed.

His uncle nodded again, unbuckling his seatbelt.

Win focused on the dashboard, then on the steering wheel. "The airbags didn't go off."

"It was an option back in '76. This car doesn't have airbags."

"Huh," Win said, having just learned something.

Then, something outside shifted. The rear door window behind Bill suddenly popped, and a million pieces of glass gave way like a landslide.

"Oh, fuck," Bill whimpered.

Calm and cool, Win said, "We'll take this nice and easy, okay?" He unhurriedly slid back, guiding his uncle, grabbing Betsy's purse.

"I should have packed a couple sandwiches for our trip across the front seat," Bill quipped.

Win chuckled.

They carefully navigate their way out. Once free, Win led the elderly man through the blasted debris. Betsy, clutching her mouth, stood trembling.

"I'm a nervous wreck!" she panted.

Win handed Betsy her purse, scanning them both for cuts or blood, up and down and left and right. There wasn't any. "Are you in any pain?"

Betsy unloaded on Bill. "LOOK AT WHAT YOU DID, WIL-LIAM! YOU ARE DONE! NO MORE DRIVING!"

She huffed, then stormed toward the front entrance at the speed of a turtle, her pocketbook swinging like a weapon of justice. "AND I DON'T MEAN MAYBE!"

Bill, dignified despite the chaos, straightened his cardigan. Win leaned in. "Are you sure you're okay?"

Bill nodded precariously, shook his head no, and went for a hug. Win gingerly squeezed his favorite uncle before each pulled away for a look.

The group inside the portico door came rushing out the front, passing Betsy.

"I'm going to miss that old girl. She was a hell of a tank." Bill sighed. "And Jesus, take the wheel! Darci's going to kill me for wrecking her house and destroying her car."

Win froze in bewilderment, studying Bill's face. The indoor entourage slowed their mad dash as the carnage came into full view.

"She custom-ordered that Chrysler," Bill added mournfully.

Winston gently suggested they head inside.

"I'm a goner," Bill whispered like a little boy about to be in trouble with his mom. "My sister's going to kill me."

Peters approached, his face drawn with concern. "Are you all right, Mr. Hicks?"

Bill nodded. Then, he shook his head. Then nodded again.

Win gestured to Susan. "Can you please help him inside?"

She nodded, carefully taking Bill's arm as they shuffled toward the house.

Winston turned to Peters and de Beaumont. "He punched the gas instead of the brake."

"Are Bill and Betsy all right?" Leland asked, visibly shaken.

"As far as I can tell," Win shrugged. "At their age, they should be examined. But I think Uncle Bill must have hit his head—he's worried about how upset Darceline will be, with no recognition she's dead."

"Oh my," Peters said, glancing back at the wreck. "I'll call Dr. Funnell. He's the family physician."

The three men and the staff stood in disbelief, surveying the crushed cars and the ruined portico. Winston realized it could have been far worse for Bill and Betsy if they'd been in anything other than that classic tank. He reached for his cigarette case.

Suddenly, they heard Peter's classic doorbell ringtone. He reached inside a suit coat pocket for his phone and answered. He listened, nodded, and said, "Yes, Mrs. McCrory. A slight mishap occurred when a guest accidentally bumped their car into the house, but all is well."

Still nodding, he said, "Yes, it was loud. And yes, everyone is alright. I would appreciate it if you could pass that along to everyone."

He listened, pressing his lips together. "Have a good evening. Thank you for calling. Goodbye."

Peters hung up and sighed. "The sound of the crash echoed across the lake. I'll have a hundred more phone calls any minute."

Leland asked Win, "Did you see it happen?"

"Yes."

de Beaumont added, "The sheriff will be arriving shortly. He'll want a statement."

"Of course," Win replied, lighting up and taking a long drag.

Peters looked at the *mishap*. "I'll deal with this tomorrow." He turned to his staff, "We have a long night ahead of us. Let's get back to work."

"I have more calls to make," Leland added, departing behind them.

Win watched as Peters bit his lips, his sadness visible. It was as though keeping his mouth shut would allow him to carry on. The two men slowly turned and walked the drive along the front of the house. Winston couldn't shake the realization that everything in Peters' life— his life's work—was literally crashing down around him.

"I loved driving that car," Peters sadly sighed, looking back at the wreckage. "It was my favorite of all Madam's classics."

Win's heart ached for him. Pausing at the front steps to smoke, he assured Peters, "I'll be in soon."

"You can smoke inside," the houseman replied.

Win grinned. "I've never smoked in my house. Aunt Darceline always had. And I guess, being in her company, in her home, she expected fellow smokers to join her. But now that she's gone, I think I'll smoke outside."

Peters gave him an understanding nod, turned to go inside, and his phone rang again.

"Mr. Peters?" Win called as he entered the foyer. "Can you please turn off the heat? It's fricking hot in there."

"Consider it done," he grinned before closing the door.

"Mr. Peters?" Win called again.

The door sprang open. "Yes, Winston?"

"Let's leave the front doors open to cool the place down."

"Of course," Peters said, fully opening both before disappearing inside to answer the next nosy caller.

Winston sat on the cold concrete porch step, exasperated.

What the fuck!

He smoked and watched another set of headlights winding through the trees. The car entered the clearing and turned on its high beams to illuminate Bill's disastrous handiwork. Win immediately recognized the powder blue '89 Jaguar XJ—Uncle Phil and Aunt Tami. They sat for a surprisingly long time, no doubt in disbelief, before creeping closer. After a couple more minutes, the Jag completed the circle drive and parked in front of the house.

Win stood to open the door for his aunt, but she beat him to it, flinging it wide.

"What the fuck happened?!" Tami screeched, pointing dramatically at the wreckage.

Aunt Tami had always been a party broad. A vivacious, larger-than-life woman in her late seventies, she still dazzled with bold makeup, white coiffed hair, and a beige sweater covered in sequins. Her navy slacks and sparkling jewelry shimmered as much as her personality.

Uncle Phil emerged from the driver's side, shouting across the roof, "What did my fucking brother do now?!"

"What a fucking disaster!" Tami declared as she grabbed her beige leather clutch and climbed out.

Winston quickly moved to help her.

"I've got it! I'm fine!" she barked, stepping out and slamming the door shut. She slowly turned toward Win, pursing her lips in a high-octane smooch mode.

Win leaned in for a kiss and tasted the unmistakable tang of alcohol as she gripped his arm for support.

"It's good to see you, Winston," Phil shouted, equally hard of hearing as his wife. He tottered around the car in his classic navy Ralph Lauren jacket and khaki slacks, pulling Win into a side hug, his breath equally laced with booze.

Win guided Tami up the concrete stairs.

"Climbing up anything is such a fucking challenge!" she grumbled three steps up. "It certainly took you a good minute to get home."

Phil clutched his nephew's shoulder for balance.

"Did you know I was coming?" Win asked.

"Oh yes, darling," Tami shouted. "Darceline told us last week that once you broke out of that mental hospital, she was flying you home."

"It was a rehab facility, Aunt Tami. I was in detox drying out," Win clarified. "And I didn't break out—I checked out."

"Rehab, mental—we don't care what kind of hospital it was, Winston. We love you and are so happy you're here," Phil bellowed as though Win was the one who was hard of hearing.

"It doesn't matter to us! We love, love, love, love you!" Tami squealed, planting another boozy kiss on him before heading inside.

"That's right," Phil declared, clapping Win on the back like he'd just scored a touchdown. "We love you no matter what you're into."

Win's jaw metaphorically hit the H-emblazoned doormat beneath his feet, feeling a sharp jolt of teenage mortification. It was as if they'd just caught him red-handed, jacking off with *Playgirl* magazine … again.

"Go on in," Win directed. "I'm waiting for Mom to arrive."

"Okay!" Tami cheered, grabbing Phil's arm as they staggered their way inside.

Winston shivered in the brisk night air, his blazer doing little to ward off the October chill. Deciding to finish his cigarette and warm up inside the Kenner Easy-Bake Oven, he strolled the circular driveway to get his blood moving. Eight hours ago, he'd been walking out of Betty's. Now, he found himself strolling around this upside-down universe.

His mind lingered on his final conversation with Aunt Darceline. He touched his chest, feeling the pendant beneath his shirt. It was a gift, a reminder, but even more than that, a lifeline. Bless her heart. She had given him the one thing he never expected: *an out*. But he wasn't out of the woods yet.

There was no panic or dread. Sadness, yes. But there was a certain ease that wrapped around him now. Life had tilted back to manageable—until, of course, thoughts of his mother hijacked his mind.

Where was she?!

That familiar question clawed its way up from the recesses of his brain. Even now, decades later, it struck with the same fury it had every time she was late. Boy Scouts, school pick-ups, birthday parties—it never mattered. She lived five minutes away, but the clock held no authority in Marci Time. Winston's resentment simmered, the embers fanned by memories of waiting and waiting.

But no. He wasn't letting that trap him tonight. Sticking his cigarette in the sand-filled wall-mounted ashtray, Win resolved to check on Aunt Betsy and Uncle Bill. About to go in, he caught another set of headlights snaking up the long drive. Relief surged through him, mingled with frustration.

Finally, goddamn it!

Mom's here!

The flood of childhood indignation rose anew, conjuring flashbacks of his eleven-year-old self—the last kid standing at the Camp Ottertail summer pick-up, fuming while the counselors exchanged awkward glances. He had been there for three weeks and was furious he'd been forgotten, abandoned.

But as the vehicle emerged, its hulking form beneath the canopy of trees made one thing clear: this wasn't his mother's sedan. It was an SUV. White decals reflected off the pathway lights.

HICKSVILLE SHERIFF.

Great.

The sheriff's vehicle paused at the mangled wreckage of Bill's Cadillac and collapsed portico. Like Phil before him, the officer inched closer, taking in the absurd spectacle before creeping toward the house. Win popped a mint in his mouth and braced himself for a hundred and one questions.

The SUV pulled up behind Phil's Jaguar. The engine cut off. The door opened.

Out stepped a trim man about Win's height, clad in a black leather uniform coat with a holstered gun and a crisp navy campaign hat. Moving with a confident stride, his boots struck the pavement with purpose. As the sheriff rounded the back of his vehicle, the porch light illuminated his face.

Win's breath was caught.

Those eyes. Blue, sharp, and utterly familiar.

"Winston? Is that you?"

Win's heart pounded. The name on the badge glinted in the light. **MCKAY.**

"Mitch?"

The sheriff's lips parted, his voice soft with disbelief. "Yeah."

Win stared, his mind racing. The teen who once reminded him of Emilio Estevez had grown into a man who could have passed as a rugged Sheen family member. Still striking. Still captivating.

"Yeah," Win echoed, unable to contain his grin.

"You're back."

"Yeah."

"Wow."

"Yeah."

The tension in the air fizzled into something warm—an unspoken acknowledgment of years lost and memories regained. Mitch broke the silence, his voice laced with genuine sympathy.

"I'm sorry about your aunt. Darceline was always very kind. And generous—the biggest supporter of our local charities."

"Thank you," Win nodded, touched by his words.

A brief silence stepped in, their eyes captivated.

"When did you get in?"

"A couple hours ago. I live in Fort Lauderdale now."

Mitch nodded. "Yeah, I heard."

Win's brow lifted. *You did?*

Catching himself, Mitch fumbled. "Well, I mean, you know … word around town."

Win smirked, amused by the sheriff's boyish attempt at cover.

"How's your wife and kids?"

"Divorced. Kids are grown. Out of college."

"Congratulations," Win replied, then winced at the awkward phrasing. "On the grown kids. Out of college."

Mitch chuckled. "Thanks."

Another pause hung between them, thick with nostalgia. Then Mitch's tone softened.

"I'm sorry about your partner … about what happened to Chris Copens. I can't imagine …"

Win swallowed, awkwardly saying nothing, replying with a slight nod.

"He was a good reporter. I liked him." Mitch's gaze turned somber. "I was watching UNN when his live news report from Afghanistan came on, and the bomb hit …"

McKay stopped, instantly regretting saying those words … to, of all people … Winston.

Win's stomach twisted. He politely nodded.

Mitch mentally kicked himself in the ass. "It was awful." He said, pursing his lips sideways, stretching his cheek … heartfelt. "I'm sorry."

A beat passed. Win pressed his lips together.

Mitch's eyes flicked to the ruins of the portico. "Looks like Bill missed the mark. Is he okay?"

Relieved to move on, Win explained, "He and Aunt Betsy are fine. I think. Mr. Peters is calling Dr. Funnell.

"Uncle Bill hit the gas instead of the brake."

"It may be time to evaluate his getting behind the wheel again before he or someone gets hurt. Or worse," Officer McKay offered with authority.

"After it happened, Aunt Betsy made that call," Win grinned.

The sheriff nodded, then suddenly shifted his gaze. "You look good," he said.

Win's heart skipped. "So do you."

Mitch licked his lips, his eyes lingering on Win. Then he reached out, squeezing Win's forearm with a lingering warmth.

"You look cold," Mitch smiled. "Shall we go in?"

"Yeah," Win breathed.

"Okay," Mitch said, his lips curving into a grin.

As they climbed the handful of steps up to the porch, Mitch stated, sounding official, "And, at some point, I'll need to take a couple of statements for my reports."

"As in plural?"

"Miss Hicks's death. And Mr. Hicks's accident."

"Of course," Win agreed, not thinking.

"We had a dozen 911 calls come in reporting an explosion on Bucks Peak," the sheriff said. "I'm surprised there's not a handful of local looky-loos up here checking everything out."

"I saw the start of it happen," Win replied, leading McKay into the manor. Mitch immediately removed his hat, holding it with both hands before him as they walked through the shotgun foyer.

"It was a hell of a crash. The car took out both support columns, and then the roof came smashing down."

They passed a small open alcove on the right with a black tufted bench inside. Mitch pointed, lowering his voice.

"What's that?"

"It's an open lift … an elevator," Win answered.

"Interesting," Mitch commented.

"Is this your first time here?" Win asked.

"Inside it is," Mitch said with a smile just before they heard yelling from the Grand Room.

"Here we go," Winston declared, nudging Mitch's forearm like they were cresting the highest point on a roller coaster before the drop.

Mitch glanced at him with wonder and intrigue. They paused at the room's entrance, looking in.

Win turned to Mitch and said with a jovial smile, "Welcome to my family of Hicks. The ones the outside world never gets to see."

"*HEY!* WHAT DID YOU JUST SAY?!" Uncle Phil shouted, grabbing their attention.

While Phil paced the room barking into his cell phone, Bill sat at the dining table, two seats away from Darceline, with Betsy across from him. Tami was also at the table, next to Bill. Leland lounged in a club chair that had been turned to face the table, tapping an iPad.

Looking down, shaking his head, Bill spoke with resignation, "I knew she'd be mad." His eyes went to Betsy's. "She's giving me the silent treatment."

Betsy sighed, leaned her elbow upon the table, and buried her face in her hand.

"She is not giving you the silent treatment, Bill. She's dead!" Tami yelled.

Mitch immediately pursed his lips to the left.

"Where are you?!" Phil snapped, pausing to listen.

"Goddammit, Marci, we're all here waiting for you …"

"No, she's not going anywhere …"

"*WHAT?! …*"

"*FIVE MORE MINUTES?! …*"

"Fine! We'll see you in about half an hour or whenever you can get your ass over here!"

He hung up with a frustrated sigh, spotted Winston, and shouted,

"Your mother wants five more minutes to finish her nap! *Then* she needs to get ready!"

Win raised both palms in a familiar gesture of resignation. This was nothing new.

Tami, however, was not so indifferent. She pointed at Darceline and exploded at Phil. "Your sister just died, and *MARCI* needs five more minutes to finish *A NAP?!*"

Phil, mirroring Winston's shrug, sighed. "She said Darceline wasn't going anywhere, so what was the rush?"

"For fuck's sake!" Tami bellowed, pushing back from the table and storming to the bar.

Betsy loudly gasped, sighed, and declared with heightened exasperation, "This entire night has made me terribly nervous. Between the car wreck and dead Darci staring at us, I am just so nervous … so terribly, *terribly* nervous."

Tami spun around, highly irritated. "BETSY!" she shouted as she reached for a bottle. "You've been nervous from the first day we met! For sixty years, you've been nervous! *EVERYTHING* makes you nervous! *WE KNOW* you're nervous! You don't have to keep repeating it!"

Tami poured herself a drink, holding it up with a final, cutting remark. "And you know what, Betsy? If you had more than one fucking sip of sherry every six months, YOU WOULDN'T BE SO HIGHLY STRUNG ALL THE GODDAMN TIME!"

Betsy responded, "I'm not highly strung, Tami, I'm nervous."

Tami lost it. "WE GOT IT, BETSY! YOU'RE *NERRVVOUUSSS!!*"

Betsy folded her hands on the table, her expression tight with disapproval. "*Well!*" she huffed.

"Hey, Mitch!" Phil yelled with a wave to acknowledge the sheriff.

Leland de Beaumont's head turned to look at Mitch and Win. "Sheriff," he greeted.

Sheriff McKay remained by Win's side and conveyed his condolences to the room. The aunts and uncles thanked him and invited him in.

Mitch took a step, then glanced back at Win, looking like he had just lost a bet and was dared to enter a big, dark cave with unseen things breathing inside. Winston gave him a kind grin. McKay smiled, then coolly made his way beside Darceline.

"Winston!" Tami yelled, grabbing his attention. "You're empty-handed! How about a cocktail?!"

Win gave her a big, polite smile, saying he was good.

"Well, pour me one! I'm empty!" Phil shouted at her.

Tami roared, "How about you, Betsy?! Are you ready for a shot of sherry?!"

Betsy dramatically sighed, rose from the table, and stormed away, shaking out her hands and disappearing into the foyer.

Win's gaze was on Mitch, paying his respects to Darceline. McKay inhaled deeply, his eyes welling just a little, giving her a nod—as anyone would when taking in the reality that someone they liked was gone. Clarke watched him look down to stare at the dining room table.

Suddenly, Winston tapped into Mitch's emotional moment, becoming overwhelmed. He clearly saw that this man deeply cared for his aunt and family.

Mitch turned his attention to Phil and Bill, saying, "I am deeply sad for everyone's loss today. Miss Darceline was a good woman."

Winston, the uncles, and aunts stared at Mitch wide-eyed, almost stunned, realizing the sheriff had obviously known Darceline in a much different, special way than they had. Win watched him with an expanding sense of awe that, after all these years, after all this time, Mitch obviously bonded with his aunt, and her passing truly affected him.

Yet, after his sincere conversation with Darceline an hour ago, in some way, Win could see where Mitch's compassion came from—because he just saw a side of his aunt he'd never seen before. His heart suddenly swelled for Sheriff McKay, his stomach fluttering.

What is this?

What is happening here?

The Rundown

Mr. Peters emerged from the swinging kitchen door, catching Leland's eye. With a slight head tilt toward Winston, he prompted Mr. de Beaumont to stand. The two men approached Win, their movements deliberate, before Leland softly suggested, "Let's step into the BS."

Win followed. Once inside, de Beaumont closed the double doors, then motioned for Winston to sit at the head of the conference table. Peters sat to his left.

"We're about to have a busy week," Leland said gravely, sitting on Win's right. With his iPad in hand, he requested Winston's cell number and began tapping it as he recited it aloud.

Leland continued. "Your mother should be on her way. I will share the events that must unfold promptly." He paused to confirm he had Win's full attention, which he did.

"Your aunt was precise in her instructions following her death. I'll review those briefly, but we face an unforeseen issue."

"I can go pick up Mom, now," Win offered.

"I'm not referring to Marci," Leland clarified, exchanging glances with Peters.

Win's curiosity sharpened, his eyes bouncing between the two men, and then Leland revealed, "Our quandary is Irene Kelley."

Irene Kelley had become indispensable to Darceline, taking on the workload Penny had once shouldered. Statuesque and commanding, with a basketball player's build and an always-on presence, she had a caring face framed by brunette waves and peach-toned skin. Behind her sharp eyes buzzed a thousand business details.

Mrs. Kelley had served as Bill Hicks's executive assistant for eleven years, securely plugged into the Hicks America machine. When hospice was brought in during Penny's final weeks, Bill was on the cusp of retirement and suggested Irene help Darceline—since his sister was now spending all her days and nights with her dying love, and essential business was inadvertently being neglected, falling through the cracks. Irene was trusted and proficient, and her competence became the keystone that allowed Darceline to stay by Penny's side.

"Where's Irene? I'm surprised she's not here," Win said.

"That's the problem," Leland replied. "She's on a ten-day Antarctic cruise with her husband."

Win registered the weight of that. Like his own Ginger Brooks, Irene was the linchpin of Darceline's world—she had access to everything. And now, with Darceline gone and Irene unreachable, they were completely locked out of Darceline's Hicks America computer.

"I've contacted the cruise line," Leland went on. "The ship's in the Drake Passage. They'll reach the South Shetland Islands tomorrow. But there's no cell service until they're back in Argentina. I've put in a request for her to call me via satellite phone."

"How do we get her home?" Win asked.

"We don't," Leland said. "Logistically, it's not possible. And even if it were, we don't have the time. We need access to Darceline's computer. Now."

Win looked to Peters.

"My access is limited to household operations and staff," he explained.

Leland added, "Now, the time difference is only an hour ahead of ours. Chances are, Irene won't get my message until the morning. Once she calls, I'll text you the passwords you'll need."

"Me?" Win asked, puzzled. "Why do I need them?"

Leland straightened. "I'm going to outline what is to happen this week. If you have any questions, please interrupt."

Win nodded.

"The three hours following Miss Hicks's death are divided into timelines. First, her siblings arrive to establish a quorum to acknowledge her passing. Second, the remaining family arrives. After the three-hour mark, her remains may be taken to the county morgue."

Win lifted a finger to interject. "What's the quorum for?"

"It's a family tradition," Leland explained. "Established in 1865 by your grandfather's grandfather. Before a coroner officially certifies the death, the family of honor—the elders—gather to acknowledge the passing."

"So, it's symbolic?" Win clarified.

"Yes."

Win nodded, satisfied.

"Miss Darceline's final wishes are simple," Leland continued. "No public viewing of the body. Cremation. Her name will be added to the family mausoleum in Hicksville Cemetery."

He tapped the tablet.

"On Wednesday, her Last Will and Testament will be executed here at Bucks Peak. Noon."

"No probate," Win confirmed.

"Correct. She established a personal trust, 'The Darceline Isabel Hicks Trust,' aka 'The DIH Trust.' Assets will be distributed without court delays."

Win suddenly chuckled, reflecting on what Steven Wolfe from Las Olas Bank shared at Marc's party about the 'mystery buyer' who bought his building—The DIH Trust. Shaking his head, he found it ironic how that conversation had sent him spiraling straight into an afternoon drift of California snow.

Once his departed gaze returned to de Beaumont's, Leland went on. "Friday, there's a Hicks America board meeting here at 4 p.m. to elect her replacement as CEO and Chairman. You will attend."

Win nodded.

"Saturday, there will be a private luncheon at the Hicksville Country Club, followed by a public procession at 2 p.m. to the cemetery for a memorial service. At 6 p.m., a private family dinner will be held at the club."

Finally, Leland concluded, "At midnight, her ashes will be taken by boat to the center of Hicksville Lake and spread. Only family members will attend."

Win raised his finger again. "Why host the board meeting here and not at corporate?"

"Miss Hicks always held them here," Leland replied. "I can arrange otherwise if you prefer."

"No, keep it status quo," Win said.

Leland nodded, then inclined his head slightly. "There are two pertinent legal instruments involved in this matter: first, the Darceline Isabel Hicks Trust, which we have previously reviewed, and second, the Hicks Irrevocable Family Trust. The latter retains majority ownership of Hicks America, LLC."

He adjusted his posture and continued in a measured tone. "Each of these trusts is governed by a dual-trustee structure: a Principal Trustee, who manages the substantive directives and intentions of the trustor, and a Legal Trustee, who ensures compliance with fiduciary obligations and statutory law. Your aunt served as the Principal Trustee of both entities. I have served—and continue to serve—as the Legal Trustee."

Leland turned to face Winston directly.

"Under the succession clause set forth in the governing document of The Hicks Irrevocable Family Trust, upon the passing of the sitting Principal Trustee, that role is to be assumed by the eldest lawful heir of the next generational tier."

Leland took a beat.

"In this case, that individual is you, Mr. Clarke."

Winston's face remained unreadable.

"Do you acknowledge and understand the transfer of fiduciary duty as outlined?"

"I do," Winston replied evenly.

"Very well," Leland said, his tone firm.

"In the presence of Jonathan Peters, acting as a witness on this twenty-sixth day of October, I, Leland de Beaumont, Esquire, Legal Trustee of The Hicks Irrevocable Family Trust, hereby designate and confirm the succession of Winston Jameson Clarke as Principal Trustee of said trust, with all rights, responsibilities, and fiduciary obligations therein conferred."

Winston suddenly found himself immersed in a thick fog, like he was entering a dream, rendering him speechless. He could hear de Beaumont speaking, but the words had seemingly lost all meaning.

Leland gave Win a moment. Uncertain if he clearly understood, he elaborated.

"To clarify, Winston, what I've just stated is not merely ceremonial—it's a formal legal act. As Legal Trustee, I am authorized by the terms of the Hicks Irrevocable Family Trust to carry out certain administrative functions. One of those is the designation of a successor Principal Trustee following the death or incapacitation of the prior holder of that office—in this case, your aunt."

He leaned forward slightly, his voice instructional but respectful.

"By naming you as Principal Trustee, I am effectuating the transfer of authority and responsibility to you, as outlined by the trust instrument. This means that you now stand in the position your aunt previously held. You will have the power to make decisions on behalf of the Trust in alignment with its purpose and provisions—including any financial distributions, business oversight, and legal obligations tied to Hicks America, LLC."

Leland glanced at his iPad, then continued.

"Additionally, you will assume what we call fiduciary duties. These are legal duties to act in the Trust's and its beneficiaries' best interest. That includes the duty of loyalty—meaning you must avoid conflicts of interest—and the duty of care, which means you must manage the trust assets prudently, with the diligence of a reasonable person in a similar role."

He folded his hands neatly on the table.

"The language I used encapsulates that transfer of legal and practical authority. This is not merely symbolic. It carries weight under the law, and your decisions from this point forward will have binding implications."

He paused, letting the full scope settle in.

"Do you have any questions about what that entails or what your duties will now include?"

Snapping back to the present as though he just reentered his body from a visit to another dimension, Win said, "*What?*" He wobbled his head, trying to focus. "Can you explain that to me again as you would to a child?"

Leland softened his tone.

"Winston, what I just said means this: your aunt used to oversee the family trust—the thing that holds the family businesses and other important matters, and Bucks Peak. Now that she's passed, you are now the one who makes the big decisions."

"*What?*" was all Win could ask again, Leland's words slapping him awake.

"Bucks Peak is now your residence," Leland added matter-of-factly.

"Wait! No… no… no!" Winston fired back, voice cracking with disbelief. "Aunt D said she was giving me an out if I didn't want this. I don't want this. I want the out."

Leland raised an eyebrow, but his tone remained steady. "Winston, as Principal Trustee, you do have the right to resign from the position. However, legal procedures—and fiduciary responsibilities—must be observed before that resignation can be formally recognized and enforced. We'll review those on Wednesday."

He tapped his tablet. "As stipulated in the trust documents, the next designated successor is Kaitlyn Hicks-Cook."

Win shook his head, not following. "What are you saying?"

"I'm saying you can step down. But not today. And not this week," Leland replied. "Should you choose to resign, Kaitlyn Hicks-Cook becomes the next Principal Trustee. That transition must follow protocol."

Leland blinked with a tight jaw. "Understand?"

"Not really," Win muttered, then let out a long sigh. "I don't know a thing about agriculture … let alone the '*vast Hicks America empire.*'" He gestured dramatically with air quotes before leaning back into his chair and looking at the coffered ceiling.

"But go on."

"There's no need to feel overwhelmed, Winston," Leland said evenly. "At present, you are not required to take immediate action. Or do a thing. All operations and holdings under Hicks America, LLC will continue functioning without interruption."

He waited for a beat. "Are you alright?"

"Yes," Win whispered, his gaze still upward.

He gave Winston a steady look. "Shall I continue?"

"Yes," he whispered again, adjusting himself in the seat by sitting up, crossing his legs, and focusing on de Beaumont.

"Okay," Leland said softly, waited another beat, then continued. "Following the reading of her Last Will and Testament on Wednesday, I shall officially announce your position to the family, at which point your status as patriarch will be formally acknowledged." Leland's tone grew solemn. "Until then, we should handle all of this, including your resignation intentions, with absolute discretion to prevent family discord or endless questions. Understand?"

Win nodded.

"Before that announcement, you and I will review everything, including a complete overview of the Trust and your responsibilities.

There will also be documents requiring your signature. Understand?"

"Yes," Win replied, the adrenaline rush overpowering him. He glanced at Peters, who was studying him thoughtfully.

"Take a moment, but only a moment, to let this settle in," Leland advised. "If you don't want this and prefer an out, we'll get you out. But it will take a little time."

Seeing the whole picture, Win pulled a cigarette from its case, placed it between his lips, and said, "In the meanwhile, I'll need the passwords to access my aunt's computer."

"Yes."

Winston bit the cigarette filter between his front teeth, comprehending fully.

Leland continued, "Now, let's tend to your mother. Marci needs to be here. Right away."

Win removed the cigarette, rubbing his temple. "You said today is October twenty-sixth."

"Yes."

Win scoffed sarcastically. "Darceline's party wraps on Halloween with the spreading of her ashes at midnight. *How fun.*"

Leland tilted his head back, stretching his neck. "That is the fifth day. So, yes."

A devilish smirk came over Win. "What a trick or treat this shall be."

The day's absurdity had topped out. Exhausted, he turned to Peters. "Let me freshen up, and we'll go get my mother."

"I'll pull a car from the garage that will be easy for her to get in and out of," Mr. Peters replied kindly, sensing Win's emotional fatigue.

"Thank you," Win said, genuinely grateful for the support.

Leland leaned in. "Winston, there will be a lot of media coverage of this tomorrow. Darceline was a very powerful, renowned, and respected businesswoman. With Irene away, I have a team drafting the official press release on her passing. Would you care to review it before anything goes out?"

"Yes, please," Win answered, ready to go outside and smoke …

until a sullen thought struck him head-on. "We may have a problem."

Leland, caught off guard, asked, "What?"

"Sally."

"Why?"

Win explained that Sally's podcast, *Back Alley Sally*, was based on a fictional character with a rags-to-riches story—except for two things: Sally is a real-life heiress who stupidly used her real name.

"She used her real name?" Leland repeated, incredulous.

"Sally Hicks is Back Alley Sally," Win confirmed. "Yes."

"Sally used her real name and lied about *once* being poor?"

"Yes." Win tightened his lips, nodding.

Leland dropped his head, clutching his forehead. "Fuck!"

"I know," Win echoed, still nodding.

"Darceline was meticulous about details, so nothing ever went astray. And now this?!" Leland fumed.

Winston asked, "Did Aunt D ever watch Sally's podcast?" No one knew.

He looked at Mr. de Beaumont. "Have you?"

Leland shook his head.

"I did for half a minute. Have you, Mr. Peters?"

Peters shook his head.

Win cleared his throat and offered a solution. "Okay. Here's what we do. We only mention Aunt D's siblings. She died childless. Yes, she built a blah, blah, blah. And yes, gave money to blah, blah, blah. There it is—without a mention of Sally."

"Agreed," Leland said, sinking back into his chair, his mind running countless scenarios. He sighed dramatically. "This could be cataclysmic."

"Let's not go there," Win countered.

"Agreed. But I'm thinking about preparations."

"Can we discuss the family's apocalypse tomorrow?" Win asked, steering them back into a direction they controlled.

"Of course. We'll keep the press release minimal."

"Thank you," Win sighed, highly relieved.

"Thank you for pointing this out," Leland replied with a small, tired smile.

"What about her obituary?" Winston asked. "Has that been written?"

Leland raised a finger to say, "Yes, Darceline wanted it short and sweet." He tapped his tablet, then read:

"Darceline Hicks.

"She died."

Looking at Winston, he added, "That's it."

Win exploded into laughter.

A coy grin from Win's outburst came over Leland, lifting his energy as he said, "Darceline once mentioned, 'If people want to know about me, they can fuck off. And when I'm dead, I'm dead. Those two pairs of words say it all.'"

Win clutched his abdomen, winding down. "I love it! *She died ... and everyone can fuck off!* How perfect!"

Winston blew that one out, moving on. "Okay, thank you."

Turning to Mr. Peters, he added, "Give me ten minutes, and I'll meet you out front."

Leland glanced at Peters, and they stood and left the room.

Win rose, returned the cigarette to its case, and walked to the bar, eyeing the decanter of bourbon—or whiskey, or whatever it was. Tempted, he grabbed a water bottle instead and downed it in a single throwback.

Everything was happening too fast.

He closed his eyes and took six deep breaths. When he opened them, his gaze was drawn to the massive flatscreen above Darceline's desk. It showed a nighttime aerial view of Bucks Peak—its winding drives, sidewalks, and twinkling lights shimmering like a Christmas village beneath a glowing tree.

The magnitude of it all hit him.

Bucks Peak was his.

Oh ... wow.

Oh ... fuck!

Pulling his phone from his blazer, Winston dialed.

"I'm sorry to call so late, Ginger," he said, his voice edged with mystery. "Something's happened. Quite a few somethings, actually."

Q&A

Sheriff McKay was gazing out one of the tall, narrow windows overlooking Hicksville Lake. Bill remained at the dining room table, with Betsy again sitting across, adjacent to the candelabra between them, with a clear view of her husband, watching him closely. Phil and Tami were perched at the bar. Winston reentered the Grand Room as Tami's voice carried across the space.

"Bill! Let it go! It was an accident!"

Betsy shook her head, her expression tight with frustration, while Bill stared blankly at the melting candles, unmoved by Tami's outburst.

Win casually strolled over to Mitch, who stood holding his campaign hat. In the glass reflection, Mitch watched Winston step beside him.

"Hey," Win whispered, looking at him in the glass.

"Hey," Mitch whispered to the window, his concern evident.

Win smiled, finding unexpected comfort in Mitch's steady presence. The faint scent of his cologne grounded him.

"Can you do me a favor?" Mitch asked, his reflection grinning.

"Of course."

"Can we have a couple minutes? Alone?"

"Sure," Win replied, the warmth of the request lingering. "Give me a minute, then meet me in the foyer."

Mitch gave Win a wink in the glass, and it felt better than any swig of whiskey he might have downed two minutes ago.

Turning away, Winston approached Betsy and eased into the seat beside her, folding his hands on the table. "Any soreness from the accident?"

A faint, weathered smile crossed her lips. "I'm fine. My waist is a little tender from the seatbelt, but no pain. I'm okay. Thank you, darling," she said, patting his hand.

"Mr. Peters and I are going to get Mom. Will you join us?"

Betsy's eyes brightened. "That's a lovely idea," she said, then leaned closer, dropping her voice to a whisper, glaring Tami's way. "I could use a break from that screaming hyena. I told that woman to get hearing aids twenty years ago, and now, we have to contend with *this!*"

Win chuckled. "I'm heading upstairs to freshen up, then we'll go."

"I'll get my coat and wait by the door," Betsy said, relieved for the distraction.

Win kissed her cheek, then circled the table to Bill. Mitch was already making his way to the foyer, and their eyes met. Win offered a slight smirk before sitting down next to his uncle.

"Any pain or discomfort from the accident?" Win asked.

Bill shook his head, silent.

Leaning closer, Win asked softly, "Uncle Bill, are you okay?"

Bill shook his head again.

Win understood—a foolish question under the circumstances. Death in the family, a totaled car, a damaged house. No one could be okay. He patted Bill's arm gently.

"Okay," Win said with quiet sympathy. "Mr. Peters and I are going to get Mom. We'll be back soon."

Standing, his gaze drifted to Darceline's lifeless form. He sighed, then followed Mitch.

Mitch stood just outside the Grand Room, studying a large 4'x6' painting of a yellow sailboat on the water, helmed by a young blonde woman with windswept hair. She wore a light blue top and smiled with her eyes closed, basking in the sun.

Win stepped beside him. "This is called *Penny*."

"It's beautiful," Mitch said, captivated. "And … it's painted in dots. Nothing but colorful dots."

"The technique is called Pointillism," Win explained with a small smile. "Aunt Betsy painted it."

"This could be in a museum," Mitch said, still awestruck.

Win glanced around at the vast collection of paintings lining the shotgun foyer. Mitch followed his gaze, taking in the space with a new-found appreciation.

"Huh," Mitch chuckled with a sense of awe. "I guess, in a way, this is a museum."

Turning to Win, he offered a handsome smile that caught Win off guard in the best possible way.

"I'm going upstairs to freshen up before I go pick up my mother," Win said, savoring the moment. "That should give us a couple of minutes."

The Sheriff and Win coolly walked through the mansion. Winston glanced at him with a happy smile, and Mitch returned the gaze— equally stunned this was happening and exhilarated by it. Like two teenagers sneaking away, they peeked behind them to ensure there were no witnesses. Win led him to his second-floor room and closed the door behind them.

Mitch carefully laid his navy uniform coat and campaign hat on the stuffed yellow chair by the door, then turned, staring at Win as if he were a dream.

"This is a nice surprise …" Win began, but Mitch stepped into his personal space, his face six—then three inches away. McKay breathed heavily through his nostrils with his delicious smile, saying nothing but everything.

Their eyes were locked. Win's breath hitched, unconsciously syncing with Mitch's. Then, Mitch leaned in, softly bumping his nose against Win's before abruptly stepping back.

"Duty calls," he declared, then strode into the bathroom.

"It's been a few hours since my last break," Mitch's voice echoed.

Winston quickly reached for his phone, confirming de Beaumont's contact information had arrived for the morning's press release. He walked to the open bathroom doorway, returning it inside his blazer, and paused.

Mitch stood at the toilet, taking a long, unhurried piss, his perfectly fitted uniform hugging his frame. Win smiled, stepping to the sink to wash his hands before grabbing a quick mouthful of mint Listerine.

He turned around, leaning against the vanity—lingering on the man he had once licked from head to toe.

Mitch tucked himself in, zipped up, flushed, and caught Win's marveling stare. He smirked as he walked over, sliding beside him at the sink to wash his hands.

Facing opposite directions, Win looked over his left shoulder—only to find Mitch's baby blues looking over his left shoulder in return.

"Is this how you swoon, Sheriff McKay?" Win cooed.

Mitch smirked like he'd been caught. Then, just above a whisper, he asked, "Are you seeing anyone?"

"No," Win quickly blurted out.

"Really?" Mitch sounded surprised, raising an eyebrow as he dried his hands.

"Really," Win affirmed, then countered, "Are you?"

"Nope." Mitch grinned, slowly reaching behind him for the mouthwash. He leaned back with the blue bottle in hand. "May I?"

"Have anything you like," Win whispered.

Never breaking eye contact, Mitch took a slow sip, swished, then seductively gurgled before spitting it out and rinsing the sink. He stepped back, wiped his mouth with two fingers, and then took another step to stand directly before Win.

"Anything?" he asked with a playful curiosity.

Win's lips curled into a smile, his eyes widening in response.

Mitch cocked his head, stepped in tightly to straddle Win's legs, and placed warm, clean hands on each side of his face. He slowly, deliberately moved in, brushing his lips against Win's—just like when they were young pups. Win surrendered, meeting him halfway, and their mouths melded, escalating from soft and lingering to deep, ravenous kisses. Their tongues tangled, their breathing heavy, their bodies pressed—until Win pulled his head back and placed both hands on Mitch's face.

"Wait," he gasped.

The only sound was their heavy breathing.

"Wait?" Mitch echoed, equally breathless.

"Yeah."

"Yeah." Mitch exhaled, suddenly aware of where they were and what was happening downstairs.

He retook Win's face again, resting his forehead against his. "Okay."

Win nodded against him. "Okay."

They stood there, breathing each other in, until the tension became unbearable, and Mitch stepped back. He chuckled, looking wild-eyed. "I've missed that."

"Me too," Win admitted, his grin matching Mitch's.

Mitch studied him intently. "You've grown into one handsome man, Mr. Clarke."

Win smirked. "As have you, Sheriff McKay."

Mitch shifted from foot to foot, unsure where to go, before finally planting his feet and crossing his arms. "Want to play a quick round of Q&A?"

Win tilted his head, intrigued. "Sure."

"Have you dated anyone since Chris?"

Win exhaled. "The only relationship I've had in fifteen years since

Chris died was with work. I became a lone wolf in advertising."

Mitch swallowed and nodded. "Your turn."

"Why did you marry Wendy?"

Mitch sighed. "I like marriage. I like having that one person you know will always be home, lighting the fire for you."

"But you liked dick," Win stated.

"I liked both," Mitch confirmed.

That was honest enough. Win smiled.

Mitch's voice softened. "Why did you leave for college without saying goodbye?"

Win swallowed hard, embarrassed. "Because I was young and stupid and wanted to leave this town as fast as possible. I'm sorry I didn't say goodbye."

Mitch pursed his lips, absorbing the explanation, the apology.

"Why did you marry Wendy?" Win pressed again.

Mitch let out a short laugh, pointing a finger at him. "I never really answered that, did I?" He took a breath. "Okay.

"You know I joined the Navy right out of high school …

"I looked for you before I went to basic training that June. But you were gone.

"Anyway, you remember Wendy and I dated in high school—boyfriend, girlfriend, with my boyfriend on the side …" Mitch tilted his head, smirking.

Win smiled, nostalgic.

"After Basic, I came home for five days before shipping out to the Pacific. A few months later, I got a letter—Wendy was pregnant.

"I flew back on my next furlough. We got married because it was the 'right thing to do.'" He made air quotes.

"She became a Navy wife, and we had a little girl. Two years later, another baby girl.

"I did what I was supposed to do."

Win nodded.

"One more Q each … for the road?" Mitch asked.

"Sure," Win agreed.

Mitch leaned in, his expression smoldering. "How many times have you thought of me since we were last naked together?"

Win exhaled. "Countless."

A charged silence stretched between them.

Win finally asked, "Why did you divorce?"

Mitch's gaze held his. "Everything I did was never good enough. Once the kids were grown and gone, all we had left were her daily complaints from dawn to dusk. And then, one morning, as I took my first sip of coffee, she launched into another list of grievances … and I realized—she wasn't good enough for me.

"I made the call."

A sadness flickered through Win. He couldn't imagine living like that—the way his parents had.

He shook off the thought with a knowing nod and a slight grin. "I like your Q&A game."

"I like standing here with you," Mitch seductively confessed. "Looking at you."

"I've got to go get my mom," Win said, reluctantly pulling himself back to reality.

"Yeah," Mitch said.

"Yeah," Win echoed.

"Okay," Mitch said, still unmoving.

"Okay," Win repeated, mirroring his hesitation.

Neither wanted to leave.

Suddenly, the haunting theme from *Twin Peaks* played between them. The dramatic overture of his ringtone struck Win as oddly fitting, and he grinned as Mitch reached into the chest pocket of his uniform shirt for his phone.

"Excuse me," Sheriff McKay said with a playful wink. "Duty calls again."

Mitch answered, his expression shifting almost immediately. Win watched as his eyes flicked to the right, his breath deepening before he released it in a slow, measured exhale. His lips pursed. He stepped back, nodding.

"Right. I'm on my way. Thanks, Bonnie."

Slipping his phone back into his pocket, Mitch met Win's gaze. "Something's happened across the lake. I need to go."

Win's brow furrowed, but he nodded. "My Aunt Betsy's waiting on me. I need to get going, too."

"I'll be back within the hour," Mitch assured him, turning to leave.

"Mitch?" Win called softly, a faint smile playing on his lips.

Mitch stopped. "Yeah?"

Win hesitated, then admitted, "I'm damaged."

Mitch's face fell. He took a slow breath. "So am I."

He turned toward the door, going for his coat and hat—but then he stopped. Spinning back around, he closed the distance between them in a heartbeat. Without a word, he cupped Win's face and kissed him with raw intensity. It wasn't rushed; it was rugged, full of meaning—a kiss meant to last until he returned.

When they finally pulled apart, Win barely managed a breath. "Okay," he whispered, his voice unsteady.

But before the word had left his lips, Mitch kissed him again—one more … for the road.

Mother

Betsy, bundled up in her coat, sitting on a high-back wing chair upholstered in tufted beige velvet fabric beside a Chinese end table topped with a silver platter filled with Andes Crème de Menthe after-dinner chocolate mints, couldn't help but watch Mitch and Winston descend the stairs, turning in unison like they were a couple. They were approaching her—no, *floating*. Mitch smiled with hat in hand and waved before heading out toward his cruiser.

Her eyes flicked to her nephew, and in a deep, sassy voice, she said, "Well, that was subtle."

"What?" Win said, grinning, stepping outside to check if Mr. Peters had arrived. He was parked behind Sheriff McKay's SUV.

Winston returned to Betsy, extending an arm for her to hold as they walked to the car.

Aunt Betsy leaned into the high-back chair, glancing at her nephew. "My, oh my," she taunted, remaining seated. "Home just a couple of ticks on the clock, and you've already got the sheriff in your back pocket."

"He's not in my back pocket, Aunt Betsy," Win corrected, clearly enjoying this as Mitch's cruiser started, then drove away.

"*Oh, Winston,*" Betsy's voice dropped low and teasing, "are you *sure* about that?"

"You are a naughty little girl!" Win scolded with a contagious smile, slowly shaking his finger at her.

With a sassy wink, Betsy stood up, taking his arm in hers. Moving into the bright lights of the porch, she glanced at Win, pausing for a closer look at his face.

"Do you have lipstick on?" She examined.

"No," he unabashedly replied.

"Then why are your lips so pink and flush?"

Winston blushed.

Betsy leaned in, rubbing her thumb under his lower lip, her voice turning sultry. "Oh, I see ... *uh-huh.*"

Winston groaned, shaking his head. "Aunt Betsy, please!"

Linking her arms with his again, she added, as he followed her lead down the steps, "Sweetheart, I may be eighty, but I sure know when someone has been *pow'd* right in the kisser."

Winston grinned, shaking his head. She was hitting all the marks.

They made their way down the steps, and Betsy grinned, lowering her voice like she was letting a scandal slip: "I heard he's divorced and not dating—any women, that is."

"And all I'm hearing is ya-dee *ya,* ya-dee *ya,*" Win said, cutting her off.

She giggled as Peters pulled into Mitch's space with an immaculate black '68 Chrysler Imperial, and Betsy made a dramatic show of admiring it. "Darceline certainly had a *thing* for her Imperials."

Peters parked and quickly dashed to open the backseat door. She smiled as he took her hand to assist. Win walked to the other side, rolling his eyes as he entered. Pulling down the black leather dividing armrest between them, Win leaned comfortably closer to his aunt.

Looking around the back seat, he said in awe, "I love how D kept every one of her cars looking brand spanking new."

Betsy's smile faded. "And then my husband kills one. Thank God she wasn't alive to see it." She turned to look out the window as they pulled away into the darkness of the winding drive down the hill.

Releasing a troubled sigh, she quietly said, "This is a disaster, Winston. Bill's driving days are done; that's a given. But it's more than that. I think he's ... slipping. No, he's been slipping."

Winston reached over to gently squeeze her hand, his expression softening. "How long?"

"A good three years," she said, shaking her head. "But tonight ... tonight was the worst of it."

Win listened intently.

Staring at the passing night outside, Betsy shrugged. "I honestly don't know what to do."

"Oh, Aunt Betsy," Win softly said, his voice filled with compassion. "Do you have any assistance, any help?"

"We've got a housekeeper, but it's not enough.

"It's become so unpredictable with him. I'm considering a professional nurse or someone who can manage more day-to-day things with Bill. He gets confused. He's there one minute, fully coherent, and not the next. I honestly don't know what to do."

She shook her head, scolding herself. *"I should have never let him drive tonight!"*

"You're doing your best, Aunt Betsy," Win said, reassuring her with a light squeeze of her hand. "What can I do? What do you need?"

"You're about to have a plateful. Don't you worry about this old dame or your demolition uncle. We'll be fine."

She gave him a sad grin, patting his hand, her tone lighter. "And if something in the wind blows your way with our County Mounty, you need to leap into it. See where it takes you."

Win was captured. Why in the world was she playing Cupid so adamantly? And *now?* After *that* admission?

Then he remembered his aunt always loved love. Forever the

matchmaker, Betsy thrived on connecting those she deemed pair-worthy as if it were a natural calling. She was relentless. And tonight, her gaydar was certainly blipping like an intense game of Ms. Pac-Man.

Sitting with her, hand in hand, Win could sense her sudden interest in him and Mitch … had magically calmed her nerves. With her heart flowing the purest of love, he leaned his head onto her shoulder, looking out the window.

Then Winston suddenly sat up straight.

"Mr. Peters," he called, "we're going to need Aunt Darceline's finest champagne. She would appreciate a toast for her third hour of honor. And I believe Aunt D would love the family sipping her best bubbles altogether."

"Of course," Peters replied, looking at Win in the rearview mirror.

Betsy clapped her hands together, delighted. "That's a wonderful idea! Let's do it!"

She suddenly giggled. "Watching me drink champagne will knock the dentures right out of your Aunt Tami's head!"

The car slowed, and they pulled into the long driveway and up to the large house where Winston was raised. Growing up, his chore was the lawn, which he kept immaculate every season that didn't snow—he worked hard to ensure it.

All three looked outside—shocked to see how Marci had utterly neglected her yard. Winston gasped. A fallen dead tree lay in a haphazard sprawl, its skeletal branches reaching out like twisted fingers toward the night sky. Patches of tall dead grass were stuffed with collections of fallen autumn leaves. There was no sign of recent care or attention, and the place looked like a rural Indiana version of Norma Desmond's dilapidated mansion in the movie *Sunset Boulevard.*

"Why isn't she using a lawn service?" Win blurted, staring at the mess.

Peters stopped, looking at them both in the rearview mirror.

Betsy was triggered, dropping heavy sighs and flicking her fingernails. "Winston, why don't you fetch your mother, and I'll wait in the car."

"Come on, Aunt Betsy. I think the two of us can handle it faster than I can on my own," he said, trying to be reassuring.

Spontaneously nervous again, she said with the dreaded fret, "I just don't know if I can go in there."

"Sure, you can," Win insisted before hopping out to dash around the Chrysler's big-ass trunk and open the car door for his dear aunt. With a hand extended for assistance, he added, "Come on. Let's go get her."

Betsy took an exasperated breath and relented, slowly stepping from the vehicle. Arm-in-arm, Win paced his walk to match her slow stride along the sidewalk covered in dead leaves and small branches. He glanced at patches of tall dead grass shooting in all directions that weren't buried in brown leaves. They loudly crunched to the front porch, discovering the locked door.

"Oh, my God," Betsy huffed.

Winston rang the doorbell, catching his aunt examining the only exterior hanging lamp that worked, lighting its filthy glass smothered in cobwebs and dead bugs.

Rolling her eyes and slightly shaking her head, Win wasn't sure if she was talking to herself or him when she whispered aloud, "This is going to be horrible. *Just horrible.*"

Impatient, she rang the doorbell again, and they heard a shriek of frustration from inside before Marci screamed, "I'M RIGHT HERE, GODDAMMIT! GIVE ME A MINUTE TO OPEN THE GODDAMN DOOR!"

Stunned, Betsy and Winston looked at one another as the sound of moving boxes, yelps, and something sliding around accompanied a moan, a bump against the door, and another moan until the deadbolt unlocked and the door cracked open a few inches, only to freeze. Win pushed on the door to open it wider, only to quickly pull back once they heard a long-winded murder scream, then Marci's voice shrieked through the house, "STOP! STOP! STOP! IT'S AS FAR AS IT CAN GO!"

Betsy and Winston exchanged a look: she was spooked; he was trying not to burst into laughter.

"Oh, my God," Betsy repeated with heightened trepidation.

More things were heard scooting about, and the door finally pulled open in two jolts—the first about a foot, the second another foot and a half.

"Would you like to go first?" Win calmly asked as if they were about to enter the Elm Street House in search of Freddy Krueger.

"No!" Betsy desperately gasped, her face filled with terror. "I'll follow you."

Winston took a crunchy step, making his way inside cautiously. Betsy clutched onto his shoulder.

"Oh, my God," he felt her breathe onto the back of his neck.

They stepped inside like two Little Debbie Swiss Rolls tucked together in an unopened package, immediately realizing that this house was not a home—it was a flea market that had lost control of its inventory. Sheer clutter filled every inch of available space. 2'x2' moving boxes, layered sandwich-style like a quadruple Big Mac, with newspapers and magazines topped with FedEx, UPS, QVC, Amazon, and HSN boxes topped with shopping bags from Kmart, Casual Corner, Walmart, Goodwill, Fashion Bug, Target, Hahn's Shoes, Mervyn's, Payless, Sycamore Shops, Kohl's, Bed Bath & Beyond, and Macy's, topped with more newspapers and magazines, and stood like unstable Jenga towers, threatening to collapse at any moment. Every surface groaned under so many violated laws of gravity and physics.

The once-grand architecture of the home and its furnishings were now buried beneath an Everest of possessions—obscured by mountains of discount-store bargains piled higher than humans, creating absolutely nothing but chaos and disorder. Furniture was buried under layers of clothing, books, and hundreds if not thousands more shopping bags and boxes from Thom McAn, Hook's Drug, Service Merchandise, Wilson's, Dollar General, Ace Hardware, Meijer, Wayfair, KB Toys, Ulta Beauty, The Salvation Army, G. C. Murphy, JCPenney, Linens N

Things, Blockbuster Video, Musicland, and Walgreens. The beautiful stairwell sconces were hidden behind tall pillars of … well, you name it—heaped from the foyer floor up to *and into* the second-floor wing because no bargain could be left behind. Clothing with price tags draped over everything everywhere, like misfit decorative tassels shunned by their curtain tieback cousins abandoned by Macy's and left for dead at HomeGoods.

Betsy and Winston squeezed through what barely passed as a walkway, forced to navigate the house as if playing a high-stakes game of Twister. Having spent his childhood here, Winston should have known where they were standing—but, alas, the house had transformed into a maze with no apparent exit, and he hadn't a clue.

Dim lighting cast ominous shadows, while the air smelled like an antique store had been locked in a sauna for a decade. The atmosphere was thick with must, mildew, and the faint desperation of a thousand impulse purchases.

Winston's heart suddenly ached over the palpable sense of isolation and loneliness his mother undoubtedly had been living in *and* the realization she was, in fact, being slowly consumed by a shrinking labyrinth of her own making, trapping her to suffocate on mere possessions.

Betsy released him once she was close to a stack of cardboard boxes that were low enough, and she could grip them with her fingertips without them toppling over. Breathing heavily, she declared in an intense whisper with the urgency of someone discovering a bomb, "Oh God, Winston … there's no place to sit."

Win stood, clutching his mouth, looking at *everything*. "Oh, my God …" he said under his breath.

Betsy caught sight of cobwebs draping from the ceiling. "Oh, my God …" she said under her breath.

Win leaned over to read the date on a newspaper from 1999. "Oh, my God …" he repeated under his breath.

Betsy looked into an open bag of bloated baked bean cans about to explode, which had to have been purchased in the 1980s or earlier. "Oh, my God ..." she repeated under her breath.

Suddenly, Winston's elbow brushed against a teetering stack of more boxes, bags, newspapers, coupons, and draped clothing, and then he heard it slide. Stopping in his tracks, he turned to watch the top half just call it a fucking day, and slowly ... ever so slowly ... avalanche against another stack of shit, that avalanched against another stack of more shit ... that avalanched against another, and then another, until the cascade found the lowest loser heap of more shit, and collapsed there until was nothing left to spew. The dumpster dominos went all out—toppling in a straight line through the middle of the house, exploding dust into the air like a deployed canister of tear gas.

Win's mouth fell open like a trap door as he stared at the newly made scattered debris field. His gaze shot to Betsy, whose jaw also dropped onto the floor.

Locking eyes, she mouthed without a sound, *"Oh! My! God!"*

Winston stared back and silently screamed, *"Fuck!"*

From somewhere deep within the jungle of junk, they heard a blood-curdling shriek: "WHAT WAS *THAT?!"*

Acoustics bounced Marci's voice through the house like a ghostly echo, making it impossible to tell where she really was. Then, from behind a towering stack of who-knows-what, she emerged.

Winston's mother—tightly wrapped in a blue terry cloth robe—appeared like a plump blueberry rolling in for damage assessment. Her once-vibrant, beautiful face was pale and gaunt with dark raccoon circles around her eyes, framed by unwashed silver hair matted to her head. She wore the unmistakable expression of a woman whose world had just been shaken.

Win was taken aback.

This was as far as she had gotten ready?

Marci gasped at the crash site. Horrified, distraught moans escaped her lips, "OOOHHH! *OOOHHH!"*

Suddenly reverting to ten-year-old guilt mode, Winston stammered, "I'm sorry, Mom. I turned and bumped it, and it slid over. I am *so* sorry."

Aunt Betsy sneezed. Winston blessed her.

Marci clutched her chest like someone had just knocked over a priceless artifact instead of expired coupons and 17-year-old magazines.

"BE CAREFUL! EVERYTHING IN HERE IS *PRECIOUS!*

"*PRECIOUS*, I say."

Winston reached out for a hug, but Marci was too deep in her forensic investigation of the wreckage. She let out another dramatic moan.

"Something *had* to have broken in there.

"It just *haaad to have*.

"*Ooohhh … just the sight of it makes me siiick!*

"I'm just *sick*, I tell you! *Siiick!*"

"Oh, my God," Betsy muttered, sneezing again.

Marci snapped, "DON'T START WITH ME ELIZABETH! I'M IN NO MOOD FOR YOUR GOD RIGHT NOW!"

Then, as if nothing had just happened, Marci slowly turned to her son, arms outstretched—finally ready for a hug. Win leaned in, gently squeezing her, and immediately felt like he was hugging a human radiator.

Pulling back, he pressed the back of his hand to her forehead. "You're warm, Mom. Are you feeling okay?"

"I'm tired," she sighed, looking like the physical embodiment of exhaustion. "And I'm tired of being tired."

Ever the optimist, Betsy smiled and asked, "Do you have a place for me to sit, Marci?"

Marci's response was swift and dramatic. "DOES IT *FUCKING* LOOK LIKE IT?! IF YOU HAVE TO SIT YOUR GODDAMN ASS DOWN RIGHT THIS MINUTE, THEN GO SIT IN THE CAR!"

Betsy gasped like she had just been slapped with a wet fish. "Well! That was uncalled for, Marci."

Winston winced. His heart went out to his Aunt Betsy.

She sneezed again. Win blessed her again.

Marci, completely unbothered, waved a hand before disappearing into the labyrinth. "Give me a minute to fix my face and put on my wig, and I'll be ready."

Betsy sneezed. Then sneezed again. And then, just for fun, sneezed three more times. Gasping like she had just run through a pollen factory, she turned to Winston, eyes filled with agony. "Oh my God, Winston … I want to return to the car!"

From deep inside the clutter vortex, Marci's voice shouted, "THAT'S PROBABLY BEST! YOU'RE SPREADING GERMS EVERYWHERE!"

Winston, ever the gentleman, asked, "Would you like me to walk you out?"

"Please," Betsy exhaled with the relief of a woman being granted parole.

Carefully navigating the maze of mayhem, Win instructed Betsy to turn around and lead them single file. It was the only way to make it out without triggering another avalanche of hoarder debris that could bury them alive. He gingerly made his way behind her, careful not to body-bump *anything*. Several slow, cautious steps later, they finally emerged into the night.

Betsy paused on the sidewalk, gulping in the fresh air like it was the first oxygen she'd had in years. "It's so much worse than last time. You can't even see the furniture anymore."

She sneezed again. He blessed her again.

Win simply shook his head, defeated. "Mom can't keep living like this. It's dangerous in there. I'll have to talk to my sister about it."

Betsy gently patted his arm. Peters, waiting by the car, stepped forward. "Everything okay?"

Winston nodded. "Mother is getting ready." Then, passing Betsy's arm to Peters like a relay baton, he sighed and turned back to the house of horrors.

Carefully maneuvering through the narrow pathway, Winston called, "Mom?"

From the depths of the junk jungle came an immediate, *rage-filled* scream: "I'M PUTTING MY MAKEUP ON!"

"Just letting you know I'm here," he called back loud enough for her to hear … *wherever that was*.

Looking around, Win could barely recognize the house of his childhood. The once-grand foyer was gone, swallowed whole by hoards of stuff from stores that *no longer existed*. The grand staircase had been reduced to a single-person squeeze-through, with mountains of crap stacked on each step, daring anyone to attempt a climb.

Marci appeared behind him *like a damn ghost*.

"Let's go," she declared.

Winston jumped. She had covered her dark circles with concealer, applied an alarmingly orange shade of lipstick, and was now sporting a wig—which *almost* gave the illusion that she had her life together.

Smiling, he leaned down to give her another hug, which she was all too happy to accept. Marci still felt too warm to him and was huffing a little. Her breathing wasn't normal.

He smiled. "You look pretty."

"Bullshit," she deadpanned, adjusting the wig with a grunt.

Win reached around her hairline to gently push her silver strands into the wig. "Turn around, Mom. Let me do the back," he softly guided.

As he did one last check, she suddenly beamed with pride. "It's a Cool Style Jane Fonda wig I bought at the Goodwill," she said proudly.

Winston gave a supportive nod. "It's a good look on you."

Marci sighed dramatically, her face twisting into a frown. "Well, I'm ready. Let's go say goodbye to my darling sister."

Winston hesitated. "Mom?"

"Yes, sugar lump?" she asked sweetly.

"—Wouldn't you like to *get dressed first*?"

She glanced down. "Oh!"

"Or go as is," he teased.

Her expression immediately soured. "Shit, now I have to put a bra on!" Marci angrily whined, shaking her head.

Bursting into a rage of disgust, she slowly rotated, punched her tiny fist in the air as if she were flipping off God, then screamed as she vanished into the clutter, "GODDAMMIT! DAMN IT TO *FUCKING HELL!*"

Paramnesia

There was nothing to say. The return to Bucks Peak was silent and heavy, the weight of Darceline Hicks' passing settling over the car like a thick fog. Winston heard his mother sniffle first, then Betsy as she turned to the window, holding a handkerchief to dab at her nose between sneezes. Even Mr. Peters let out the occasional discreet sniffle. For the moment, Win's own eyes remained dry.

As they pulled into D's driveway, Marci broke the silence. "Betsy, just so you know … I couldn't reach around to snap my bra on, so I'm going without. My bazongas are hanging like tree limbs, ready for Edward Rice Burroughs's Tarzan to have a good swing."

Betsy gasped, literally clutching her pearls. *"Oh, Marceline!"*

Winston grinned, hearing his mother chuckle from the exact response she was hoping to get from her sister-in-law. In the rearview mirror, he caught Peters shaking his head, his expression plainly stating this wasn't his first rodeo with these two women.

"I need both of you strong men to help me up those steps," Marci announced once they parked behind Uncle Phil's classic import.

Peters turned to Betsy. "I'll help you inside first," he said before stepping out and walking around the car.

Win watched his aunt exit the Imperial on her own, steady and sure-footed despite her size. Betsy had spent her entire life on her feet—cooking, cleaning, continually moving. His mother, on the other hand, was the opposite. Decades of sitting on the couch, ordering from shopping channels around the clock had left her body stiff and uncooperative.

Like back at her house, while getting dressed, Marci had needed Winston's help to pull up her black stretchy slacks, slip on her flat shoes, and put on a black and green Bob Mackie tweed jacket that could no longer button. Her oversized black top draped her enormous, unsupported chest—a fact she seemed to take more humor in than anyone else. And now, seeing her pale, overheated, and struggling to move, Win knew she would need assistance at every turn that evening.

Bookending her, he and Peters helped her up the steps at a snail's pace, pausing after each footstep to catch her breath. They had just stepped inside when Marci dramatically announced, as if she had just been felled by the vapors, "I need to sit. I can't go on. I need a minute."

After carefully placing her in the same high-back wing chair Betsy had been in earlier, Mr. Peters patiently asked, "Marci, would you like me to angle the chair by your sister so you can face her?"

"That would be nice, Jonathan," she wheezed, sounding worse by the minute.

The house was still oppressively warm. Winston removed his blazer and draped it over the empty chair in the entryway beside her.

She gave him a tired smile.

"Would you like some water?" Win asked gently.

"Maybe later," she said, reaching for his hand. "I want to ask you something."

He squeezed her fingers lightly and crouched beside her so they were at eye level.

"Did you and Darci have a chance to talk before she …"

"Yes," he answered before she could finish, reassuringly smiling.

Darceline's siblings were the only ones allowed to call her 'Darci.' Per D, no one else on the planet had the privilege—not even Winston.

"Did she give you the option to stand down?" Marci asked.

"Yes."

Her face contorted with emotion, a joyful wince as tears welled in her eyes. She swallowed hard and whispered hoarsely, "Good. She said she would."

Wiping her eyes, she asked, "Did Darci tell you why?"

He nodded. "My heart broke when she told me about Violet."

Something inside Marci cracked. She choked back a sob. "No one will ever know how painful it was for Darci to step into Daddy's shoes and surrender everything she wanted in life—including her true identity. Your uncles and I had it made while my sweet sister had to make it on her own, all alone."

She pulled a crumpled tissue from her jacket to blot her nose. "I am so happy she found Penny. I believe she healed her loss of Violet."

Win felt himself tear up again, noting how his mother and her twin could sometimes pair words identically.

"I haven't mentioned our conversation to anyone," he said softly.

"There's no need," Marci gruffly said, dabbing at her eyes.

"I know you thought it was unfair how we got you home, but Darci felt an extreme urgency to see you in person," she continued. "She could always sense things. And she must have known her end was near."

Winston nodded, his throat too tight to speak.

For a moment, mother and son simply looked at one another.

"I love you, Mom," he whispered.

"I love you, Sugar Lump," she whispered back, pulling him into a hug.

When they finally pulled apart, Win stood, removed his glasses, and wiped his eyes. "Shall we head on in?" he asked, slipping them back on.

Marci inhaled deeply, releasing it like she was about to tackle an impossible feat. Scooting to the edge of the chair, she gathered her strength to stand. At a slow, deliberate pace, they strolled the long foyer toward the Grand Room, pausing several times for Marci to catch her breath.

Phil and Tami were on a yelling time-out when they entered. The family sat in an uneasy silence. Mr. Peters and Mr. de Beaumont stood by the bar. All eyes followed Winston as he guided his mother to a chair facing her sister.

Win crossed the room and stood beside his Uncle Bill, now settled into a club chair beside a loveseat. The houseman and lawyer discreetly slipped into the kitchen, granting them privacy.

Marci leaned forward, silently weeping, placing her hand on her sister's.

No one said a word. Not a single mention of "no touching."

"Bless you, my darling sister, for being the strong one," Marci spoke hoarsely. "We all know the sacrifices you made for this family. I will always love you. And … well … I guess I'll see you on the other side soon enough."

Winston scanned the room. There wasn't a dry eye in sight—except for Uncle Bill, who sat unmoved, watching his two sisters.

As sniffles circled the room, Win bowed his head in silent prayer, thanking his Aunt Darceline again for *the out*.

A few minutes of silence passed before Marci dried her eyes and asked, without looking up, "Is everyone here for a quorum?"

"Yes," Phil replied in a normal voice.

"Yes," said Betsy.

"Yes," Tami added.

Bill suddenly broke into a grieving sob, burying his face in his hands. Marci turned in her seat, gazing at her brother before slowly rising and shuffling over to the black leather loveseat beside him.

"Bill?" she asked gently, sitting.

He continued to weep, his shoulders shaking. Betsy stepped beside him, rubbing his upper back in slow, soothing strokes. Finally, he nodded, sat up, and cleared his throat. Wiping his eyes, he choked out, "Yes. I'm here."

Marci looked at her son. "Winston, you will be the one to explain this family tradition to your sister and your cousins."

Winston met the expectant gazes of the family before nodding.

Marci took a breath and began, her voice solemn. "We, thy family of honor, acknowledge and confirm the death of our matriarch, Darceline Isabel Hicks. We are forever grateful for her servitude and generosity to our family and wish her peace in the heavenly otherworld. And it is so."

Win's uncles and aunts echoed, "And it is so."

That's IT?! Winston's mind reeled.

THAT'S the family tradition? 'And it is so?!'

What the fuck?!

He reached for his cigarette case to step outside and cool this mental fit down while he hyper-chain-smoked.

Then—clop, clop. Clop, clop. A rhythmic sound echoed from the foyer.

As it grew louder, Win watched Betsy dramatically motion for silence, tapping her ear and pointing toward the entryway. Her mouth formed the words, *"Listen!"*

Clop, clop. Clop, clop. Clop, clop.

And then, as if summoned, an enormous six-point buck appeared. It strode into the Grand Room's entryway and stopped. The buck's gaze was fixed on the back of the chair where Darceline sat. A stunned hush filled the room. Unable to see, Marci slowly rose, shuffling forward until she saw it.

A wheezy gasp of elated surprise cooed from her lips. *"Ooooo ..."*

The buck stepped back, exhaled a deep, throaty grunt, then dipped its head, turned, and walked out the way it had come.

Marci clutched her chest. *"Ohhh, my ...* The handsome buck! He was Darci's favorite."

Win exhaled in amazement, the experience returning his Zen. "Incredible."

"Wow!" Tami roared, eyes wide.

Bill chuckled, shaking his head in disbelief.

"He just walked in, said goodbye, and left!" Phil declared, laughing. "Ha!"

Marci staggered back to the loveseat.

Betsy, still frazzled, blurted, "How on earth did he get in?!"

"The front doors are open to cool the place down," Win admitted.

"I'm closing them," Betsy huffed, marching toward the foyer. "We don't need all of Darceline's woodland creatures waltzing in to pay their respects while I'm in the ladies' room."

"Why not, Elizabeth?" Marci called after her. "Her land is their land! She loved them, and they loved her!"

Tami quipped dryly, "That'll certainly give her nerves something to tinkle over."

Marci let out a wheezing giggle, but her laughter quickly became labored breathing. Sweat glistened on her brow. "It's so hot in here," she complained, struggling to catch her breath. "Win, help me out of this jacket."

As he carefully removed it, she sighed. "My sister, the waif, was always cold. But goddammit, if she didn't keep this place blazing enough to scald a lizard!"

Marci suddenly wobbled, her breathing heavier. "I need to lie down."

Winston quickly helped her settle onto the loveseat, tucking a pillow beneath her head. Stepping back, he noticed how her short frame fit perfectly, the furniture cradling her as though it had been waiting for this moment. He fetched a glass of water and placed it beside her on a coffee table.

Peters entered from the kitchen, and Winston caught his attention with a tilt toward the foyer.

Win met up with him and quietly asked, "Is Dr. Funnell on his way?"

"He should be here any minute."

"Good." Win exhaled. "Can you have the kitchen bring out some coffee?"

"Right away. The chef has prepared an array of hors d'oeuvres for the buffet."

"Thank you."

de Beaumont stepped into the foyer. "Was the family tradition held?"

Winston nodded.

"Fine. I'll make the next tier of calls."

As he turned to leave, Win added, "Leland, please call my sister first. Our mother is ill, and I feel she needs to go to the hospital."

Peters mentioned the doctor was on his way to de Beaumont. Leland agreed.

The gentlemen nodded and parted ways. Win returned to his mother's side. Her eyes were closed, her breathing still ragged. The family exchanged uneasy glances.

Bill pointed to Marci with raised eyebrows, his expression asking, *What's wrong with her?*

Winston shook his head. "Dr. Funnell is on his way," he reassured.

Tami stood, lifting an empty glass. "Anyone for a drink?"

Win's mind immediately shouted, *Yes!*

His uncles and Betsy followed her to the bar. Winston, meanwhile, reached for his cigarette case—opting for one vice over another—and turned to step outside.

Before he could leave, Marci choked out, "Winston?"

He immediately turned back. "Yes, Mom?"

Her eyes remained shut. "Son?"

"I'm right here." He sat beside her, resting a hand on her warm forearm.

She fluttered her lids open, locking eyes with him. Her voice raspy, as she whispered, "I have something to confess."

Win leaned in closer.

"I did something horrible to your father … and I have to tell you what it was."

He stayed silent, waiting.

Marci swallowed hard. "When you were in high school—before I filed for divorce—we went to the club for bridge. I wasn't on my game. We lost. Max was furious.

"We quarreled in the car. We argued while undressing. Then, somehow, we ended up on the second-floor landing. He went downstairs. I was so angry—I ripped off my wig and threw it. He came storming back up, rage in his eyes … and … and …"

Win tilted his head.

"And then I pushed him," she choked out. "And he fell backward down the stairs.

"That's how he dislocated his shoulder."

"What?" Win blurted. "No. That's not what happened."

"Yes, son. I tried to kill your father."

"No. That's not true. I was there."

"Honey, we were alone in the house."

"No. You may have thought so, but I just got home from the bowling alley. I was in the kitchen when it happened."

"That's not possible."

"It is. I saw everything, Mom. I saw the whole thing! You came screaming from your bedroom and stopped on the landing. Dad was behind you. There were words. He went down the stairs. You screamed. He laughed. You ripped your wig off and threw it. It hit one of the sconces along the stairs—a piece of glass fell. He laughed, then ran up the stairs to where you had more words. And then you stormed off to your bedroom.

"Dad turned to go downstairs … and he slipped on the piece of sconce. Boom, boom, boom. Down he went."

Marci was in astonished shock. "You were there?"

"I was there."

"You saw it happen?"

"I saw the whole thing."

"I didn't push him?"

"No."

Her eyes widened, turning to stare back at the ceiling. Slowly, her lips quivered, and then she exhaled deeply—as if releasing years of pent-up guilt.

With a choked sob, she whispered, "Your father told his divorce attorney I pushed him down the stairs."

"That's not what happened," Win soothed.

Tears rolled down her cheeks. She looked at her son, confirming, "I didn't try to kill him?"

"No."

Marci looked back at the ceiling in disbelief. "I didn't do it … I didn't do it."

He leaned close, whispering, "Let it go, Mom. You did nothing wrong. Dad fell down the stairs all by himself. I drove him to the emergency room, where they popped his shoulder back in, and I drove us home."

She quietly cried, nodding, soggily repeating to herself with overwhelmed relief, "I didn't do it. I didn't do it."

Sensing her deep anguish, Winston laid his head next to hers to softly reverberate, "No. You did not do it. You did not do it."

"I *didn't* do it," his mother gasped, suddenly remembering, her eyes widening. Marci took a deep breath with an abrupt sense of clarity. She rolled her head to look at Winston.

A peaceful smile spread across her lips. "I can let go."

Win's stomach dropped. That frightened him. He sat up with a sudden concern. "Mom—"

Marci folded her arms across her chest, staring at him with adoration.

"Mom, you can let *it* go."

Changing the subject, he primed with enthusiasm, "Hey, Sissy is on her way … she'll be here any minute."

"That's good," Marci wheezed. "I want to see my baby girl sitting

beside my baby boy.
    "Then I can let go."

Ben Fun

Once his mother closed her eyes to rest, Winston reopened the front doors Betsy had shut and grabbed his blazer from the high-back chair, slipping it on. He began pacing the drive around the fountain, smoking—uneasy about what his mother had said. After several drags, he spotted headlights flickering through the trees and hoped it was his sister. He made his way back to the front porch to greet her.

A new white Yukon Denali pulled up the drive and around the circle without slowing to inspect Bill's wrecked car. A striking woman in her late thirties with sleek black hair smiled from the passenger seat. This was not his sister.

The driver, a sharp salt-and-pepper type who looked like the lead in a medical drama titled *Diagnosis: Hot,* popped out. He walked around to open her door and took her hand. Together, they approached Winston, dressed in business casual, their smiles subdued.

"Hello, I'm Dr. Ben Funnell, and this is my wife, Amanda," the man greeted. "My apologies for the delay. We were having a late supper at the club."

"Hello, Doctor. Amanda." Winston extended a hand. "I wish this were under better circumstances. Thank you for coming."

"Our condolences," Amanda offered, her smile tinged with sorrow. "Miss Darceline was the most generous woman I've ever met."

Dr. Funnell added, "My wife is President of the Hicks America Foundation."

"I've worked closely with your aunt for many years. We'll miss her dearly."

Winston gave Amanda a soft, polite smile. "Thank you for sharing. Aunt D certainly cherished her philanthropy." He turned to Funnell. "Doctor, my mother has a fever and has been panting all evening. She can't seem to catch her breath and has been clutching her heart. This isn't mere grief—something is physically wrong with her."

Dr. Funnell's expression turned serious. "Right." He broke from his wife, hurrying to the rear of the SUV to retrieve his medical bag.

"Head on home with the kids," he told Amanda before kissing her goodbye.

"Okay." She turned to Winston. "Again, my deepest condolences. I hope your mother feels better."

"Thank you." He smiled cordially, watching her move to the driver's side.

After taking a long final drag, Win stepped to the wall ashtray, snuffing out his cigarette. Dr. Funnell stepped beside him as he exhaled the last plume of smoke. Once inside, Winston discreetly popped a mint into his mouth.

"Dr. Funnell, were you Darceline's primary physician?" he asked as they walked.

"Yes."

"My aunt and I had just sat down for dinner when she started one of her coughing jags. A minute later, she was gone. The time was around 7:45, in case you need to record it."

The doctor listened intently as Winston continued. "She's still seated at the dining room table. Per her wishes, she will not be touched or moved for three hours."

Dr. Funnell quirked a brow. "May I be blunt?"

"Of course."

"Miss Darceline had requested me to personally call her time of death when she expired. How am I to do that without touching her?"

Winston smirked. "Try not to let the staff see you." He shook his head. "It's a thing. I touched her neck to check for a pulse, and they lost their minds."

"Oh." The doctor sputtered.

"Exactly." Winston gestured toward the Grand Room. "My mother is on the sofa by the windows on the left."

"I understand," Dr. Funnell said, though his expression suggested otherwise.

As they stepped inside, Winston mentally noted how Dr. Funnell, Mitch, Leland, and Mr. Peters were the only ones who didn't reek of alcohol. A sudden screech of tires outside made him glance toward the open doors.

Win led the doctor into the Grand Room to his aunt.

Dr. Funnell immediately noted, "She's sitting up."

"Yes."

"She's not listing to one side or slumped over."

"No. She's in the exact position she was when she died."

Intrigued, Dr. Funnell let out a thoughtful hum.

Winston observed as the doctor studied Darceline. His gaze settled on her hands, still loosely gripping the arms of the mammoth chair. "How unusual."

He looked at Winston.

"When the body dies," he explained, "the brain stops sending signals to the muscles, causing them to relax and go limp." His focus returned to Darceline. "Yet your aunt's posture remains upright and perfectly vertical."

Dr. Funnell leaned in, stretching his neck for a closer look. "Hmm."

Winston decided to leave him to his medical deductions, excused himself, and turned toward the foyer. He spotted his sister crouching on the front porch through the open doors, hurriedly gathering spilled items from her oversized steamer trunk purse. He smiled as he approached.

"Willow?" he called.

She flinched, whining in startled frustration, "Geez Louise, Winston!" before sighing and abandoning her purse altogether. She stood and threw her arms around him, hugging him tightly.

They held onto each other before she pulled away, her breath laced with alcohol. "My head is spinning. I can't believe Aunt D is gone. What's wrong with Mom? And I'm so glad you're here."

Winston smiled at her adorable scatterbrained nature, realizing how much he'd missed her goofiness. He took in her beautiful face—hazel-blue eyes, perfect lips—and her long, naturally blonde hair flowing in the nighttime breeze. She was tan from hours in a sunbed, dressed in tight skinny jeans that accentuated her slim figure. A men's white sleeveless tank clung to her perky chest, layered under a fitted denim shirt, fastened by a single button at her stomach.

This fabulous-looking middle-aged broad gave him a delighted grin and said, "Hey, Mom finally spilled the beans—you checked into rehab. Was it for pills and booze?"

Winston pressed his lips together in a smirk before replying, "Jack and coke."

"*Ooohhh!*" Willow gasped theatrically. "The dynamic duo got ya, huh?"

"Yeah."

She pursed her lips, tilting her head before pulling him into another hug—this one longer, tighter. Slowly pulling away, she looked him over and asked, "Why *are* you here?"

Wilhelmina

Winston's baby sister was a stunner, the kind of beautiful who turned heads at gas stations and made old men forget why they were holding the pump. She grew into a full-fledged social butterfly, using humor not just as a coping mechanism for the minefield of crushed eggshells in the Clarke household but also as a strategic distraction from the whole "spoiled Hicks heir" reputation. Four years younger than Win, Wilhelmina quickly observed her brother's winning strategy: be funny, be kind, and people won't care if your family name is plastered on half the county's real estate. She became a masterful jokester, gifted with the talent of telling the cleanest and filthiest stories—sometimes in the same sentence.

From day one, Max and Marci drilled the gospel of hard work into their kids. No free rides. If Winston wanted to spend money, he earned it by mowing lawns and detailing pontoon boats for lakefront neighbors. Conversely, Wilhelmina embraced the noble art of babysitting, wrangling kids like a teenage Mary Poppins—if Mary Poppins had a fondness for bubblegum lip gloss and a never-ending stash of Skittles.

When she hit the magical age of sixteen, Sissy and/or Willow, as she was known, took her first 'real' job at the Hicksville Country Club as a hostess. It was cute initially, smiling sweetly at well-to-do patrons in pastel polos and pearls. But then came the polite laughs at golf jokes and the unbearable frequency of the phrase "My usual table, dear." After a year of that nonsense, she defected to the bowling alley across town—Balls & Beers—where the dress code was 'whatever doesn't smell like chicken wings,' and conversations involved fewer stock portfolios and more 'hold my beer and watch this.'

Darceline had her eye on Willow's hustle. Six months into the gig, Sissy was promoted to closing manager on the Balls side of the business. "When you turn twenty-one," Aunt D said with a mischievous glint, "you can slide over to the Beers' side if you like."

School, however, was Willow's arch-nemesis. She survived it like a prisoner tallying days on a wall. Max and Marci were crushed when she nixed the idea of college. Darceline, however, delightedly waved a metaphorical pom-pom. "If you're not going to Indiana University, you might as well run a bowling alley," she declared, practically ready to commission a gold-plated name tag for her niece.

During her early Beers years, Willow married a mechanic who had recently moved to town, working for Uncle Phil at the Hicksville Marina. His name was Todd, and the only thing attractive about him was his good looks—it turned out he had more fists than feelings. After three years and enough of the black eyes, she kicked him to the curb with a divorce and reclaimed her maiden name. As a single mom of three rowdy boys, she made a name for herself as the county's funniest bartender, slinging jokes as quickly as she poured shots.

On her twenty-fifth birthday, Win called her in the late afternoon to give her some well-wishes and a couple of good laughs. In return, she gave him the story of a lifetime.

Aunt Darceline had invited Willow over for a private birthday lunch. After some bourbon-soaked laughter, D presented her niece with two gift-wrapped boxes. One was tied with a blue ribbon, the other with green. Ever the dramatic matriarch, Aunt D lit a cigarette, informed Willow that the blue ribbon gift was a birthday present, and asked if she would like to buy the green ribbon box for one dollar—payable only by check. Both amused and curious, Willow pulled out her checkbook from her king-sized purse and was always up for a good game of *Let's Make a Deal!*

Upon opening the first gift, Sissy found a crisp white polo with the Balls & Beers logo nicely embroidered on its front. Classic. But in the second box? A Bill of Sale for the bar and bowling alley. For $1, she becomes the proud owner of Balls & Beers.

"And what if I had said no?" Sissy had asked her aunt, still basking in the Oprah-level shock.

"Then you'd have a lovely polo shirt," Darceline quipped with a devilish grin.

Winston howled when she recounted it, swearing he could practically hear Aunt D's voice through the phone. On that special day, Sissy had officially bowled a perfect game in the family legacy.

Lighting another cigarette, Winston perched on the front step like a man awaiting a court summons. At the same time, Sissy corralled the chaotic contents of her Hermès Birkin purse—which, by the looks of it, had recently attempted to flee. Out tumbled not one, but two hairbrushes, a travel hair dryer (because you never know when a power blowout will strike), a pack of gum that had clearly staged a rebellion, several pens, a Kindle reader gasping for air, a stack of Post-its with cryptic half-finished notes, her pocketbook wallet packed with receipts, a makeup bag made of clear see-through plastic showing its contents cram-packed in, half a dozen random colored hair scrunchies, a protein bar, a small hammer ('for emergencies,' she insisted), a small air pump for a volleyball or bicycle tire, and, just to keep things interesting, a silver handgun that winked in the moonlight like a mischievous party trick.

Win kept his thoughts to himself, though he did mentally assign odds on which item would next fall victim to the Great Birkin Purge. Grinning, he asked, "May I ask how this particular disaster occurred?"

Willow sighed, the universal sound of a woman who had seen some shit. She reached for his cigarette, taking a drag. Letting her keep it, he pulled out another and lit up.

"In my rush to get into the house, I forgot my phone in the car. So, I set the bag on the step. By the time I came back, it had toppled over like a drunk bridesmaid and puked its guts out all over the stairs."

Winston chuckled, missing the way she turned everything into a dramatic adventure.

"Oh, sure, laugh it up, Giggles. Next time, I'll just let the gun shoot its way out," she sneered, wrapping an arm around his back and leaning into his shoulder. "How I've missed that laugh."

He smiled. The two smoked.

"Where are the boys?" Win asked, knowing his nephews were grown men in their twenties.

"It's Monday night football, and the bar's packed. The four of us were jamming nonstop. I didn't tell them what happened—just that I was needed at Aunt D's and to lock up after closing."

Winston nodded and said, "This will be a rough week."

"Who's here?" She asked.

"Mom, and the aunts and uncles. The doctor just arrived to call Aunt D's death and have a look at Mom. The rest are on their way."

"What's wrong with Mom?"

Win shook his head. "Aunt Betsy and I went to pick her up. She felt feverish and couldn't breathe properly—like she was gasping for air. She's inside lying down."

"Has she made it all about her yet?"

"No," he said thoughtfully. "Actually, Mom said something earlier that jarred me. I think … I think Mom's ready to go."

Willow scowled, releasing him. "Go where?! Her twin sister dies, and she's ready to get up and leave?"

Win placed a hand on her knee, looking her in the eyes. Then he pointed skyward. "She's ready to go."

Willow's expression faltered. "What?"

Win nodded.

"Oh, fuck," she groaned. "So, she *is* making this all about her."

He shook his head. "I don't think so, Willow. I think she's really sick. And … Darceline's death has given her some sort of peace. Or maybe she just doesn't want to fight anymore. I don't know."

"We'll see," she muttered skeptically.

"Yeah," Win sighed, knowing she may be right.

Her voice softened. "I can't believe it. Aunt D's really gone," she whispered, shaking her head as her eyes welled with tears, taking another drag.

"Yeah," Win sighed, his face turning grim.

Willow, of course, could never leave things solemn for too long.

"Nobody dies for years, and two kick the bucket within an hour on the same day," Willow said heavily.

Win blinked. "Wait. Who else died?"

"Remember Cheri Yoder?"

He didn't.

"She would've been Cheri Delabarre in high school—the grade after yours."

"Oh," he nodded, smiling at the memory. "Yeah, I remember Cheri Delabarre. How is she?"

"Flatlined."

"What?"

Willow stared at the water fountain. "She stroked out or had a heart attack drunk screaming 'SHUT THE FUCK UP!' at her neighbor."

Win's brow furrowed. "*Ooo.* … that's an ugly way to go out."

"Yeah. Before Leland called me, word started buzzing around the lake: Cheri Yoder keeled over."

Win quipped, "Sounds like she's the one who shut the fuck up."

Willow pulled out her phone and sighed. "My phone's been blowing up. The whole county is talking about it."

She read aloud a message, shaking her head. "'How tragic. This town has lost one of its greatest champions.'"

Win frowned.

Willow smirked and read another: "'Our undefeated Fartgasm Champion is gone and is undoubtedly shitting herself about now.'"

Win's jaw dropped. "Do I even want to know what that means?"

"Probably not," Sissy said, sensing he really didn't.

After taking a long drag, she exhaled. "What a clusterfuck."

"Like your purse?" Win retorted, barely able to contain the smirk tugging at his lips.

"Don't start," she shot back, dragging from the cig like Bette Davis would in a dramatic black and white film.

They smoked in silence until Winston turned to her. "When was the last time you went to see Mom?"

"I popped in Thursday to clean her kitchen and bathroom. Why?"

He blinked. "Why?! That place is dangerous! Mom can't live like that. No one could."

Willow exhaled, looking exhausted. "Look, I've spent *years* trying to get her to stop hoarding. Do you know how many hours I've wasted arguing with her about it? So, one day, I just gave up. Now, I just do what I can—her laundry, cleaning what I *can* get to, stacking the crap she buys higher and higher because there's nowhere else to put it."

Win exhaled sharply. "We have to do something. She *can't* live like this."

Willow gave him a slow, sarcastic smile. "Wow. What a thrill it is to have you back. And now that you're here, I am more than happy to share Mom's funhouse with you."

She stood. "In fact, you can have Mom's crazy place all to yourself. Welcome home, big brother."

Win reached over, gently patting her shin. "Hey, I'm not criticizing you."

He stood beside her. "I appreciate everything you've done for Mom. I can only imagine what you've been through.

"But I'm here now. And I'll help however I can. Okay?"

Willow exhaled, giving him a relieved smile. "Thank you. It's been *hell* dealing with her."

Win pulled her in for a firm hug. "I understand … but I *don't* understand. If that makes any sense."

Willow chuckled, knowing exactly what he meant. They both nodded in quiet agreement.

Then, like her brother, ever the one to break up awkward moments with a splash of humor, she smirked. "So, what's with Uncle Bill's car fucking the house?"

Win laughed. "He hit the gas instead of the brakes."

"Oh, shit."

"Yep."

Suddenly, Willow squinted at him. "You really *are* sober?"

"Yeah."

"Well, fuck!" she huffed. "Here I was thinking I'd have my boozing buddy back to get through tonight, and that guy isn't even here. *Fan-f'n-tastic!*"

With an over-the-top groan, she picked up her suitcase-sized purse, stubbed out her cigarette, and stormed inside.

Win shook his head, chuckling. "Yep. Half a cigarette was all it took before making this all about *you*, Sissy."

Then, headlights swept across the front lawn. A two-tone silver and dark red Mercedes-Maybach S-Class SUV glided up the drive, parking behind Sissy's truck.

It appeared his sister wouldn't be the only one inflicting loud, jarring needle scrapes across an LP tonight—Cousin Sally just pulled up.

Win exhaled with a sarcastic thought, *"Terrific! The human version of a 'Mayday' signal has arrived in her chariot."*

Uncle Tilly

While Darceline Hicks navigated uncharted waters as the new leader of Hicks America—stepping into the role immediately after the sudden death of her father, Theodore, it was a given that her youngest sibling, ten-year-old Tillson Hicks, or "Tilly" as he was called, would remain at the homestead with her, Phil, and Bill. Ever since their mother had died from complications during Tilly's birth, Darceline, Marci, and their brothers had stepped in to help raise him. At the same time, Theodore focused on running the family businesses.

Not two weeks had passed since Darceline had lost her battle with the elders, having to give up Violet, when her Aunt Edna—Theodore's only sister—arrived unannounced one Saturday afternoon with her husband, Abraham. Tilly was out playing around town, leaving Darceline alone to host them. After serving tea in the parlor, she kept her unease in check, knowing Edna was the very woman who had once threatened to have her committed for what she called a "temporary phase in lesbianism."

"We believe the boy should come live with us," Aunt Edna began.

Darceline's jaw tightened. "His name is Tilly. And he'll be staying here."

Abraham leaned in, his voice devoid of warmth. "Tilly is coming to live with us. You do not have the time to be a mother. Phillip and William do not have the time to be fathers. The three of you did a commendable job helping your father raise the boy after your mother died, but you are not his parent. Nor are *you* fit to raise a child at this time—given your confused identity."

Edna interjected smoothly, "Our children are closer to his age. It would be a far healthier environment for him."

Darceline stiffened. "You know this isn't what our father would want. And …"

Edna cut her off. "As his deceased father's sister, I will be filing a petition for guardianship tomorrow."

Before Darceline could respond, the sharp ring of the telephone interrupted them. Franklin, her butler, answered.

"Ma'am?"

"Yes?" she replied, not taking her eyes off Edna and Abraham.

"There's a call for you. It's the community hospital."

Darceline stepped into the hall to take the call, gripping the receiver tightly as the nurse on the other end explained: Tilly had been climbing the side of a silo at their farm off First Avenue. He had made it up to the ladder, fifteen feet high before his hands lost their grip. The youngster fell, breaking his left arm. Otherwise, he was fine.

Slowly, Darceline hung up the receiver, exhaling. It couldn't have happened at a worse time. Bracing herself, she returned to the parlor, where her aunt and uncle sat in smug silence.

"Tilly fell," she informed them. "Broke his arm. I need to go."

"Well, that's that," Edna declared, standing as if the matter were settled.

Abraham followed. "Yes. That is that. The boy is coming with us."

H

Tilly had always been a rambunctious child—more so now that he identified as an orphan. He constantly tussled with his cousins, his energy relentless. Edna and Abraham found his behavior intolerable and punished each infraction with added chores around the farm.

To give their family a break from Tilly's antics, Abraham persuaded Paul Davis, a local volunteer fireman, to take the boy under his wing for a few hours each week and introduce him to the workings of the fire department. It was a chance for Tilly to learn something new—and maybe even consider volunteering himself one day.

When he turned fifteen, Edna decided it was time for a change. On a sunny day in late May of 1960, after schools had let out for the summer, she arrived at Bucks Peak with a freshly baked apple pie and a smile, seeking a favor. As Darceline had done with every skeptical man under her leadership, she led her aunt into her office, where phone books were stacked on the seat of her chair, elevating her above her small desk. It was a calculated move where she would look down upon those who questioned her authority sitting before her—a silent but undeniable reminder of who was in charge. It was a strategic little trick, but it served its purpose for the petite woman of 4'8".

Lighting a cigarette, she exhaled a slow stream of smoke over her aunt's head. Edna, shifting uncomfortably, realized for the first time just how completely her niece controlled everything.

"Abraham and I think Tilly should get a summer job off the farm," Edna began. "Though we could use the extra hands, we feel it's time he learns about one of our enterprises. He enjoys tractors and combines, so we thought you might open the door for him at the farm machinery dealership. He could sweep the floors or do whatever a hard day's work requires."

Darceline took a long drag before answering, her voice steady with the confidence of a woman who, after years of her own hard work and sweat and angry tears, had become the respected family matriarch. "Of course. Whatever you feel is best."

Edna hesitated, then humbly cleared her throat. "There is one additional request."

Darceline arched a brow, signaling her to continue.

"Now that Phillip is managing the marina and has moved into his new house, William is in West Lafayette for school, and Marceline is settling in with Max as a newlywed, Abraham and I think it would be best if Tilly returned to the homestead. To live with you."

Darceline leaned forward. "You want Tilly to come home?"

Edna swallowed. "Well, we've always considered our house his home, but …"

"But now it isn't," Darceline finished for her.

Edna pressed her lips together. "Abraham and I …"

"Abraham and you *what?*" Darceline's gaze was sharp, unyielding.

Edna faltered. "We feel we made a mistake taking Tilly in."

"Do you?" Darceline's voice was razor-edged. "And why is that?"

"He's …" Edna started, then hesitated.

"He's *what?*" D pushed.

"He's …"

"Go on. *Say it.*"

"He's unhappy," Edna finally admitted. "He's never gotten over the loss of his father. Or coming to live with us. He's been a wild child, and we think he needs to be here. Back in his real home."

Darceline leaned back, exhaling smoke with slow satisfaction. Watching Edna squirm was a rare delight. This was the woman who had not only made the love of her life disappear but also demanded that she extinguish a part of herself.

Oh, how the tables had turned.

But she didn't let her pleasure show. Instead, she held her stern expression, dragging out the silence, savoring the moment. Let the old bitty squirm a little longer.

And so, Darceline smoked the rest of her cigarette in silence with great relief, scowling as she watched her wretched aunt surrender.

The morning Tilly returned to Bucks Peak with a suitcase in hand—now a tall young man—was the first time Darceline openly wept since the night he was taken away as a boy. She pulled her brother into her arms, holding him tightly, never wanting to let go.

Birthdays and holiday visits over the years had always ended in painful goodbyes, sending him back to Aunt Edna and Uncle Abraham for weeks or months. But this reunion was different.

He was home for good.

"I am so, *so* sorry I ever let them take you away from here, my darling brother." she sobbed into his chest.

"It wasn't your fault, Darci," he comforted her, pulling her in tighter, tears of joy rolling down his cheeks. "I know they took me away on purpose."

They held each other for a long while until Tilly finally pulled back. His face was set with conviction.

"There is one thing I have discovered about myself while under their roof," he said. "I never want to have kids. *Never.*"

Darceline smirked, wiping tears from her cheek and his. "Then keep that pecker of yours packed inside your trousers. That's all you have to do."

When Tilly turned sixteen the following year, he had grown even taller and more handsome, carrying himself with a newfound confidence that Darceline nurtured daily. In his second summer working full-time at the farm machinery dealership, he advanced from sweeping floors to mastering every facet of farming equipment—service, parts, and sales. His humble yet magnetic charm had secured him three significant sales of top-of-the-line corn row crop headers to local farmers. The commissions were enough for him to purchase his first vehicle—on his own.

Darceline was standing on the front lawn, hands on her hips and eyes lifted in quiet admiration, taking in the way the fresh coat of white paint made the house gleam like a polished shell in the light, giving the old place a kind of dignity it hadn't had in years. Up on a tall ladder, George, her ever-patient handyman, was brushing the final strokes along the second-floor bedroom window, whistling softly to himself. The scent of paint lingered in the warm air when an engine's low, throaty rumble broke the silence.

A brand new, white Dodge Power Wagon pickup rolled up through the trees of Bucks Peak, drawing D's curiosity as it parked. Inside was Tilly, with a beaming smile, who quickly hopped out to join her as she approached for a look at the black interior inside.

"I just picked her up from a dealer in Elkhart," he boasted.

Though Darceline was proud of his hard work and financial independence, she couldn't understand why he had chosen such a plain, bulky truck.

"Now, I know what you're thinking," Tilly said before she could speak. "Why did I choose this instead of a sportscar? Okay, hear me out ..."

He excitedly lit a cigarette and handed one to Darceline, giving her a light with his metal butane lighter before continuing.

"First, it's last year's model, 1960, so I got a good deal on the price compared to all the '61s on the lot. *And* it's a four-wheel drive to get up Bucks Peak in the winter snow."

She smoked and listened, nodding.

"But I realized something—we can go days without a single farmer entering the store. They don't just mosey in to buy big-ticket equipment. They might think about it, sure, but most never take the time to stop in.

"And it got me thinking—farmers just don't know how the latest and greatest machinery can boost their harvest, increase bushels per hour, or let them cover more acres in a day, saving them time. So, I thought I'd get out and tell them about it."

He took a drag and exhaled, eyes gleaming with excitement.

"The last sale I made was to a guy with three hundred acres down by Nappanee. I borrowed Tommy's plain four-door Chevy and drove around the county roads. I saw him working on an old crop header and stopped to talk for three hours. Eventually, he agreed to come in and see what we had. And when he did, he bought the most expensive header on the lot.

"As I walked him out after, he said, 'You know what sold me, young man? Sure, you're a great salesman, but what really caught my eye was when you pulled up in a simple car, dressed in simple clothes, and took the time to listen to what I had to say. *That's* what sold me.'"

Tilly gestured toward the Dodge with pride. "I know farmers. They're no-nonsense folks who don't care for Flash. If I rolled up in a fancy sports car, I'd lose them before I even opened my mouth. This"— he patted the hood—"is my way of bringing the business to us."

Darceline tilted her head, intrigued. "How many other salesmen do this?"

"What? Go out and bring customers in? No one."

Her brow lifted. "That was your idea?"

"Yep."

She studied him for a moment, then smiled. "Do you like what you do?"

Tilly grinned, his confidence unwavering. "Yeah. I think I'm really good at this."

Darceline hugged him. "I believe you are."

Pulling back, she added, "So, this is your company car … company truck."

"Exactly," Tilly smirked. "She's gonna make me a lot of money."

Darceline nodded approvingly. "I can see that. But when school starts in two weeks, you'd better keep your grades up."

"I will."

"You know the deal—work as long as you keep a B average."

"I know the deal," he said with a playful wink.

"I'm gonna go in and change before taking her for a spin," he added, bounding inside.

Darceline watched him go, her heart swelling with pride at his creativity, determination, and success at sixteen. Tilly deserved to revel in this self-made milestone for as long as he could. She sighed happily, her gaze drifting to the old barn.

That settled it—she would wait to give him the brand-new, custom-ordered 1961 Chrysler 300G convertible, hidden behind a freshly stacked wall of hay bales. The sexy red beauty, with its tan leather bucket seats and white soft top, was a back-to-school present for all his hard work that summer. Christmastime now sounded better. Or, maybe she would keep it for herself … considering she always wanted a convertible.

Then, suddenly—

"DARCI!" Tilly's frantic scream jolted her.

He stood at the front door, eyes wide with alarm, before dashing inside.

Darceline's cigarette fell from her hand as she bolted after him, her stomach twisting as she saw thick black smoke creeping across the hallway ceiling the second she stepped into the foyer.

Tilly was dialing the phone in the parlor, calling the fire department.

Darceline's instincts took over.

"EVERYONE GET OUT OF THE HOUSE!" she bellowed, sprinting through the first floor, checking every room for her staff. Her young housemaid, nineteen-year-old Susan, was in the dining room polishing the silver, standing with a cloth and tablespoon in hand, frozen.

"Should I grab the silver?" she asked in panic.

"No!" Darceline instructed. "Put that on the table and go outside!"

And Susan did.

Darceline ran into her office to find her secretary, Louise, frantically loading her arms with ledgers. "LOUISE!" she shouted.

"I know!" Louise yelled.

"The house is on fire!"

"I know!"

"You've got to get out!"

Panic-stricken, Louise cried out, "But I don't have everything …"

Darceline dashed to her side, shouting, "TAKE WHAT YOU GOT!"

Louise stood looking around for what else she needed to seize. "But what about the …"

D grabbed her by the arm and pulled her into the hall. "GET OUT OF HERE!" she screamed, thrusting her hand toward the front door. *NOW!*"

As Louise scurried to go, D rushed to Tilly, who was hanging up the phone. "Check upstairs! Make sure no one's there!" she ordered.

Darceline charged toward the kitchen where the black smoke was rolling from, but she stopped cold when she reached the doorway.

Francetta, the cook, was on the floor, unconscious.

Flames engulfed the stove, racing up the wall and setting the window curtains ablaze. The fire roared, hungry and unforgiving.

"FRANCETTA!" Darceline screamed.

The woman was tall, broad, and heavyset—there was no way Darceline could lift her alone. She yelled for Tilly.

Dropping to the floor, she grabbed Francetta's wrists and pulled with everything she had, her high heels skidding uselessly against the polished wood floors. Cursing, she kicked off her shoes, reached under her skirt, unfastened her garter belts, ripped away her knee-high stockings for better traction, and dug her bare feet into the floor, dragging Francetta inch by painful inch in a quarter circle toward the hallway to drag her out.

"TILLY!" she screamed, pulling with every ounce of strength.

Smoke thickened, a choking black that burned her throat. Heat seared her exposed skin. Glass shattered somewhere behind her, and still she pulled.

"*TILLY!* I NEED HELP—*NOW!*"

The fire raged, devouring the kitchen whole. Wooden cabinet doors began to sizzle, and flames roared like a living monster.

Darceline yanked on Francetta's dead weight again and again, screaming, "MOVE, GODDAMMIT!" as if brute force and willpower alone could save them both.

Something exploded on the counter.

"TILLY!" She panic-screamed.

It didn't matter that the heat of the fire was becoming unbearably intense, and the black smoke was thick and heavy, causing her to choke; Darceline was not leaving Francetta there to burn.

"*TILLY!*" she shrieked, desperation clawing at her throat.

Then—

"I got her! Get out!"

Tilly rushed in through the swirling smoke, grabbed the front of Francetta's black uniform dress, and dragged her to the hall. He crouched, hoisted her into a fireman's carry, and hauled her toward the front door.

Outside, he gently laid Francetta on the grass.

He turned immediately to his sister. "Are you okay?"

Darceline wasn't thinking about herself. Her eyes scanned the grounds and found Esther and Susan standing stunned. "Thank God you got out!" she gasped.

She dropped to her knees beside Francetta. "Is she breathing?"

Tilly leaned over Francetta, examining her, and noticed that her face and dress were singed as though she had been hit with a flash fire.

"No."

Without hesitation, he began CPR.

George had climbed down the ladder with a white droplet of paint on his nose, paintbrush still in hand, and gathered by the housekeepers and Louise—still clutching ledgers. Tony, the gardener, ran up from the side of the house to join them. All stood in horror at the sight of Francetta on the ground, unresponsive.

Darceline forced herself to stay steady. "Is everyone accounted for?"

"Where's Franklin?" Susan cried out.

"He went for groceries," D answered, scanning each face,

confirming everyone was there.

Tilly pressed on. For several long minutes, he kept working—breath, compressions, breath, compressions—until finally, blessedly, Francetta coughed. She rolled onto her side, struggling for air with wheezing gasps between choking coughs.

Relief washed across everyone.

Darceline exhaled hard, sinking down beside Tilly and hugging him fiercely. She reached for Francetta's arm, squeezing gently. "You're okay."

Francetta sat up suddenly, her eyes wide in horror. "Oh!" she gasped.

Everyone turned, following her gaze, and saw it:

The house—Darceline's house—was no longer a house at all. In less than five minutes, it had become a living inferno.

They watched, motionless, as the fire devoured the manor whole. The sounds were staggering: the brittle, furious crackle of flames peeling paint and timber, the hollow shudder of floors collapsing one after another. Windows exploded outward with sharp, brutal pops, sending glass spinning.

Inside, hidden from sight, entire rooms fell—portraits, chandeliers, beds, chairs, books—crashing down in a shattering, thunderous chain.

The fire roared louder now, a beastly howl that overpowered everything. It sucked air hungrily into its heart, growing hotter, angrier, wilder.

The heat pressed against them even at a distance, forcing them to move farther back across the lawn.

Darceline, her face soot-streaked, watched in stunned silence. She could almost hear the house still breathing—the slam of a door upstairs, the creak of a rocking chair, a piano key struck by a passing finger—all swallowed now in the relentless, hissing rush of fire.

Darceline's gaze rolled across the pink burns on Francetta's face. Taking her hand, she asked, "What happened?"

Francetta blinked several times before saying, "I turned on the oven for the pork roast. After a bit, I smelled gas, so I opened the door to relight the pilot light, struck a match, and everything blew."

Rubbing Francetta's back, Darceline said with relief, "I am so thankful you're alright."

Phil's car raced up first, prompting D to stand. She saw her butler, Franklin, quickly pull in behind him. With the shocked 'Are you okay's' out of the way, she asked Phil for a cigarette. Several other neighbors soon roared in, jumping from their cars to freeze in eye-stopping awe.

Everyone silently watched. The walls groaned and twisted, then collapsed on themselves, plunging into the deep cellar and shooting embers high into the sky. The smoke twisted, black and endless, carrying the smell of scorched linen, varnish, old paper, and something deeper—the scent of endings.

Darceline stood barefoot in the grass, a loose white blouse billowing over a navy skirt that fluttered in the smoky breeze. Her toes curled into the lawn, grounding her as her knees threatened to give way—but she did not fall. Her chest felt hollow, carved out by grief, as everything she had ever loved turned to ash: Violet's tender letters, the family photographs, her grandmother's antique Fabergé brooch.

A few minutes later, the fire truck finally arrived—Hicksville County's only one—just in time to see flickering tongues of orange and red peep from inside the enormous fire pit.

The fire chief approached, hat in hand. "Miss Darceline, we scrammed as fast as we could—each coming from different farms. If only …"

She cut him off. "Paul, even if you'd been here when it started, there was no stopping it."

His jaw clenched. "Yeah, but dog-gone it … this was your home."

Taking a long drag from her cigarette, Darceline hid her anguish, consoling the firemen. "Everyone is safe," she said firmly as a tear broke away. "That's all that matters."

The freshly painted beautiful white house wasn't burning anymore. It was *gone.*

H

Since Max and Marci were expecting their first child, Darceline and Tilly moved in with bachelor Phil while Bucks Peak was being rebuilt from the ground up. Tilly thrived, both academically—graduating high school early that following spring—and professionally, earning a promotion to Senior Salesman at Hicks Farming Equipment, *"Just off Indiana State Road 21, in Hicksville!"*

With his shiny new title, Tilly was asked to attend the Midwest Farm Tractor & Combine Show in Quincy, Illinois, hosted at the Floyd Miller Farm. That week, his boss had plans to take his family to Coney Island for vacation, so Tilly stepped up to represent. It was the first of many agricultural shows and conventions Tilly would attend throughout his illustrious career in farm equipment sales.

Then came Kansas City in 1964.

There, in a haze of diesel fumes and promotional flyers, Tilly laid eyes on Millicent Geere. Radiant. Charismatic. As the official spokesmodel and roving ambassador for the Don Geere Manufacturing Co., she was *the* face of ag machinery—a title she held with sparkling conviction and great-smelling hair.

The great-granddaughter of founder Donald Geere, Millicent wasn't just part of the family business—she *was* the business. With the wit of Katharine Hepburn, the confidence of a linebacker, and the wardrobe of someone who knew how to mix business with bourbon, Millicent broke every mold that dared to contain her. She was a legend in steel-toe stilettos, a master of the pitch, and, if need be, a bar-fight finisher.

Her motto? "Sell hard. Party harder."

Enter Tilly Hicks, walking into the Don Geere Showcase Arena like he was the blue-eyed farmhand stud. He spotted her—laughing, radiant, and making three Iowa general managers fall in love with her and their new row crop tractor. Tilly waited for his moment, then stepped forward to introduce himself.

"I'm Millie Geere," she said, extending her hand for a shake, falling hard that second, eyes twinkling. "Can I buy you a drink, Tilly Hicks?"

Tilly and Millie were perfect matches—like torque and horsepower, grease and overalls, and gin and tonic. Neither wanted children. Not even a four-legged fur baby. They loved travel, smoky bars, hotel room service, and the freedom to catch flights to see each other every other weekend. They wanted to marry but had no proposal yet because of the obvious question: Where would they settle?

Tilly was a Hoosier through and through. Millie was Kansas City royalty. So, naturally, they decided to leave their futures to the highest authority known to humankind: a coin toss.

Tilly pulled out a shiny new quarter to flip for the first toss at the Starlite Lounge near the Indianapolis airport between whiskey sours and chain-smoked Marlboros. Millie called heads and won the right to toss the coin—and the claim to heads for the game.

With the coin in hand, she paused and said, "No backing out."

"No, ma'am," Tilly grinned. This game was about to change their lives.

Round one: Heads get to propose. Millie won.

They laughed, drank, and chain-smoked.

Round two: Heads for a big family wedding, tails for elopement. Tails it was—they were eloping.

The third round was the biggest of all, making their hands tremble. It would decide where they'd build their life together. Kansas City or Hicksville. One toss. One life-altering decision. Twenty-five cents would call it.

They ordered two more drinks. Then, two more. Then, two more.

The coin was tossed. Kansas City or Hicksville. Tilly won.

He looked at her seriously for the first time all night. "No backing out?"

"No, sir!" Millie said, eyes gleaming. Then she raised her glass and asked with a grin, "Tilly Hicks, will you marry me?"

At the time, Darceline was preparing to open a second Hicks Farming Equipment dealership on the southside of Indianapolis. When Tilly approached her about becoming the sales manager for the new location, she hesitated. As talented as he was, she didn't believe he was quite ready for a management role—at least, not to launch a new store. (Besides, she wasn't keen on him moving three hours away.) Instead, she transferred her current general manager to the new location and promoted Tilly to GM of the Hicksville store.

He and Millie immediately flew to Las Vegas, where they were hitched by an Elvis impersonator with a serious sideburn situation at the Little White Wedding Chapel—the same place Paul Newman and Joanne Woodward were married in 1958—and called it a honeymoon.

While packing for their flight home, Tilly handed Millie a tiny gift box, grinning like a man who'd nailed the romance game. She tore off the wrapping like Christmas morning and opened it to find … a delicate pair of silver eyebrow scissors.

"I'm getting a vasectomy so you can ditch The Pill."

Millie practically levitated. She clutched the metaphorical scissors, declaring she would treasure them forever.

But news of the elopement hit the Kansas City society pages like a bomb. Even though Mr. and Mrs. Geere personally knew and respected Darceline Hicks, Millie's mother, a pearl-draped socialite fond of legacy and appearances, was livid by the defiant act. Her father—powerful, calculated, and the current head of Don Geere Manufacturing—called it an "alcohol-induced mistake" and insisted on an annulment. Her parents gave her an ultimatum: annul the marriage or be fired and disinherited.

Millie didn't flinch.

She chose Tilly.

Equally stubborn, Millie's parents turned their backs on her, heeding her to never return. The Hicks family embraced Millie with open arms—more so now that she was shunned from her own tribe.

Tilly bought a beautiful spec home on Hicksville Lake that Max had designed and built and was about to put up for sale. The two love birds settled in, Tilly was snipped, and they lived happily ever after—well, for at least five years until Millie unexpectedly became pregnant.

The news devastated them both.

Tilly returned to his urologist demanding an explanation of why the vasectomy failed. The doctor spelled out as he sat on the examination table, "Rare recanalization after a vasectomy typically occurs within the first few months following the procedure, though it can happen years later in sporadic cases. This occurs when the severed ends of the vas deferens spontaneously reconnect, creating a passageway for sperm to travel again, which can potentially lead to pregnancy.

"Which, in your case, Tilly, I believe is what happened."

Tilly blinked, having no idea what the doctor said. "What does that mean?"

"The tube we cut that transports the sperm reconnected over time, allowing the sperm to pass through again."

"Shit!" Tilly said, shaking his head. "Can we cut it again?"

"Yes."

"Then let's do it *again*. I am not having children."

They kept the pregnancy a secret from the family and began searching for underground doctors in Chicago who performed abortions since it was illegal at the time. Eventually, they found a reputable provider and scheduled an appointment.

Millie had a lifelong passion for dolls, curating an exquisite collection of vintage Madame Alexanders and antique porcelain figures from France and Germany.

The Saturday evening before their trip to Chicago, as she waited for Tilly to close the dealership, she finished her first bottle of merlot and opened another. She wandered into the guest room she had converted into a shrine for her dolls, sinking into a rocking chair to admire their delicate beauty. As she sat there, sipping her fifth glass of wine, she suddenly questioned whether they were making the right decision.

Tilly arrived home around nine, having stayed late to finalize a $100,000 tractor/equipment sale with a farmer and his wife. It took the entire day, but he closed the deal with Mr. and Mrs. Soybean and was ready to celebrate.

He rolled in with a grand smile. Millie lay stretched out on the sofa in the living room, smoking a joint. Tilly gave her a soft kiss before taking a hit himself. He removed his tie, headed toward the bedroom to change, and asked about her day.

"I'm about to ruin yours," she exhaled, tapping ash into an ashtray.

Tilly slowed to a stop in the hallway, tie dangling from his hand, and slowly returned, pausing as he studied her expression.

"You changed your mind," he said, his voice heavy.

"I changed my mind," she confirmed in a weighty tone.

They locked eyes, both absorbing what this meant.

Tilly walked over and sat at the edge of the sofa, near her legs. She held out the joint, and he took it, inhaling deeply before passing it back. As he exhaled, he reached for her glass of wine on the coffee table and took a sip.

Leaning sideways to look at the woman he loved, Tilly smiled and nodded.

"Then I've changed my mind, too."

Cousin Sally

Sally was born on a humid July afternoon—the kind where the Indiana air clung to the skin like a wetsuit. But she didn't cry much, not like other babies. Even then, it was as if she understood that quiet was expected.

Tilly and Millie brought her home to their immaculate ranch house on the shores of Hicksville Lake, where everything gleamed like it was constantly threatened by a surprise *Better Lake Homes* photoshoot.

Millie treated Sally like one of her porcelain dolls—delicate, untouchable. Her nursery was painted the softest shade of pink, and a crystal chandelier hung from the ceiling. Rows of Millie's beloved dolls lined all four walls on built-in shelves two feet below the ceiling, their glass eyes watching over Sally like unblinking babysitters. But unlike those dolls, Sally could breathe. She could feel. And she longed to be more than a pristine decoration.

Millie brushed her daughter's teeth daily and fussed with Sally's natural blonde hair, curling the fine strands into perfect ringlets. Satin bows and lace-trimmed dresses became her daily uniform.

"A lady must always be presentable," Millie would say, adjusting the ribbons.

Tilly would nod in agreement, though his focus was rarely on Sally. His days belonged to the dealership, and his evenings to a night of drinks with Millie over a joint before and after dinner to bookend their rituals.

Playtime? Forbidden. The perfectly manicured lawn was not a playground—but a "statement." Dirt was a criminal offense. Grass stains were practically an act of domestic terrorism. While her cousins rode bikes down the street and leaped through sprinklers, engaged in daring bouts of driveway chalk artistry, or rode the school bus together, Sally was confined to the "indoor play experience," which mostly involved sitting near breakable objects and practicing *not breaking them*. She watched from behind the ivory curtains of her bedroom window—or from the passenger seat of her mother's car, chauffeured to and from school like precious cargo. Somewhere out there, five-year-olds were digging for worms, but Sally? Sally was training to be the Queen of Absolutely Nowhere Fun.

Her only companions were her reflection in the full-length floor mirror in her bedroom and the silent gaze of the video camera Millie gifted her on her fifth birthday.

"Practice your poise, darling," Millie would coo as Sally stood before the camera. She would stand tall, chin lifted, imitating the regal positions her mother demanded. The camera's red light blinked steadily, capturing every perfect pose and forcing a smile. In those moments, Sally ceased to be a child. She was a doll, just like the ones that lined the walls. And dolls did not speak.

Loneliness became her shadow. She named her reflection "Sad Sally" and whispered secrets to the mirror. She practiced conversations with the camera lens, imagining an audience that might one day listen. But no one ever did.

Hicksville Lake was the town's pride, joy, and summertime social hub—where boaters showcased their drunk driving skills, pulling water skiers and whipping children off their boating tubes speeding around bends. Tilly and Millie's pontoon boat was a floating cocktail lounge, and Millie took her hosting duties very seriously. With oversized sunglasses, a permanent adult beverage in hand, and a laugh that always identified where the real fun was happening, she basked in the glow of lakeside gossip.

Sally, on the other hand, was banned from the boat. "The water's not safe for children," Millie would say—this coming from a woman who once flipped a golf cart attempting a *Dukes of Hazzard* jump over a small sand trap.

Sally was left behind, her nose pressed against the glass of her bedroom window. She watched her cousins whoop and holler, zipping across the water like aquatic daredevils. She traced patterns on the glass, imagining herself racing a Jet Ski against … anyone.

And then there were the infamous afterparties. When Tilly and Millie invited the grownups to their home's walkout basement after sunset for cards, muffled chatter and bursts of laughter seeped through the floor. Sally was to remain upstairs, a silent ghost in her own home.

One crisp fall day, Tilly and Millie were invited to join some fabulously eccentric friends who owned a hot air balloon—for "cocktails in the sky." They loved it so much (the altitude? the Prosecco? who's to say?) that they promptly bought their own and began drifting off to hot air balloon festivals across the country like two stylish aviators on a floating grand tour.

Meanwhile, Sally was always left behind with a rotating cast of caretakers: Aunt Darceline and "Aunt" Penny, Aunt Marci and Uncle Max, or Uncle Phil and Aunt Tami—who once accidentally fed her a dog treat.

"We'll be home in a few days," Millie would always say sweetly, pressing a dramatic kiss to Sally's forehead like she was setting off on a glamorous but slightly absurd spy mission.

Tilly and Millie especially adored their annual trips to New Mexico for the Spring Hot Air Balloon Celebration. Every April, the skies above Albuquerque burst into color as the event drew dreamers, adventurers, and sky-gazers from around the world. That year, they arrived early, towing their teal-and-lavender balloon—affectionately nicknamed *Cloud Dancer*—behind them in a trailer for the two-day drive.

They'd attended festivals for over a decade, but this one differed. A rare meteor shower—The Eos Stream—was forecast to streak across the Albuquerque skies for six days and nights. Astronomers called it "an unrepeatable cosmic ballet." The news sent ripples of excitement through the ballooning community.

On the second evening of the shower, Tilly and Millie launched *Cloud Dancer* at dusk. It rose above the desert floor alongside 500 other glowing balloons. Below them, Albuquerque twinkled; above, meteors began carving silver streaks across the deepening blue heavens.

At 2,500 feet, they felt untouchable—drifting in still air, wrapped in the hush of night and surrounded by silent bursts of celestial fire from other ballooners. Millie pulled two champagne flutes from a picnic basket, popped open a bottle of Taittinger Comtes, and poured them delightful bubbly to celebrate the magnificent view.

But at 2,610 feet, as they tapped their glasses, space, and Earth made a fatal handshake.

Two pieces of space debris, no bigger than large marbles, had survived reentry—slipping through the upper atmosphere without disintegrating. Traveling side-by-side at over 300 miles per hour, they struck.

The first sliced through the left side of *Cloud Dancer's* envelope.

The second punctured through just below. It was a swift one-two death-kill. What began as a rip became a tear and then a roar. The balloon's silk canopy shredded like tissue in a hurricane.

From nearby baskets, horrified onlookers watched as *Cloud Dancer* crumpled midair, its vibrant fabric flailing like a wounded bird. The balloon dropped almost vertically, the silence broken only by shrieking wind—and a final, thunderous impact deep in the sand dunes below.

News of the accident went global before sunrise. Tilly and Millie's shocking deaths reverberated through Hicksville like an earthquake.

And Sally, fifteen years old, frozen in the center of it all, was now orphaned by both parents—just like her father.

Having lost their own mother when they were half Sally's age, the Hicks siblings swooped in, descended upon her like an abducted child finally found and returned home—filled with overwhelming love and sorrow. Darci, Marci, Phil, and Bill gathered with Sally, each eager to share her grief and assure her that she wasn't alone.

Although Darceline had been named her guardian by Tilly and Millie, she gave Sally the choice of where—and with whom—she wanted to live. But having spent her life in near solitude, the thought of living with her cousins was, if anything, a little frightening. Instead, she chose the place closest to the familiar: Darceline's sprawling mansion, where she could wander the halls like a wisp of smoke, vanishing into one of its many rooms to be alone.

Sally stood at the edge of an uncertain world for the first time.

She left the dolls behind at her parents' house but brought her two dearest companions: the full-length floor mirror from her bedroom and the new camcorder her mother had given her on her fifteenth birthday. One day, as the red light blinked and the camera captured her reflection in the gilded glass, Sally saw something she hadn't before.

Not a doll.

Not a reflection.

But a young woman.

Darceline understood better than anyone the weight of trauma Sally carried. With a withdrawn teenager now living under their roof, Darceline and Penny tried patiently, gently, to reach her. They searched for ways to inspire her and draw her out from the fortress of books where she had buried herself.

Despite their efforts to gently insist that she play with her cousins or swim in the pool, Sally rarely left the mansion's vast library except to eat and sleep.

Then, one day, Penny had an idea.

She suggested Darceline take Sally on a tour of the original Hicks America offices on Main Street in downtown Hicksville.

Darceline, thrilled at the thought, jumped at the opportunity. She watched with quiet satisfaction as Bill proudly guided Sally through the agricultural building, explaining the labs' work testing soil and crop samples and the company's research into environmentally friendly fertilizers.

Next, Bill handed her off to Dean Davison—the Chief Financial Officer of Hicks America. Dean walked Sally through the accounts receivable, payables, and payroll systems. Then the tour continued across the street to the headquarters of Hicks America Finance Corp.

They climbed the stairs to the second floor and entered the brokerage division.

Sally froze.

Before her eyes was an entire wall of sleek digital monitors glowing with real-time market data. The screens—divided into vibrant grids—tracked commodities like crude oil, gold, wheat, and natural gas. Bright greens signaled gains; sharp reds, losses. Numbers flickered: current prices, percentage changes, trading volumes, bid-ask spreads. At the bottom, a ticker scrolled continuously, streaming global headlines, exchange rates, and breaking financial news.

For the first time that day, Sally spoke.

She asked a question.

Then another.

And another.

Within minutes, she and Dean were deep in conversation—questions and ideas bouncing between them, her eyes alight with curiosity. It was as if something inside her had flicked on the "Life" switch.

Darceline clutched Bill's arm from the sidelines, her heart swelling with joy and relief.

At last, it seemed Sally had found her spark.

Market trading.

H

Never allowed to grow into a social butterfly—like her mother, her father, or the rest of the Hicks—Sally's isolated upbringing had robbed her of the communication skills needed to connect with others. People assumed she was simply shy, but they didn't know the truth: she had been taught not to speak, engage, or make a sound unless asked to.

Sally never responded, no matter how hard her classmates, teachers, or cousins tried to draw her out. And when she did, it was barely above a whisper. Eventually, they stopped trying and left her alone.

Young Sally took that as rejection. She began to resent the people who had once reached out to her. Over time, her disappointment twisted into a quiet disdain for people, further deepening her isolation.

Darceline called Sally into her office one morning to break through the shell and had her sit across the desk. From her high-backed leather chair, D looked at the young woman with a firm but not unkind expression.

"Now that you're sixteen, you're not spending another summer holed up in the library the way you did last year," she said. "Like your cousins and your daddy did at your age—you're going to work."

Sally remained still, her eyes widening. Spending time with strangers, being expected to talk to them, maybe even depend on them, filled her with dread.

"Where?" she asked cautiously.

D smiled. "Anywhere you want. What sounds interesting to you?"

Sally thought for a moment. She hadn't expected to be given a choice. The question alone startled her.

"I'd like to be a commodities broker," she said. "What about at the office downtown?"

Darceline lit a cigarette and exhaled a slow ribbon of smoke. "That requires a solid finance, economics, and market analysis foundation. What do you know about any of that?"

"I've read a few things," Sally replied.

"Like what?"

To Darceline's surprise, Sally began explaining how commodities are classified, the key factors influencing their prices, and how derivatives like futures and options are used in hedging and speculation. She even mentioned the importance of global trade dynamics, weather patterns, and geopolitical events on supply chains.

D leaned back in her chair, a wide grin spreading. "I'll have Dean set up an interview. But it's up to you to get the job. Think you're up for it?"

A flicker of something new passed over Sally's face. Excitement. She smiled. "I can do that."

Sally landed a position as an assistant to a junior-level trader. She would be there two years before she turned eighteen, the legal age to become a commodities trader. To her, this was a dream apprenticeship.

That winter, with her plan to graduate high school a year early in the spring, Darceline and Penny began pitching university after university, hoping one might ignite some interest in Sally.

Then, one snowy January evening over dinner, Sally looked up from her plate and said plainly, "I don't want to go to college. And when I turn eighteen, I will take the Series 3 National Commodities Future Exam, become a commodities trader, and work full-time at HAFC."

Darceline and Penny exchanged a glance. Surprised to hear Sally didn't want to go to college but not surprised by her career choice, all D said was, "Okay."

$$\mathcal{H}$$

After graduation, young Sally was in heaven working full-time with the commodities traders. The experience fulfilled her in ways she never imagined, and she saved every cent of her paycheck.

Sally kept a private journal where she tracked hypothetical commodity trades—bets she would've made if she'd been brokering her own money. She made a deal with herself: once she'd "earned" her first imaginary million, she'd quit her job and day-trade for fun.

The following year, on her eighteenth birthday, she was summoned to the BS office and invited to sit at the conference table with her aunt and their lifelong attorney, who was nearing the end of his life. He explained that now, as she was of legal age, she would assume ownership of the assets in her parents' estate trust. And so, on that day, Sally Hicks became an heiress—receiving Tilly Hicks's sixteen percent ownership of Hicks America.

Sally was grateful—but she had no intention of touching a dime. She was making a good salary at HAFC and planned to keep working.

"Do you mind if I move back to my house?" she asked, turning to Darceline.

D and Penny had grown fond of having her in their home. Neither wanted to see her go. But knowing it was time for Sally to truly step into her independence, Darceline nodded.

"Of course not."

"But I'd like to renovate first," Sally added. "Can I stay here with you and Penny until they finish?"

Her aunt smiled. "Of course."

Two years later, Sally hit her first imaginary million in her Monopoly-style trading diary—but decided not to quit just yet. She enjoyed the rhythm of office life: waking early, strategizing with her fellow traders, and forecasting the day's market winners and losers.

For the first time, she felt a sense of camaraderie outside her family, and for the first time, people listened to her when she spoke.

Then, the day she turned twenty, she noticed a faint wrinkle forming on her forehead while getting ready for work.

It was devastating.

Sally called in sick. Her second call was to a renowned plastic surgeon in Chicago, scheduling a consultation for the next day. During the drive, she couldn't stop checking her reflection—so much so that she tilted her rearview mirror permanently toward her face to keep one eye on the road and the other on herself. That mirror would never be adjusted again.

The consultation was equally traumatic. Seeing Sally's youthful face's flawless symmetry, the surgeon refused to operate. But to ease her distress over what she described as a "flaw" and "age spot," he offered a compromise: a cutting-edge wrinkle reducer, a non-surgical injectable to smooth out minor lines. It was temporary, he warned, requiring ongoing maintenance.

Sally didn't hesitate. She loved the results. That appointment marked the beginning of her obsession—with staying flawless forever.

A year before the COVID pandemic, Sally thought about launching her own market-trading podcast. She would convert her parents' old party basement into a sprawling office and recording studio.

But she knew the truth: no one wanted trading tips from a wealthy heiress. So, she invented a persona—a self-made woman from humble beginnings who clawed her way to millions through grit and sharp instincts. The podcast would be subscription-based, but she needed a hook—something irresistible enough to make people pay ten dollars a month without hesitation.

One day, while waiting in the drive-thru line at a coffee shop in Hicksville, she ordered a triple espresso with a splash of vanilla syrup. As she inched forward behind the car ahead, she glanced to her right and noticed the back alley behind the grocery store. A refrigerated truck was backing into the loading dock. The building had no signage—just a blank, looming structure.

That's when it hit her.

A game. A mystery. A reward.

Each podcast would end with a guessing challenge. Sally would present a photograph of the nondescript backsides of iconic buildings—no signs, no clues, just architectural details. Whoever correctly identified the building first would win $100,000.

By the time she took her first sip of espresso, Sally Hicks had a name and a concept: *Back Alley Sally*.

She spent the next six months traveling the globe, snapping pictures of the grand façades and gritty back entrances of skyscrapers and landmarks in major cities. By the end, she had a curated collection of nearly three hundred buildings for her weekly guessing game.

When she finally launched the show, it skyrocketed. Within four months, *Back Alley Sally* had racked up 300,001 subscribers, each paying $10 a pop for her hotshot trading tips and the magnetic, rags-to-riches persona she beamed through the screen. At last count: 776,348 credit cards were auto-charged monthly for their fix of her charisma. She was closing in on her next goal: a million paying fans.

Sally was living the dream she'd craved since childhood—people were finally listening. She had the audience, the influence, and the numbers—everything she ever wanted.

At least, on paper.

Because none of them really knew her. Not one.

They knew the character—the poised, savvy Sally in soft lighting and flawless makeup, who never missed a beat, and always knew what to say. But the woman behind the mic? The one sitting alone in her soundproof basement at 6 a.m., tweaking thumbnails and checking analytics—she was still waiting for someone to ask how she was doing.

Week after week, year after year, she broadcast to hundreds of thousands ... completely alone. Slowly, the shy, awkward little girl she'd once been reemerged, this time cloaked in expensive silk and exhaustion.

Sally started drinking to dull the ache of isolation. Then drank to deal with the hangovers. Eventually, it was just part of her routine—same as checking the subscriber count.

Like her mother, she was a party animal every single day, but with a tortured twist: hers was a one-woman social. Daily. 365.

Egads

Standing on the front porch at Bucks Peak, Win smiled politely and nodded at Dano—Sally's driver, houseman, and bodyguard—as he parked her Maybach. The meat-rack Samoan stepped out with the precision of a butler in a luxury car commercial—his perfectly tailored black suit, crisp white shirt, and black necktie unshakably pristine.

"Hello, Mr. Winston," Dano said, moving toward the backseat.

"Hi, Dano," Win greeted, watching as the man leaned into the car, deciphering Sally's slurred words with practiced ease.

Dano scooped Sally out like a life-size Barbie without pause, her stiff, petite frame pressed to his chest. He carried her past Win and up the steps, placing her gently on her feet. He carefully positioned her hand on the doorframe for balance and stepped back to assess whether she could remain upright.

Sally had crammed herself into a slim hot pink dress that clung to every curve—including a pair of projectile breasts now blotched with martini stains. Her long blonde hair spilled over bare shoulders, framing a freshly plumped face: cheeks ballooned like golf balls, lips jutted like a crimson duckbill. Hiding behind massive black bar sunglasses, she looked like someone in a redacted photo—obscured for legal or national security reasons.

"Take the shoes off! I can't move in these things," she begged Dano, wobbling. "Or I'll be stuck here like a Walmart greeter."

Dano knelt to remove her stilettos. Sally slurred, "Damn it, I spilled my martini on the drive up the hill … now I look like one of my implants malfunctioned."

Once her pantyhose-clad feet touched the limestone foyer, Dano paused to ensure she wouldn't topple.

"Would you like to return home to change?" he asked, deep and calm.

"After all it took to get me here?!" she snapped. "No, but fetch my pink princess slippers from the trunk."

Sally raked a diamond-encrusted hand through her hair—only to get one of her oversized rings tangled in her locks.

"I'm stuck! I'm stuck!" she shrieked, flailing.

Unhurried and methodical, Dano freed her with surgical precision. He then quickly returned to the car.

After a round of profanities, Sally finally noticed Win and squinted behind her shades.

"Well, if it isn't our very own Pinky Tuscadero," he joshed, dusting off the old nickname Willow had used for her since junior high.

"Winston?" she garbled, focusing on his voice.

"In person."

Dano returned with pink slippers decked in diamond-encrusted sunflowers. He knelt again to slip them on.

Standing, he said to Winston … as though, for some reason, Winston needed to know, "I'll wait in the car until she's ready."

Win stepped closer.

"Is that a burning cigarette you're bringing into my personal space?!" Sally barked.

He popped it into a nearby ashtray. "Not anymore."

Satisfied, she leaned in for a slow, drunken cheek-tap kiss, never releasing her grip on the doorframe.

"You look fabulous," Win said with a smirk.

"Oh!" she groaned. "With this black-and-blue bruising around my eyes? I'm still sore from my last procedure!"

"You're wearing sunglasses," he replied cheerfully. "I can't tell."

"I am?" she slurred, reaching up—only to smack herself in the face. "Ow! Son of a bitch!"

Win sighed. Some things never changed. Sally had always been as clumsy as his sister.

Fidgeting with her dress, she commanded, "Be a dear and unhinge me from this door. Escort me inside."

"My pleasure, Mi Lady," Win said, taking her arm and pivoting her around.

They made it six slow steps into the foyer.

"Shall we invite Dano to join us? He's practically family," Win offered.

Sally froze. Her chin lifted, big lips tightening. He could feel the weight of her glare behind the sunglasses.

"Never tell me what my employees should or shouldn't do," she said coldly. "It's none of your goddamn business. Agreed?"

Startled by the venom in her tone, Win blinked. Dano had been with her for years—a loyal fixture in their family chaos. But the sweet girl he remembered was now swimming in bitterness, booze, or both.

"Of course," he replied evenly, swallowing his dismay.

Eleven steps later, she froze again.

"Oh, fuck."

"What now?"

"I have to piss like a racehorse."

"Luckily," Win said, gesturing, "we're right by the bathroom."

He rotated her toward the door, led her inside, and placed her hand on the wall before turning to leave.

"Where are you going?" she demanded.

"I'm leaving you to take care of business."

"You can't go."

"What?"

"I can't get out of this fucking dress by myself!"

Win's jaw dropped. "What do you want me to do?"

"Unzip me, help me step out of it, get my ass on the toilet, and then get the fuck out."

"I'm not pulling your panties down."

"I have pantyhose on!" she barked. "I can do that part!"

Sighing, he pointedly looked away, unzipped her dress, and carefully lowered it.

"Where should I put this?" he asked, staring out the door.

Sally shuffled toward the toilet. "Just fucking hold it! You'll have to put me back in the goddamn thing!"

"What?"

"I can't get back into it by myself!"

Flabbergasted, Win neatly folded the dress over his arm, stepped out, and closed the door. He paced. After a few minutes, he was ready to give up, find Willow, and let her finish this.

But the door swung open.

He turned—instantly regretting it.

Sally stood naked, her breasts in full launch mode, her basement waxed totally clean, and her calves hogtied by her pantyhose—looking like a nude S&M Barbie doll wearing censorship sunglasses.

"Oh my God …" Win muttered, horrified, spinning away.

"I need help," she said.

"Yes. You do," he deadpanned, looking at the glass doors to the back deck.

"Serious help."

"I can see that."

"Winston, help me."

"Just take the pantyhose off."

"I want them on."

Win shook his head. "I don't do pantyhose. That's where I draw the line."

"Then what do I do?"

"Pull them up or take them off."

"I can't pull them up."

"Then take them off."

Sounding like the idea was hers, Sally slurred, "Me thinks I'll take them off."

"Great idea," Winston replied, rolling his eyes.

She nodded, then looked down at her tangled legs.

Sally frowned. "How do I do this?"

Win exhaled sharply, turning toward her, eyes on the floor, annoyed. "Close the door. Hold the handle. Take off your slippers. Step out. Or sit down and pull them off. You can figure that out, right?"

Sally hesitated, looked to the right and left of the bathroom entry, then slowly scooted her way backward inside and shut the door.

Win pressed a hand to his forehead. "Oh God, help me!"

He began pacing, loudly talking to himself. "This is exactly like when I was six … on the school bus with Mom …

"Fuck! I can't unsee this! I'll never be able to unsee this!"

Inside, Sally yelled, "Who are you talking to, Winston?"

He spun to face the door to fretfully yell, "I'm talking to myself, Sally!"

The door flung open again. Still naked except for the sunglasses, Sally drunkenly asked, "What can't you unsee?"

Win looked to the floor and whimpered, "Oh, Jesus … where's a drive-by shooting when you need one?"

"I'm ready to be redressed," she demanded.

Head down, Win walked sideways over, shaking out her pink dress, turning its backside open for Sally to easily step in. She did … after two failed knee-lift attempts, nearly tipping over on the third try. But on the fourth, she managed to step one foot in after the other without crashing into him, taking them both out. He slowly pulled the dress up for her to slide her arms into until Sally ordered he give her a minute to tuck her nipples in properly before he zipped up the back.

"I need a fucking drink after that!" Sally slurred, clutching his arm.

"*So do I!*" Winston snapped a sarcastic retort, shaking his head, *way beyond ready* to pass the pink lush off to anyone as quickly as possible.

After several slow steps, Win looked at her blonde head bobbing like a peacock back and forth as she put one foot in front of the other. His mind immediately heard Shirley MacLaine break into song, "If all my friends could see me now …"

Sally staggered to the Grand Room. Win suggested she sit with Darceline in the chair facing her.

"Me thinks not particularly," Sally replied, eyeing their deceased aunt. "It would be a one-sided conversation anyway. And I have nothing to say."

Win glanced at Darceline, understanding her point—but still, for him at least, he felt his time with her brought absolution. He thought maybe, just maybe, Sally would like to seize the moment for some of her own.

Instead, she quipped, "This is rather macabre. Isn't that right, Cuz?"

Was it? He hadn't the time to even think …

Before he could respond, she asked if he'd heard Cheri Delabarre had died.

He sighed. "Willow mentioned it when she arrived."

"Yeah, I'm sure it's all around the lake by now." Sally said thoughtfully, "That woman could really blow it out her ass," and broke into raucous laughter.

As Win prepared to ask what *that* meant, Sally slowly turned like a ballerina on a jewelry box, winding down her laughter. She tugged on his arm; she was ready to get to the bar.

With one foot trying its best to get ahead of the other, she began complaining, "I have always loathed how this place reeks like a casino. Even with all the air purifiers Aunt D has pumping, injecting fragrant chemicals everywhere, trying to cover up the smell of stale cigarette smoke, I feel like I'm walking through a filthy ashtray right now."

Win said nothing, counting her steps to get her to an open bar seat on Phil's right. After two failed attempts to climb it at the speed of a sloth, she commanded, "Winston, grab my ass, lift me up, and put me into this goddamn thing."

With one arm firmly behind the bend of her knees and the other around her lower back, Winston said, "On three—one, two, and three," and lifted the ninety-pound woman up and placed her onto the pedestal.

"Well done, Winston," Phil said, raising his scotch.

Win stepped back to ensure Sally was secure and not about to slide off, then watched his uncle lean in to inspect Sally's face.

"I see you've added a little weight below the eyes and above the chin, Sal. Are each of your lips up to a full pound a piece?"

Scanning the bar for someone to serve her, she slurred, "I thought you died."

"Nope," Phil grinned.

Sally looked directly at her uncle. "Who's bartending? I'm empty-handed."

Phil raised an eyebrow. "Say, what's with the sunglasses? Looks like someone started crossing out your face with a fat black Sharpie marker."

Sally removed them, revealing her blue and purple bruised eyes.

"Holy fuck, kid! Did you laugh too hard and punch yourself in the face with your top lip?"

Sally blinked slowly, firing back, "Are you having a stroke?"

"Nope," Phil countered again with a devilish smirk.

Win watched the two glare at one another for five seconds before both burst into laughter and fell into a loving hug. Win adored the fondness these two shared for one another. Phil was an excellent surrogate father to Sally after Tilly died.

He was the only one who could serve Sally a slice of humble pie and make her genuinely laugh—even at herself.

The only one.

Wunnerful, Wunnerful

With cousin Sally securely planted at her barstool throne, gulping down her signature gin martini with a whisper of vermouth Winston made to her specific order, it was still too hot inside. Time again to shed the blazer. He strolled to the dining table and draped it over a chair away from Aunt D, glancing at the buffet. It was stocked with silver platters of ham and cheese sandwich quarters with the crusts trimmed, spinach dip, crackers, fresh vegetables and fruit, various chocolates, and a wide array of cookies. A large coffee urn steamed beside the drinkware at the far end. He grabbed a white cup with gold trim and poured himself a fix.

Looking across the room, he saw Sissy standing behind Dr. Funnell, who was deep in examination. Winston approached quietly, stepping in behind his sister. Willow turned to glance at him, then down at the black coffee in his hand and let out a disapproving *"Hmmf!"*

"What is it, Doctor?" Win asked.

"As I was just explaining to Marci," Dr. Funnell replied calmly, "she appears to be in congestive heart failure. I want to get her to the hospital immediately."

"No," Marci choked out.

The doctor looked to Willow and Winston, hoping one of them might persuade her. Win nodded and motioned toward the foyer—his go-to spot now for private council. They followed him out while he gulped the hot coffee for a quick jolt.

"Your mother's adamant," Dr. Funnell said. "She won't leave until her sister has been taken to the morgue. She insists on remaining by her side until that happens.

"I'd like to order an ambulance to wait out front—ready to transport her when she agrees."

Winston and Sissy exchanged a look, then nodded.

"Order it," Win said. "But no sirens. No lights. Discretion is best."

"Right," Sissy added.

"Okay," the doctor nodded.

Then, turning back to Win, he said, "I've officially called the time of death for your aunt at 7:45 p.m.—confirming what you said."

"Will the coroner send an ambulance to pick her up?" Sissy asked.

"The county has a vehicle. I'll arrange everything," Funnell assured.

Willow straightened and declared, "I'm going to grab myself a little cocky-tail before I sit with Mom," and pranced off to join the bar crowd.

Funnell mentioned stopping by the restroom and returning to Marci. Winston walked him to one in the foyer and then went looking for Peters.

The entry to D's professional kitchen was nearby. Win stepped inside and immediately noticed changes—everything appeared freshly renovated.

The kitchen was vast, open, and gleaming. High ceilings and wide aisles allowed multiple chefs to work simultaneously. New stainless-steel appliances—commercial-grade stoves, ovens, grills, and fryers—lined the space. The layout was optimized for flow: prep, cook, plate, clean. The walk-in fridge and freezer were still where he remembered, as was the wine cellar, now even more impressively stocked. White custom cabinetry covered every wall. Above a swinging door into the dining area, a flat 30-inch monitor showed six camera angles around the property: the front gate (inside and out), the driveway, the front door, the back door, and a blank square where the portico camera once operated.

The kitchen buzzed with staff at work. A chef sat typing on a laptop. Peters wasn't in sight. Winston finished his coffee and placed the cup into one of the massive industrial sinks.

"May I help you, sir?" a voice called.

He turned to see Susan, eyebrows arched, wearing a polite but tired smile.

He asked after Mr. Peters. She said he'd just stepped out. "Try the BS," she suggested. "Either that or his office."

Winston thanked her and exited through the swinging door, reviewing the Grand Room. No Peters. No Leland. He headed to Darceline's office and found them both seated at the conference table, papers scattered before them. They looked up and smiled as he entered.

"Dr. Funnell is asking when he should arrange Aunt D's transport," Winston said.

Peters checked his watch. "That would be 10:45 p.m. In ninety minutes."

"I'll let him know," Win said.

Leland asked, "How's your mother?"

"The doctor says she has congestive heart failure. She must go to the hospital but refuses to leave until Aunt D is picked up."

"Does she need oxygen?" Peters asked.

"I'd say yes."

"There are a couple of tanks in the med room. Let the doctor know."

Winston remembered that little room—when Miss Penny took him there to mend a cut when he was a boy.

"I will, thank you."

Then Peters added, "Winston, would you mind if I gave the staff the day off Saturday? As a day of mourning for Miss Hicks? Me included."

"Oh, absolutely," Winston nodded. "Of course."

"Should you need anything during your stay, call my cell. I believe you have the number from your last visit."

"I do. Thank you." He smiled and turned to go.

"Winston?" Leland called after him. "Are you all right?"

"I'm overwhelmed," Win admitted. "It's been a long day—and it's nowhere near over."

"Have you eaten anything?" Mr. Peters asked.

"No. Well—three or four bites of salad before my aunt ..."

"May I suggest you fix a plate from the hors d'oeuvres in the dining area. You should eat something."

Winston was running on fumes. "I will," he smiled, heading back toward the Grand Room to check on his mother.

He paused at the buffet and loaded a plate: two ham and cheese quarters, a pineapple chunk, and three cookies. He popped a cube of cheddar into his mouth, grabbed a cloth napkin, and headed to a chair beside Marci, chewing as he set the plate on the coffee table across from Bill and Betsy.

Scanning the room, he spotted Sissy at the bar, seated next to Tami, talking loudly. Winston quickly noted that his sister had her priorities in order.

Betsy glanced at his plate and smiled. "That looks good. I think I'll grab something for Bill and me."

"I want to see what's there," Bill said, following her.

Winston settled onto the loveseat next to his mother, reached for a chocolate chocolate-chip cookie, and broke it in half. Starving, he ate one piece in a single bite. Then, leaning close to Marci, he held up the other half.

Her breathing was labored. He could tell she was struggling.

"Mom, I love you," he whispered.

"I love you too," came her soft reply.

"Would you like half a cookie?" he asked gently. "I've got a plate of things you might like."

Marci opened her eyes, licked her lips, and saw the piece in his hand. Like a child, she opened her mouth. Winston placed the cookie gently on her bottom teeth. She took a bite and chewed slowly.

He handed her the glass of water from the coffee table. "Have a little drink."

She lifted her head, and he carefully helped her sip, steadying the glass so it wouldn't spill. After two tiny swallows, she leaned back. He offered another bite of cookie, but she shook her head—she was done.

"Thank you," she whispered, her voice barely audible.

"Let's get you to the hospital," Winston whispered tenderly, trying to coax her.

"No," she moaned and closed her eyes.

"The rest of the family is on their way," he said softly. "The house will be full soon."

"All I need is twenty more minutes to nap," she murmured. "Then I'll get up."

And with that, she drifted again.

Dr. Funnell joined them, coffee in hand, remaining on his feet.

Winston stood beside him. "10:45 is correct," he confirmed.

Dr. Funnell tapped his Apple Watch. "Thank you. I'll make the call."

"Doctor?" Win asked.

"Yes?"

"Thank you." He smiled faintly. "The rest of the family will be arriving shortly."

Funnell nodded.

"It'll get loud," Win added. "If you prefer, feel free to relax in the office across the foyer."

The doctor smiled. "Once I've made the call, I'll return to sit with Marci. I'd like to monitor her until we get her to the hospital."

Pointing toward the foyer, Winston asked, "Did you know there's a medical room in the house?"

"No. Darceline always came to my office for her appointments."

"Mr. Peters said there's a tank of oxygen. It may help Mom. Let me show you."

"Excellent," Dr. Funnell said, visibly relieved to finally be of more use.

Winston led him down a side hallway to a closed door on the left. He flipped on the lights, revealing a bright, spotless room around an examination table. Shiny metal cabinets lined three walls. The fourth had a sink, a small desk, and a chair.

Crossing to a tall cabinet labeled **OXYGEN**, Winston opened it to reveal two small oxygen cylinders on carts. On a shelf above were sealed packages of tubing kits and breathing masks.

"This is perfect," Dr. Funnell said, clearly pleased. "I'll bring one out to your mother."

"Thank you. And please help yourself with anything in here you need tonight," Win offered, already halfway out, craving a cigarette and fresh air.

"Thank you, Winston," the doctor replied warmly.

Winston headed for the back porch. He reached for one of the tall glass doors to open, then heard a murder scream pierce the manor from the open front entrance. He spun and bolted in that direction, meeting Peters and de Beaumont as they burst out of the BS lounge, drawn by the same shriek.

They all converged at the front entry just as Kaitlyn Hicks-Cook— thirty-one, explosively pregnant, and full-throttle furious—stormed into the house like a woman possessed.

The trio jumped back as she roared, "WHERE IS MY GRANDFATHER?! I JUST SAW HIS CAR!"

"He's … he's … he's …" Leland stammered, blindsided.

"Uncle Bill is in the Grand Room!" Winston shouted defensively.

"HOW COULD HE?!" Kaitlyn cried out, charging past them. "HOW COULD HE?!"

Before they could follow, in rushed her husband, Chase, carrying their towheaded five-year-old son, Stevyn. Behind them came Kaitlyn's parents—Jeffrey and Michelle Hicks—Winston's cousins, all appearing horror-stricken.

A sinking feeling came over Win; the rest of the house was about to be equally horrified.

Only Stevyn was calm, face blank as he peeked over his father's shoulder to stare at Winston with sky-blue eyes.

Jeffrey briefly shot his gaze at Win. "Are Mom and Dad, okay?"

"They're okay!" Win answered quickly as they continued their dash after Kaitlyn.

Just then, Dr. Funnell entered the foyer, dragging an oxygen tank with one hand and balancing his coffee cup, tubing, and a mask in the other. He stopped short, eyes wide. "What's happening?"

As Win followed Kaitlyn's crowd, he said over his shoulder, "Doctor, you're about to see things you just can't make up."

Inside the Grand Room, the scene went slow-mo.

Kaitlyn stormed straight for her grandfather. Betsy sat at the end of the bar, Bill to her right, mid-sandwich. To his right were Sissy, Tami, Phil, and Sally—Sally bobbing as she attempted to focus on her surroundings.

Within spitting distance of delivering her second child, Kaitlyn steamed around the bar, stepped behind it, and faced Bill directly. Both hands slapped the polished limestone countertop with a sharp smack.

The room froze.

"WHAT HAVE YOU DONE?!" she screamed.

No one moved. The entire house fell into a shocked silence.

"I BEGGED you six months ago to stop driving!

"I PLEADED with you two weeks ago to stop driving!

"AND WHAT DO YOU DO?!

"You get behind the wheel and destroy the one thing I wanted more than anything you could ever give me!

"I CANNOT ... *CANNOT* ... BELIEVE YOU TOTALED THE CADILLAC YOU SAID I COULD HAVE ONE DAY!

"I just saw it outside!

"Grandfather, *I AM SO VERY ANGRY AT YOU RIGHT NOW!*"

And with that, Bill burst into tears.

Kaitlyn took a step back, raised her hands high above her gargantuan breasts and globe-sized baby bump, and let out a primal, ten-second scream—every ounce of fury poured into it.

Sally, eyes closed and waving an empty martini glass, slurred to no one in particular, "This is a private aircraft, goddammit! Who let the crying baby on board?!"

Sissy leaned forward across Tami and fired dryly at Sally, "And the duck goes, '*Quack! Quack!*'"

A sputtery laugh hacked out from Marci's corner. Win turned to see his mother sitting upright, grinning wide as she wheezed through deep, rattling laughter—clearly enjoying Kaitlyn's performance.

"THIS IS ABOUT A CAR?!" Tami screamed at Kaitlyn.

Winston turned as Tami launched in: "You're blowing full-on shitballs over a fender bender, AND ALL YOU CARE ABOUT IS YOU WON'T GET GRANDDADDY'S CADDY?!"

Michelle interjected gently, "Tami, I think—"

Sally cut her off, slurring with mock offense, "Did someone just call me a quack?!"

Phil, red-faced and pissed, barked, pointing at Kaitlyn. "NOW LISTEN UP, MISSY! We are here because my—our—sister is DEAD!"

He whipped his finger toward Darceline. "No one gives a flying fuck that you didn't get what you wanted. So, zip that little trap, or you can march your ass out the same way you came in!"

Marci cackled louder now—raspy, unfiltered. She fell back into her pillow, clutching her chest like it hurt to laugh that hard.

Winston exchanged a look with Willow, returning to Kaitlyn to see what might come next. Kaitlyn gave the room the 'Marc Monarch chin-up pursed lips pose.' Win smirked.

Dr. Funnell silently rolled the oxygen tank to Marci's side, calm in the chaos. Little Stevyn wriggled down from Chase's arms and shuffled over to stand beside Win, staring at him.

Sissy wrapped an arm around Bill's shoulders and snapped at Kaitlyn, "By the way, your grandparents weren't hurt. Super thoughtful of you to ask."

Kaitlyn shot Sissy a scathing, wicked glare, showing her fangs.

Willow whooped, "Well, isn't that a pretty look for the Hicksville Chamber of Commerce President and CEO!"

"Go to hell, Wilhelmina!" Kaitlyn growled.

In full Lawrence Welk mode, Willow announced, "Isn't she fabulous, ladies and gentlemen? And here she is again … featuring another one of her delightful tantrums … our very own—*Pouty Preggo!*"

Phil and Tami howled with laughter.

Kaitlyn let loose again—a second blood-curdling murder scream that could scare the fuck out of Jamie Lee Curtis.

"OH, SHIT!" Marci craggily fired off before launching into her next round of even-rougher-sounding laughter from across the room.

Time to shut it down.

Winston strode to the bar, raised his hands in a time-out gesture, and said evenly, "Everyone, please. Please. This is not the time or place."

"I AGREE!" Sally shouted. "Someone remove that goddamn screaming baby from this flight!"

Win looked at his sister, deliberately clamping his lips together, implying she shut it. She stuck her tongue out.

"Please, Kaitlyn, calm down," Betsy pleaded softly. "You're eight months pregnant and should not be this upset about a car."

"I'm nine months and one day pregnant, Grandmother," Kaitlyn snarled. "And I have every right to be upset about whatever I damn well please!"

They all watched in stunned silence as she grabbed a bottle of Cabo Wabo, yanked out the cork, and took a swig.

Dr. Funnell scurried across the room to Winston's side, concerned. He leaned in and gently urged, "Kaitlyn, with all due respect, you shouldn't be doing tequila shots. Not in your condition."

Kaitlyn lowered the bottle, eyes blazing.

"With all due respect, *Doc-Tor*—DON'T TELL ME WHAT TO DO!" she roared, then took another long pull from the bottle.

Entirely numb to the situation, Kaitlyn's husband, Chase, wandered around to enter the other side of the bar and began pouring himself a scotch.

"I'll have one, too," said Jeffrey to his son-in-law. "Make it tall, a couple of cubes."

"I give up," Michelle sighed, emotionally spent. "Same for me, please."

"*Chaaassse?!*" Sally called out loudly, slurring. "Where have you been, Chase? I need a refill. Mine's empty. Just fill her up with gin." She tried to flick her martini glass with her index finger, missed entirely, and flicked the air.

"Top me off with the Dewar's, will ya?" Phil added, sliding his glass of ice down the bar.

Wanting to get to pounding down his own cocktail, Chase scrambled to fill the orders.

Betsy let out a worried moan. "Kaitlyn, why don't you sit down? You're making me terribly nervous."

Tami rolled her eyes to the ceiling and screamed, "OH MY GOD!"

She turned on Kaitlyn. "Betsy's goddamned nerves finally calmed the fuck down, AND YOU BARGE IN SCREAMING ABOUT A WHOLE LOT OF NOTHING—*FIRING HER UP ALL OVER AGAIN!*"

Tami clenched her teeth into a furious sneer, growl-scolding, "*Get your ass out from behind the goddamned bar and go sit down. Preferably across the state line!*"

"DON'T YOU TELL ME—" Kaitlyn started to belt before Phil snapped, pointing a finger at her.

"*HEY!*"

Kaitlyn stopped cold. She stood huffing and puffing like an angry caged tiger, clocking her eyes at everyone she would maul if released.

Dr. Funnell looked at Winston, clearly expecting him to intervene. Win gave a sigh and a look that said: *If her husband, parents, and grandparents can't rein her in, what do you expect me to do?* The doctor shook his head and went back to Marci.

"FUCK!" Kaitlyn screamed. "This tobacco castle is always a thousand damn degrees—I need to get outside and breathe some *real* oxygen!"

She stormed out of the room as fast as she had stormed in.

Tami shouted after her, "That's right, Kaitlyn. Chill out!"

Willow cracked up.

Sally, slouched behind Phil, slurred irritably at Tami, "Did you just tell *me* to chill out?"

Tami leaned around Phil and laughed right in Sally's face. Phil joined in, grinning like it was amateur night at the circus.

"Sally, honey," he said, "they're trying to get the baby off the plane. Try not to get in the way—and fasten your seatbelt while you're at it."

"*Oh … that … fucking … baby,*" Sally mumbled, then began making lip-smacking sounds children use to imitate a fish.

Winston looked down at Stevyn, standing silently beside him, peering up with wide, curious eyes.

Win greeted him with a friendly smile. "Hi."

"Hi," Stevyn replied.

His small voice snapped the whole room out of *The Kaitlyn Show*.

Bill turned on his barstool for a better look at his great-grandson, then shifted his gaze to his sister's body, quietly wiping his eyes. Betsy followed his line of sight—Stevyn to Darceline. Phil and Tami did the same. Willow stepped away from the bar, moving toward her mother. Jeffrey, Michelle, and Chase observed Stevyn's focus on Win, then rolled their gazes to D. Sally was hunched over her martini glass, both hands gripping the stem, her duck lips suckling on its rim.

The room appeared to have settled.

Until they all noticed Darceline's death stare—still fixed and unmoving—locked directly on the bar—upon *them*.

Betsy, triggered, started flicking her fingernails anxiously, resisting the urge to loudly confess how nervous this was making her. She bit her tongue, eyes darting to Tami.

But even Tami looked rattled. She raised her hand over her mouth and leaned into Phil, tapping his leg. Cupping his ear for only him to hear, she whispered, "You should do something about that."

Phil stood and slowly walked over to Darceline. He bent to inspect her face, squinting at her frozen, piercing gaze.

Then, turning to the room, he pointed to his own eyes with two fingers and swiveled them toward everyone else.

"I don't know what the hell to do about this. Does anyone know where she keeps her sunglasses?"

Bill, Betsy, Jeffrey, Michelle & Satan

Bill Hicks never thought a basketball game would change his life. He was a Purdue University sophomore majoring in Agricultural Sciences and deeply committed to soil quality, crop rotation, and Boilermaker basketball. On a cold February evening, he and a couple of classmates piled into his Mercury coupe and drove from West Lafayette to Bloomington to see Purdue take on Indiana University.

They arrived early and found their seats in the packed assembly hall. As Bill stood chatting with his buddies, a group of sorority girls walked in, laughing and buzzing with energy—and in the center of the pack was her: Elizabeth 'Betsy' Allen.

Betsy had strawberry-blonde hair, a red scarf that matched her lips, and eyes that looked like they'd seen more than college parties. She majored in Fine Arts and was passionate about painting, museums, color, texture, and everything. And wouldn't you know it—her seat was beside Bill's.

He scooted over politely. "Hope you don't mind sitting next to the enemy," he said, grinning.

She smiled right back. "As long as you don't start shouting 'Boiler Up' in my ear."

"I make no promises," he teased.

They flirted gently, like two people who already knew they'd met someone important. They cheered for their teams when they scored, leaned toward each other when the ref made a bad call and shared glances like they'd been doing it for years. When halftime came, Bill turned to her.

"Would you like a Pepsi?" he asked casually.

"Sure," she said. Then added, "May I tag along?"

They walked together, winding through the crowd, balancing drink orders and popcorn, but more importantly, slipping into a conversation that just *clicked*. They talked about the weather, how weird college mascots were, and how both dreamed of traveling the world.

By the time the second half started, they'd barely looked at the court. It wasn't even about Purdue or IU anymore. It was about them.

As the buzzer rang to end the game, Bill turned to her and, with his soft voice and hopeful eyes, said, "Would you like to go out sometime? You know, when we're not supposed to hate each other?"

She giggled, nodded, and said, "I'd like that."

Their love grew like long-distance love must: slowly but deeply. They went on weekend drives, had long phone calls, exchanged books and little gifts, and made it through papers, exams, rivalries, and questions about the future. Betsy dreamed of working in a big city as a museum curator, while Bill had always imagined running his family's agricultural company back home.

But love does something to dreams. It doesn't crush them; it just *repaints* them.

By the time they both graduated, they'd fallen in love with more than just each other—they'd fallen in love with the idea of building a life together. Bill introduced Betsy to his sister, Darceline, who was also a lover of art and was looking to start a collection of paintings for the new home she was building at Bucks Peak. Betsy and Darci hit it off, taking weekend trips with Bill to art museums around the Midwest, like the Art Institute of Chicago.

Betsy was offered and accepted the job as Darceline's personal art consultant. She was still surrounded by beauty and culture, just a different kind than she'd imagined. She never looked back.

Bill became President of Agriculture for Hicks America. He loved the land, the science, the grit. But more than anything, he loved coming home to Betsy—who always had paint on her fingers and laughter in her eyes.

They agreed early on to raise one child and treat them like the crowned prince or princess of a cornfield kingdom. When Betsy became pregnant, they both cried. After Jeffrey was born, the world seemed brighter and more fragile.

Betsy embraced motherhood with the ferocity of an artist discovering a new medium. She painted less and watched more—watching over Jeffrey as he napped, watching the sky for storms that might spook him, watching Bill's face for reassurance she was doing it right.

It wasn't long before the nerves started.

It began as a flutter. A tightness in her chest when Jeffrey cried too long. A shortness of breath when the phone rang unexpectedly. An invisible tremor, like the floor beneath her feet, might shift at any moment.

Her doctor called it a mild postpartum condition—common, manageable—and prescribed her a gentle sedative to take "as needed." Betsy tried it once or twice. But the numbness it brought felt foreign, too far removed from the woman she knew herself to be. She didn't want to float. She wanted to feel, even if feeling meant riding out a storm or two.

So, she sought other paths.

Betsy found peace in water, gliding through laps at Darceline's pool in early morning summers when the air still held a hush. She joined a yoga studio and learned how to breathe and stretch her limbs into postures that matched her inner hope for balance. On Thursday nights, she danced—tapping, twirling, and waltzing her nerves into a rhythm.

The exercise helped immensely. Her episodes became fewer and softer, but they never entirely disappeared. Now and then, a moment would swell—a misplaced toy, a sound in the night, or even the sudden thought of something terrible that never happened but *could*. In those moments, she'd pause, eyes unfocused, heart racing.

Bill never made a fuss.

He was a man of the land. Earth-bound, steady, calm like fields before a harvest. When she had an anxious day, all it took was the familiar sound of the gravel of his voice as he told her about his meetings with seed reps or how the alfalfa crop looked promising.

Bill didn't try to fix it or suggest more solutions. He was simply there, gentle and rooted. His presence in the room was like an anchor tossed into uncertain waters. As he spoke about pH levels and new irrigation plans, Betsy would lean her head on his shoulder and feel her pulse slow to match his. They found their rhythm.

With Jeffrey, Betsy had always been the spine of the household—the one who kept everything standing tall, smiling, and well-fed. She managed mornings, packed lunches, permission slips, and bedtime prayers. She took to motherhood like a gardener takes to soil—hands-on, full-hearted, and attentive to the most minor seasonal changes.

Jeffrey was their pride and joy and grew up under the warm canopy of her care. She drove him to Cub Scouts, stayed through every Pinewood Derby, helped him polish his shoes for Boy Scout ceremonies, and cheered like mad the day he earned Eagle Scout. She baked cupcakes for school birthdays and volunteered as a classroom mom.

Bill proudly made it his life's work to introduce Jeffrey to the wonders of farming—because nothing says bonding like a father-son chat over manure management. Jeffrey was a brown-haired science whiz who loved it. He memorized the periodic table for fun and could talk about soil pH like most kids talked about cartoons. He was 4-H royalty, gleefully swapping fertilizer facts with farm kids who treated tractor specs like gossip.

Jeffrey met Michelle Davison in high school on the first day of tenth-grade biology. They bonded over the shared joy of dissecting frogs without gagging. Her family had recently relocated from Seattle after her father, Dean, accepted the CFO position at Hicks America. Romantic sparks flew somewhere between the formaldehyde fumes and a 4-H pig show. Before long, Jeffrey and Michelle were inseparable—like peas in an agriculturally optimized pod.

Their vow to abstain from sex until marriage collapsed entirely on prom night. After partying with other science nerds in a run-down barn off a county road—with a few lifted bottles of Boone's Farm Strawberry Hill wine—they wandered into a grassy field with a blanket and gave in to their teenage hormones.

Their sudden wedding the week after graduation surprised the whole family, but all four parents insisted once Michelle's pregnancy came to light. Bill and Betsy gifted them a lovely starter home in one of Max's subdivision wonders. Dean and his wife provided a monthly stipend for them to live on.

Michelle's pregnancy was difficult, and her labor was nearly fatal. Kaitlyn was a large baby for Michelle's petite frame. A rare complication required an emergency C-section when Kaitlyn's head wouldn't fit through the birth canal. Michelle lost a dangerous amount of blood and spent her daughter's first days in the ICU, unable to hold or even see her. When she finally came home, Michelle was handed a baby who never stopped crying.

Jeffrey juggled community college and diapers, while Michelle adjusted to a baby who seemed born enraged—and determined to let the world know it.

While Jeffrey and Michelle settled into their new life with Katilyn, the house changed for Betsy. The rooms echoed. The calendar opened up. And though Bill still came home every evening to share his department's discoveries, Betsy found herself walking slower, thinking more, and reaching for paint brushes she hadn't held in years.

And so, she began to paint again.

At first, she painted from memory—small scenes of Jeffrey as a boy chasing fireflies, Bill sitting on the porch with muddy boots, and their old golden retriever asleep beneath the kitchen table. But soon, she began painting portraits of the Hicks family—honest, affectionate renderings that made Darceline gasp and declare them heirlooms.

But the crown jewel came one summer afternoon at Bucks Peak.

It was a July day, warm enough to soften the breeze but not enough to steal it. The kind of day that seemed to hum with life. Hicksville Lake glimmered beneath a perfect sky, and from the beach, Betsy watched Darceline's love, Penny, in a yellow sailboat, carving clean lines across the water like a brushstroke on glass.

The boat itself was called *Sweet Nothings* and flashed in the sun. Penny helmed it with grace, barefoot and windswept, laughing with her eyes closed as the breeze kissed her cheeks. She wore a light blue top, loose and airy, and in that moment, Betsy saw something that felt eternal.

Betsy took her Nikon 35mm camera everywhere she went, always looking to capture something extraordinary she could recreate with her brush. She took dozens of photographs—Penny at the tiller, the sail stretched high, the light turning the lake to silver lace. But there was one shot—one perfect shot—that held everything. Penny mid-turn, hair blown back, face tilted skyward, smiling not for anyone but herself.

Betsy didn't paint it right away. She studied it for days. When she finally began, she chose something rare, something deliberate: pointillism.

She wanted the painting to feel alive, not just to show the scene but to *shimmer* the way it had shimmered in real life—sunlight broken into dots, joy broken into fragments of color. Every feeling, every breath of wind, placed one speck at a time.

The mural was enormous—four feet by six feet—and covered a

third of the studio's wall. Betsy wore soft cotton gloves to keep her hands steady and stood for hours daily, dipping her brush into tiny puddles of color: cerulean for the water, gold for the sail, peach and sunbeam for Penny's radiant skin.

Dot by dot, she conjured it into life.

The boat leaned gently in the wind, its sail taut and proud. The water sparkled in impossibly small blue, white, and lavender bursts. Penny's hair flowed in strands of honey and wheat, her face aglow, eyes closed in a kind of sunlit serenity that made anyone who looked at the painting feel like they, too, were out there on the lake—wind at their backs, warmth on their faces, time suspended.

She titled the piece simply: *Penny*.

When she unveiled it to Darceline, the house went quiet.

Even Darceline, who was rarely at a loss for words, stood before the mural with tears in her eyes. "It's *her*," she whispered. "You didn't just paint her, Betsy—you *captured* her."

And it was true. The painting held not just a person but a moment, a memory, a breath of joy suspended in paint.

Even Penny herself teared up.

It became the centerpiece of Darceline's collection—the painting visitors asked about, marveled over, and returned to again and again. But to Betsy, it was never about the praise. It was about honoring someone else's love—taking one perfect summer day and turning it into forever, one dot at a time.

But the vibrant colors in Betsy's world soon changed to darker, bluer hues once menopause arrived—bringing with it a new level of nervousness that didn't go away once the hot flashes ended. She became easily and more frequently triggered. But like she had chosen when she was younger, Betsy continued to ride her waves of anxiety prescription-free.

By toddlerhood, Kaitlyn had elevated tantrums to an art form. One memorable Christmas, three-year-old Kaitlyn didn't get what she wanted from Santa, scaled the tree like a deranged squirrel, and hurled ornaments at Jeffrey and Michelle in a raging fit. Wilhemenia babysat once when she was four. Kaitlyn threw a temper tantrum so seismic she screamed at the top of her lungs until she passed out—simply because Willow didn't bring with her the flavor of ice cream Kaitlyn demanded. Her outbursts became so unpredictably disruptive that Jeffrey and Michelle stopped taking Kaitlyn to the country club—or were quietly told not to bring her again, which may have been the case.

Desperately concerned their child had a physiological defect, triggering her disastrous and violent behavior, Jeffrey and Michelle had Kaitlyn tested by a neurologist in Indianapolis. The results: she was a perfectly healthy child with an unhealthy and unruly disposition. There were prescriptions for that.

Within weeks of starting a new mood stabilizer, eight-year-old Kaitlyn transformed. She now insisted on being called Katie. She was calmer, manageable, and even likable.

The entire Hicks clan exhaled. Grandparents resumed spoiling her, like when Bill took her to the A&W Drive-In for a root beer float on her sixteenth birthday.

"You'll be driving soon," he said, watching her stir the melting vanilla ice cream into the root beer from the front seat of his white Fleetwood.

"When I get my license, can I have your car? I've always loved your big Cadillac, Grandpa."

Bill smiled, knowing Jeffrey had bought her a new Volvo, one of the safest cars on the market. "Well, one day, when I'm done driving it, it's all yours. I promise."

Katie never forgot that day.

She blossomed into a beautiful, popular young woman. During her junior year at Purdue, still undecided on a major, she met Chase—a sweet, kind, gentle, soft-spoken agriculture student who was essentially a carbon copy of her father and grandfather. They fell in love.

Chase was welcomed into the family with open arms. After graduation, Bill offered him a promising role at Hicks America, working alongside him and Jeffrey. Still unsure about her academic direction after three years, Katie put college on pause and moved back to Hicksville to be with him.

Chase and Katie wed. She was happier than ever—so much so that she quietly stopped taking her medication, convinced she no longer needed it. No one noticed at first—a few snide remarks here, a dramatic exit there.

Then she got pregnant. With the hormonal surges and chemical shifts, her moods turned sharp, nasty, and erratic. Bill and Jeffrey told Chase it was just pregnancy. It would pass.

Michelle wasn't so sure. In her gut, she had always believed there was something dark in her daughter—something unnatural, something evil.

She grew increasingly uneasy as Kaitlyn's old tantrums and violent episodes resurfaced. Michelle invited her to lunch and gently asked if she was still taking her fluoxetine "happy pills."

"I'm pregnant, Mother. I've stopped taking anything not prescribed by my OB-GYN," she said flatly. "And you can stop calling me Katie. I go by Kate now."

The way she said it sent a piercing chill down Michelle's spine. Kate's voice was deeper, her tone cold and clipped. Something was off. Something was wrong. The woman sitting across from her was not Kaitlyn, savagely stabbing walnuts out of a chicken salad with surgical precision—like each nut had the name of someone on her enemy's list. She wasn't Katie either.

Michelle dreadfully realized she was afraid of her daughter again— *whoever, or whatever*—she had become.

Kate gave birth to a son on a gray Tuesday morning in March. She named him Stevyn—with a 'y'—because she wanted the name to look more "distinguished" on future business cards. The birth was smooth, clinical, and handled by the best OB-GYN team the newly built Hicksville Hospital had to offer. There were no tears, joyful weeping, or dramatic music swelling in the background. Kate held the baby once, sniffed his head, and promptly handed him to Chase like she'd just unwrapped a birthday gift she had no intention of keeping.

On the other hand, Chase was instantly a devoted father, never looking more alive or competent. Within days, he had a system for sleep, swaddling, bottle prep, and bathtime. He kept spreadsheets for pediatric milestones and color-coded Stevyn's wardrobe by size and season. While Kate paced the house talking to her career coach and designing her "future public persona," Chase sang lullabies and learned how to make puréed carrots taste like joy.

Motherhood, as it turned out, bored Kate to tears. She referred to breastfeeding as "prisoner duty" and maternity yoga as "cult aerobics." Her body bounced back in record time thanks to genetics, vanity, and a personal trainer named Lyle, but her enthusiasm for parenting didn't rebound with it.

By Stevyn's six-month checkup, she had made a proclamation.

"I'm not cut out for this," she told Michelle over coffee. "I have too many leadership qualities to waste them on playdates and poop."

Now well-versed in Kate's maternal detachment, Michelle sipped her coffee and said nothing.

Kate set her sights on something better: The Hicksville Chamber of Commerce. Its current president, Myrna Templeton, had held the role for over a decade and ran it like a retirement hobby. Kate considered that an insult to capitalism. She began a one-woman campaign to expose the Chamber's "obsolete leadership" through carefully leaked rumors, accusations of financial mismanagement, and one anonymously submitted (but clearly Kate-authored) op-ed titled "Time for New Blood in Hicksville."

By the time Myrna announced her "early retirement," Kate had already networked onto the interim board. A month later, she bulldozed her way into the presidency, complete with a glossy headshot in the town paper and a quote about "redefining what it means to lead with boldness." No one dared argue.

Back at home, Chase thrived in his role as a full-time dad. Stevyn was a happy child—giggly and emotionally secure. He never threw tantrums, bit other children, or once hurled an ornament across a room. Other mothers would sidle up to Chase at the park, asking for parenting advice, mistaking his serene presence and encyclopedic child development knowledge for the product of some exclusive parenting class. It was just Chase being Chase—pure-hearted, patient, and ridiculously overqualified for diaper duty.

Then, when Stevyn turned four, Kate got pregnant again.

It was not planned. Nor was it welcomed.

When she saw the two pink lines, Kate began a months-long tirade that would've made Rose Nylund in *The Golden Girls* look like Alex Forrest in *Fatal Attraction*. "Another parasite," she declared to Chase, holding the test like it had personally betrayed her.

She griped through every trimester. She hated the nausea. She hated the bloat. She hated "the gendered tyranny of maternity fashion" and referred to her OBGYN as "Dr. Doom." She swore her fetus was "leeching her will to live" and regularly told people she was only having this baby because Chase still "believed in love and God and all that corn-fed bullshit."

It was a HicksSat-1 transmission that shocked and scared the hell out of Bill Hicks on April 4, 2004, and changed everything.

A massive dust storm had swept across Iowa and Illinois, catching most by surprise. But the satellite data revealed something far more troubling than a passing weather event: entire swaths of land—

including some of Hicks America's most profitable farms—had lost up to two inches of topsoil in the storm. The implications were chilling with corn and soybean planting just two weeks away.

Bill couldn't help but think of the stories his father used to tell about the Dust Bowl of the 1930s—blackened skies, withered crops, families forced off their land. Now, staring at the data, it didn't feel like history. It felt like prophecy.

His first call was to Darceline. "I don't want to wake up in five years and find we've built an empire on dust," he told her. "We're going to find a better way to farm."

Determined to uncover the root causes of the erosion, Bill ordered his department to dig deeper. The storm was just the spark. The real culprits were decades of conventional farming practices—over-tilling, monocropping, and pesticide chemical dependency—that had stripped the land of its resilience. The soil wasn't just damaged. It was dead: exposed, depleted, and vulnerable.

After months of study and collaboration with scientists, agronomists, and Indigenous land stewards, a straightforward solution emerged: regenerative agriculture. This holistic approach aimed to halt erosion and restore the land's health by minimizing soil disturbance, integrating cover crops, rotating diverse plantings, and fostering biodiversity.

When Bill shared his findings with his sister, Darceline didn't hesitate. She gave the order: every acre Hicks America owned—over 500,000 in total—would transition to regenerative farming practices. The move was bold and risky, unprecedented at such a scale. It meant retraining workers, retooling equipment, and perhaps most challenging, reshaping a deeply entrenched farming culture.

By 2007, the transformation was complete. Every Hicks America farm was producing organic, regeneratively grown food. Yields stabilized, then climbed. The soil, once brittle and lifeless, darkened with renewed vitality. Earthworms returned. Birds followed, and with them, bees—pollinating at levels never seen before. And a new wave of consumers arrived too, hungry for chemical-free food grown harmoniously with the earth.

What began as a crisis became a movement. Bill hadn't just saved their farms from another Dust Bowl—he had reshaped the future of his family's legacy.

Though not everyone welcomed the change. One of the nation's largest agricultural pesticide manufacturers took particular offense—especially after Hicks America declined to renew their multi-million-dollar contract.

Phil, Tami, Jasmine, Jackson & Dalton

Third-born and eldest son, Phillip Hicks, was tall, broad-shouldered, and strikingly handsome, with light brown hair and piercing blue eyes. Phil possessed a natural athleticism that could have taken him far. He might've been the star quarterback or a champion track athlete in another life. Coaches saw the potential and tried to recruit him, but his afternoons weren't spent beneath the stadium lights. Instead, Phil clocked in at the family marina on Hicksville Lake, juggling school, work, and the daily lessons of responsibility.

But Phil found his freedom when the lake sparkled under the summer sun. He was a natural on the water—graceful, fearless, and in total command—whether carving glassy waves on a slalom ski or launching off wakes behind a roaring speedboat. Locals often gathered to watch him pull off impossible tricks, his tanned, muscular form cutting through the water effortlessly. He was the undisputed king of the lake—and every young woman in Hicksville knew it.

Phil wasn't just a showman but a solution-finder with an inventive streak. Instead of heading off to college, he took over the Hicksville

Marina and began dreaming up innovations for the marine world. In 1963, he unveiled the Hicks Partay Barj—a revolutionary new kind of pontoon boat that turned heads and made waves. Word spread quickly beyond Hicksville, and soon, boaters across the Midwest were placing pre-orders. By 1964, Hicks Marine was born, complete with a factory across the street from the marina dedicated to manufacturing and pontoon assembly.

The Hicks Partay Barj was ahead of its time—a floating paradise designed for leisure and fun. It featured two built-in coolers, one at the bow and another at the stern, each with a clever drainage system funneling melted ice directly into the lake. One cooler usually held beer and soda pop, the other food—but for diehard partygoers, both were strictly beverage zones.

Insulated cupholders lined the rails to keep drinks ice-cold, and removable ashtrays made cleanup a breeze. On the back deck, a custom-built propane grill turned every outing into a lakeside cookout. And for music? An eight-speaker AM radio system with a towering five-foot antenna brought rock 'n' roll straight from WOWO in Fort Wayne—forty miles away. Whether it was the Beatles or Elvis echoing across Hicksville Lake, the Partay Barj was the ultimate vessel for summer revelry.

But Phil didn't stop there. Riding the wave of the Partay Barj's success, he set his sights on land. His next big idea? The Hicks Partay Golf Kart.

This wasn't your average golf cart with seating for four—it was pure luxury with all the flair. Built-in coolers and cupholders were just the beginning. Removable ashtrays accommodated smokers on the green, while a sleek cabinet housed a full-service bar: ice bucket, glass rack with four lowball glasses, and compartments for premium spirits. And, of course, there was still room for four golf bags. It was a hit at country clubs across the country.

Phil had transformed the family marina into the beating heart of innovation. The Hicks name became synonymous with style, comfort, and fun—on water and on land. His vision ensured the party never stopped, and his legacy as a pioneer in the marine and recreational industries was just the beginning.

By night, Phillip lived just as boldly. He partied with his pals in laughter as mischief filled the summer air. The marina and factory weren't just his workplace—but his playground. Though his charm made him a magnet for women, he never led anyone on. His heart was wild, untethered—until he met Tami Thompson.

Tami was radiant. With cascading chestnut hair and striking green eyes, she was a vision of Midwestern beauty. Her elegance and confidence carried her to the Miss Michigan stage in 1966, where she proudly placed as first runner-up. But even the glitter of the pageant world paled next to the spark she felt with Phillip.

They met on a sun-drenched afternoon at the lake. Tami had come with friends. Phil, ever the showman, pulled off a daring ski jump that sent a spray of water glittering in the air. When he emerged with his trademark grin, their eyes locked—and the sparks were instant. Tami was more than a beauty queen. She was sharp, witty, unafraid to challenge him, and just as skilled on a pair of skis—water or snow.

Their courtship was a whirlwind of moonlit boat rides and stolen kisses on the marina docks. By the following summer, they were married in a lavish lakeside ceremony that brought the whole town together. Not long after, they welcomed twins—Jasmine and Jackson—who inherited their parents' magnetic charm, athletic prowess, and stunning good looks.

Phil took pride in fatherhood, raising his children with the same values he'd grown up with—hard work, resilience, and devotion to family. Though the shadow of his father's early death still loomed, Phillip forged his legacy—rooted in joy, ingenuity, and love. He left a wake that would never fade on the water and in the heart of the community.

Jasmine and Jackson were born three months after Winston. From the start, they were breathtaking—blessed with buttery blonde manes, forest-green eyes, and bronze skin that seemed to tan flawlessly when they stepped into a sunbeam to fetch the mail. Jasmine arrived first and was kind but commanding. She asserted dominance over both Jackson and Winston from day one. She basked in the attention her beauty naturally drew, while Jackson, though equally striking, sought validation in quieter ways.

Thanks to Max's architectural brilliance, Phil and Tami built a sprawling estate across the lake from Winston's parents. A seven-minute boat ride, a one-mile walk, or a breezy bike ride connected the two properties. Marci and Tami often arranged playdates, and the trio of cousins spent their early years toggling between golf lessons at the country club and chlorine-scented afternoons at the pool, burning energy and soaking up the sunshine.

At sixteen, Jasmine and Jackson took jobs at the Hicksville Country Club. Jasmine thrived as a hostess, relishing the admiration she received—it was essentially a paid fan meet-and-greet. Jackson, meanwhile, got certified as a lifeguard and spent the summer poolside, perpetually tanned and shirtless—a fact not lost on Hicksville's teenage girls. After Labor Day, he transitioned to part-time work at his father's Partay Manufacturing Plant after the pool closed, assembling pontoons and golf carts after school.

Twice crowned prom queen and eventually named second runner-up in the Miss Indiana Hoosier 1984 pageant, Jasmine wore her beauty like a birthright. Unlike Cousin Sally—whose growing collection of facelifts and fillers resembled an avant-garde art installation—Jasmine aged with enviable serenity. Thanks to her plastic surgeon husband, Robert, and a curated arsenal of dermatological treatments and moisturizers, her glow endured without a scalpel. She continued to command every room she entered, loving her fans as much as they adored her.

She met Robert Wright in college after a sorority-sponsored roadside cleanup left her with a sprained ankle. Robert, a devastatingly handsome ER resident, tended to her injury, and sparks flew. Not one for the party scene, he invited her for coffee instead of cocktails. One cup turned into another, and he proposed on their sixth date over decaf. They agreed to marry after his residency once he'd opened his plastic surgery practice.

Now President of Hospitality for Hicks America and a board member, Jasmine had long been eyeing Darceline's Chairwoman seat. Years of strategic alliances and quiet power moves had set the stage for an intriguing showdown at Friday's board meeting.

Jasmine and Robert had three children—two daughters and a son. Like Winston before them, the girls, Jean and Joan, fled Indiana when they were old enough, putting as much distance between themselves and the family legacy as possible. Meanwhile, their brother Dalton became a TV icon, the poster child for Hoosier Beef meat products.

Jackson, born two minutes after Jasmine, was the yin to her gleaming yang—humble, self-effacing, and deeply grounded. He inherited his parents' athleticism and excelled at every sport he touched, but his heart belonged to the water. Hicksville Lake was his sanctuary; later, the ocean became his obsession. A spring break trip to Hawaii changed his life. One surf lesson on natural waves, and he was hooked. He dropped out of college, moved to Oahu, and trained with surfing legends. Within a few years, he carved out a name on the pro surfing circuit—racking up wins, sponsors, and sun-bleached glory.

But at twenty-eight, during a competition on the coast of New South Wales in Australia, Jackson's luck turned. A mistimed move sent him crashing into a reef, shattering both legs. Several surgeries and a grueling rehab followed, but the ocean no longer welcomed him the way it once had. Phil, then President of Recreational Products at Hicks America, convinced his son to come home and join the family business. Though corporate life wasn't his natural element, Jackson took on a management role in the Marine Division, overseeing six marinas across five states.

One of those marinas was in Pompano Beach, just north of Fort Lauderdale. Whenever work brought him to town, Jackson and Winston made it a tradition to catch up over seafood and drinks, savoring a sliver of their old, carefree days.

Jackson never married and never wanted to. Commitment gave him hives. But his reputation as a ladies' man was practically international folklore. Women chased him not just for his dangerously handsome face but sometimes in the hopes of securing a slice of his undeniably premium gene pool. Ever the philanthropist, Jackson was happy to donate—liberally, if not wisely.

He left behind five children across three continents, each proudly named Jackson by their mothers, as if branding a limited-edition line of denim. His parenting style could best be described as "direct deposit." There were no birthdays or awkward holiday calls—just the comforting arrival of a check in the mail, like a festive little ghost saying, "Happy whatever, kid."

While Jasmine thrived on external validation, Jackson possessed something rare—a psychic ability he described as "spiritual octane." In moments of emotional intensity, and only when physical touch was involved, he could receive a message, vision, or affirmation that the person in front of him needed to hear. It didn't happen often. He never told his parents. Or anyone. But when he and Winston were twelve, spending the weekend with Darceline and Penny while their parents went to a Chicago concert, he confided in his cousin.

"Read my fortune," Winston said, holding his hands out palms up.

"It doesn't work like that," Jackson replied. "It only happens when I'm really happy, or sad, or upset."

"Like when?"

"Like at Sally's birthday party last summer. Aunt Millie was tickling me and wouldn't stop … and then … I saw her driving a golf cart really fast. She went over a bunker, flew out, and landed in the sand trap, and the cart crashed and flipped. The next day, it happened."

"Did you say anything?" Winston asked.

"No. But it happened."

"Wow."

Over the years, Jackson continued to share these moments with

Win—some were affirmations that changed lives, and others were warnings that may have saved them. Winston always listened, never judged, and believed entirely in Jackson's rare, untamed gift.

$$\mathcal{H}$$

Jasmine and Robert's youngest was Dalton. Like so many others in the family, he was blessed with dazzling good looks and magnetic charm; he was a joyful infant—a bundle of boundless energy and sunshine. His early childhood was much like any other's until, around age six, his exuberance took a sharp turn. Sudden, repetitive movements and unexpected vocal outbursts led to a diagnosis: Tourette Syndrome. But in true Hicks fashion, the family shrugged it off as a minor inconvenience, best ignored.

With medication and unwavering family support, Dalton's tics eased, and the Hicks household adapted with a masterclass in nonchalance. If Dalton barked, twitched, or shouted a rogue word during dinner, the forks didn't pause, and the smiles didn't fade. It was just another night at the table.

Meanwhile, Darceline had been expanding the company's stake in the beef industry. Hicks America already owned cattle ranches across Montana, Texas, Iowa, and Indiana—ranging from cow-calf operations to large-scale feedlots, where high-energy diets prepped cattle for slaughter. When a struggling slaughterhouse and meat processing plant in Valparaiso popped up at a bargain price, Darceline pounced. Her plan? Leverage their beef pipeline to launch a national commercial brand: Hoosier Beef—steaks, hamburgers, hot dogs.

And then there was Dalton: devastatingly handsome, photogenic to the point of satire. He wasn't just camera-ready—he was a photographer's dream. Darceline declared he should be the face of Hoosier Beef, a role seemingly custom-designed for a cherubic child who could bite into a burger like a religious experience.

Jasmine loved the idea of Dalton becoming a star. She gave her full blessing and written authorization. Darceline didn't hesitate.

Dalton's first assignment was a backyard cookout commercial. The role was simple: chomp dramatically into a hamburger, moan with joy, and flash a smile so bright it could melt grill grease. Then, with blue eyes twinkling and ketchup on his cheek, he'd deliver the line: "Hoosier Beef tastes so good. *Thanks, Dad!*"

It was like Shakespeare—only juicier.

Hoosier Beef struck gold. Dalton's image became iconic. Over the years, his character evolved from an adorable burger boy to a full-blown teenage heartthrob, aged to perfection like the prime cuts he sold. Eventually, the campaign introduced a love interest—the quintessential girl next door, all glossy hair, freckled cheeks, and the wholesome ability to make a burnt hot dog seem charming.

In the commercial, the two flirted at barbecues and exchanged meaningful glances over steaks, and, after years of slow-burn romance, America was treated to their on-screen wedding. Somewhere, a bald eagle probably wept.

The next era of Hoosier Beef ads rebranded around newlywed bliss. Dalton—shirt unbuttoned just enough to hint at a six-pack that likely had its own fan club—sauntered across the patio with a platter of perfectly grilled steaks. His glowing wife giggled by the grill. The commercial's climax? Dalton turned to the camera with a twinkling grin and purred: "Hoosier Beef."

Cue the flirtatious wink from his on-screen bride: *"Why, you are, honey!"*

Today, Dalton Hicks is etched into America's collective memory—equal parts heartthrob and hamburger evangelist. As iconic as Jimmy Dean, with fewer sausage jokes, Dalton remains the undisputed showpiece of backyard barbecue dreams. Whether flipping a steak or flashing that grin like he's harboring a juicy secret, he remains the sizzling soul of Hoosier Beef.

And he hated every minute of it.

Sugar & Spite

Looking down at five-year-old Stevyn—the Hicks prince-in-waiting—Winston squatted to meet his gaze.

"Do you know who I am?" he asked.

Stevyn tilted his head like a curious puppy, blinked once, and offered nothing.

"My name is Winston. And my mommy is Aunt Marci, who's lying on the sofa resting. She's not feeling very good today."

Winston gestured toward his mother, but Stevyn stayed locked on him.

"The last time I saw you, you were no bigger than a football," he smiled. "And now look at you. All grown up."

"Yeah," Stevyn replied. "I'm in school now."

"That's great," Win chirped.

Then, without warning, Stevyn hit him with the emotional equivalent of a rogue dodgeball.

"Aunt Darceline died. That's why we're here. Is that why you're here?"

Win nodded, lips pursed sideways, saying nothing—trying to keep the mood light while internally reeling from the kid's uncanny ability to cut through social pretense like a tiny philosopher.

Stevyn took a deep breath, eyed the buffet, and asked, "Are there cookies over there?"

Grateful for the pivot, Win grinned. "There are! Would you like to get one?"

A small smile wiped away the little storm cloud hovering over Stevyn's face. He nodded eagerly.

"Let's see what's there, shall we?" Win said, rising.

They marched to the buffet like two knights on a noble quest for confectionery glory. Win picked up the platter stacked with six kinds of cookies and lowered it to Stevyn's eye level. The boy inspected them with the intense focus of a bomb squad technician. Finally, he plucked a thumbprint cookie filled with strawberry jam and savored the victory.

"Would you like a plate so you can add a few more?" Win offered.

Stevyn shook his head.

Win handed him a folded white napkin. "Something to drink?"

Another shake.

"Thank you, Winston," he said, strawberry jam smeared across his lip like war paint.

"You're very welcome, Stevyn."

Feeling rather accomplished—and now starving—Win grabbed a chocolate chocolate chip for himself. He turned toward Jeffrey and Michelle, who had been watching with warm smiles, enjoying their grandson's first conversation with the family's new patriarch.

"I think I'll go say hello to your grandma and grandpa," Win told Stevyn through a bite of cookie. "Want to come?"

"Okay. But I call Grandpa *Grampy*," he corrected.

Michelle and Jeffrey slid off their barstools, arms open for hugs. Behind the bar, Chase—handsome, confident, sipping scotch like a man who knew exactly when to start drinking—stepped out for greetings.

"When did you get into town?" Chase asked, looking like a golf pro moonlighting as a bartender at Cindy's rooftop in Chicago.

Before Win could answer, Sally's voice rang out from the bar.

"I got back a month ago!" she bellowed, swiveling her chair to face them. "Two days after they kicked me off the yacht in Aruba. And for what?! I have *never* been disorderly a day in my life!"

Sally slowly rolled out of her seat and face-planted onto the carpet with a dignified thud, as if her body had forgotten to stop when the chair did.

"Man overboard!" Willow leaned back and hollered, nailing the comedic timing.

Betsy sniggered. Tami burst into laughter.

Phil looked down at Sally, shouting, "Told you to buckle up, honey!"

"Hold on, Pinky!" Willow yelled. "The Coast Guard is on its way!"

Betsy liked that one—upgrading to a chortle.

Win quickly stuffed the cookie between his lips as he and Jeffrey lunged into action, scooping up Sally.

"I'm fine!" she slurred indignantly. "Just put me back!"

They carefully returned her to the barstool. Win slowly turned the chair toward the counter, pulled the cookie from his mouth, and suggested she lean on the bar for support. Jeffrey stepped back, hands cupped like a safety net, ready in case she fell off again.

"Sally, dear, why don't you lay your head down for a little nap?" Tami suggested sweetly with a drizzle of sarcasm.

"Who just said I should be put down?!" Sally screeched, glaring at no one in particular.

More laughter.

Michelle motioned toward a quieter corner near the windows. They settled into a cluster of club chairs, Win facing Darceline.

Michelle asked, "When did you fly in, Win?"

"About an hour before D died," he replied.

The mood dropped from "comedy roast" to "sad family drama" in a heartbeat.

"We'd just sat down to dinner when she had one of her jags," he added.

Michelle looked uneasy. "She coughed to death?"

Win nodded, popping the rest of his cookie into his mouth.

"Damn," Jeffrey said, shaking his head. "My biggest fear was she'd die in front of me from one of those sloshy coughs."

Waving a hand theatrically, Win replied, "Sorry, Jeffrey! *My* biggest fear won that prize today. You're off the hook."

Michelle let out half a chuckle. Jeffrey cracked a half smile. Chase pursed his lips. Stevyn stood beside his grandmother, silently finishing his cookie, still watching Winston.

"What brings you to town?" Jeffrey asked.

"Ha!" Win barked, glancing at Darceline. "That's a whole story I'll share another time … but this morning, I was minding my own check-out from rehab in California, and next thing I know, Aunt Darceline's got me on her jet flying home."

Then, with a cookie-laced grin, Win shifted. "How are *you* two?"

Jeffrey and Michelle exchanged a look, then threw back half their drinks like synchronized swimmers.

Win paused mid-chew, deciding not to address the pregnant elephant in the room. He swallowed and went for something low-risk.

"Tell me, Chase—what's new? How's work?"

Chase grinned. Jeffrey shot him a wink.

"Well, I'm in line for a promotion," Chase said.

"Congratulations!" Win cheered. "Tell me more."

Chase glanced at his father-in-law, who answered for him:

"I'm retiring. And this young man is stepping into my shoes."

Win smiled at them both. "Nice."

"I'm retiring, too," Michelle added, flinging herself into the plot twist. "Friday's my last day."

"Mine too," Jeffrey said as if it was a corporate exodus holiday.

Win beamed. "Congrats, you guys. I'm so happy for all three of you!"

He watched them triumphantly finish their scotches and mentally noted how they tossed their drinks back, suggesting a promotion and retirement was only part of the story.

Before Win could speak, a piercing "OH!" sliced through the room.

Heads whipped toward the source like a pack of meerkats on alert. Phil and Tami's twins, Jasmine and Jackson, stood before Darceline's body. Jasmine adorned a polite, semi-sad, nonreactive, composed expression. Jackson, meanwhile, wore a heather-blue performance hoodie tightly showing off his chiseled torso and slim button-fly Turkish denim jeans with the cuffs rolled just above his khaki OluKai Nohea Moku boat shoes, sporting a pair of sunglasses on his head backward—was shell-shocked, his hand clamped over his mouth, eyes brimming. As he collapsed into the chair facing D, bursting into sobs, Jasmine scanned the gathering as if she were tallying who was there, like a game of Who's Who.

Jasmine was stunning—yes, and she knew it—but not in a way that begged applause. Now in the full bloom of midlife, her beautiful presence held gazes as she entered or crossed a room. Her skin glowed. Her makeup was strategic and understated: the softest liner, a whisper of blush, and a luminous nude gloss lipstick. She wore a dark green designer dress that was a precision-tailored power piece, hugging where it should, easing where it must, and pulling the dazzling bright green from her eyes like a magical illusion. Her long, rich hair fell over her shoulders—luxurious, radiant, intentional. It moved with her, like it, too, has something to say.

Jasmine never had to assert herself. She'd already won long before the conversation began.

Looking around for reinforcement from any other possible a-emotional in the room, Jasmine was relieved to see the closest equivalent possible—Sally—but quickly let that idea go once she caught sight of her stirring her martini with her tongue. But to Jasmine's surprise, she spotted Win and made her way over.

Winston saw his beautiful-as-ever cousin and stood for one of her trademark light-touch hugs with a brief, barely-there pat on the back. A second later, she stepped away and flashed him a million-dollar smile.

"I love your hair," she said with a wink. "Makes you look younger than me."

Win thanked her as Jeffrey, Michelle, and Chase rose for their versions of hug charades.

Then Jasmine crouched in her designer dress to open her arms for Stevyn. He ran to her and wrapped his tiny arms around her neck. She gave him a full, genuine squeeze and looked up at Michelle with a smile. "Oh my gosh, you're growing so fast!"

Apparently, kids were the only ones allowed a real hug from Cousin Jasmine.

A deep, rattling cough hacked through the lounge. All eyes turned to Winston's mother.

Michelle squinted. "Aunt Marci doesn't sound good, Win. What's going on?"

He shook his head. "Dr. Funnell suspects congestive heart failure, but she's refusing treatment until Aunt D is taken away. Stubborn as ever."

Jasmine gave a disapproving little nod. "Classic Aunt Marci."

"He brought in an oxygen tank from the medical room," Win added, glancing around. "But looks like she hasn't touched it."

"I'll handle it," Jasmine said, breaking away toward Marci.

Win turned back to Jeffrey, Michelle, and Chase. "I'll check on her too, then step out for a smoke. I'll catch you guys in a bit."

They nodded, concern shadowing their smiles.

Jasmine was leaning over Marci by the sofa, her tone firm. "You need to go to the hospital."

"No," Marci rasped, eyes shut.

Seated beside her, Sissy gently stroked her cheek. "Mom, please."

"No."

"You sound worse, Mom," Win said, glancing at Dr. Funnell.

"I'm okay," she lied.

"How's your breathing, Marci?" the doctor asked gently.

"Difficult."

Win knelt beside his sister. "Mom, we've got oxygen. Let Dr. Funnell help you, please."

Marci turned her head toward her deceased sister. "No."

Win took a slow, steady breath. "Okay. But the mask goes on if the doctor says you can't breathe on your own. Deal?"

Marci opened her eyes and gave a slight nod.

"Good," Win said, kissing her cheek.

He met Funnell's gaze and gave a confirming nod. Then, standing, he announced, "I'm going out back for a cigarette."

Marci patted his hand, murmuring, "Okayyy … honeyyy."

Jasmine took a seat facing Marci and sighed with exasperation as Winston turned to leave. He asked if her husband and kids were on their way, pulling out a cigarette.

She smiled and said as though she were filing a report, "Robert's at a medical conference in Zurich and flies back on Thursday. The girls are in New York. Dalton should be here any minute."

Win noticed Jasmine didn't have her furry companions. His cousin never went anywhere without her two Italian Greyhounds, Teddy and Bear, trailing gracefully at her heels like living extensions of her wardrobe. With sleek coats and regal posture, they moved with the practiced poise of creatures who knew they belonged. Whether she was stepping into a café, browsing a bookstore, or attending a gallery opening, the dogs were always there—silent, observant, impeccably behaved. They weren't just pets but part of her aesthetic, like the perfect handbag or a signature scent. Professionally trained, Teddy and Bear would settle beside her wherever she paused, sitting with such composed patience that it felt like they were waiting for their following command.

"Where are the pups?" Win asked.

Jasmine sighed. "When I took them in for their checkups at the vet last week, they somehow put on ten pounds each—which is unacceptable. So, off to the K-9 Spa they went and will come home once they're no longer fat," she replied with disgust as her eyes dipped to Win's torso before dropping to her phone, where she began tapping away.

Win smirked, thinking she sounded like their Aunt Darceline obsessively focused on someone else's body perfection—or lack thereof—dogs included. He nodded, walking away with a fag in hand, ready to light.

Stepping into the foyer, Dalton nearly mowed him down, rushing in like a man on fire. Hoosier Beef skidded to a stop, startled. "Win?" he gasped, gripping Winston's arms.

"Hi," Win replied, steadying them both.

"You're here?"

"I'm here."

Dalton shook his head, desperation creeping into his voice. "Aunt Darceline's really dead?"

"Yes," Win said softly.

Dalton staggered back, covering his mouth with both hands. "Oh my God."

Win stood quietly, watching his devastatingly handsome second cousin glance past him into the Grand Room, then turn back with a look of haunted disbelief.

"She's in there?" Dalton asked.

Win nodded.

Dalton exhaled like he'd been holding his breath for years. His arms flailed as he let out a sharp, shaky laugh. Then, out of nowhere, a broad, gleeful grin took over his face.

"Oh my God, I'm free!" he elated.

Win blinked. That was … not the reaction he expected.

Dalton spun in a slow, euphoric circle, shouting, "I'm free! I'm free! I'm free! I'm free!"

Then he stopped and threw his arms around Win, hugging him tightly.

Shocked, Win returned the embrace, trying to make sense of

whatever this was. He half-wondered if Darceline's death had triggered an episode with his Tourette Syndrome. He wasn't sure.

"You're alright, Dalton," Win said gently. "You're okay … everything's okay."

Dalton jumped back, running a hand through his hair. "I'm not having an episode, Win."

"Then what is this?" Win asked calmly.

Dalton's eyes dropped to the cigarette in Win's hand. "You heading out for a smoke?"

"Walk with me," Win said.

Opening the back door, he felt a slight whoosh of wind blow through the house with the front door open. Thinking it was best for the mansion and everyone in it to cool down a few more degrees, Winston opened the right glass door and reached behind to latch it with a hook on the baseboard. He opened the screen door onto the wide, lengthy porch overlooking the lake, holding it open for Dalton.

Win fired up and took in a deep drag. He watched Dalton lean upon the railing by his side, gazing across the lake for a long, silent stare.

Patient, Win smoked, saying nothing … ready to listen.

Finally, after a long, soul-emptying sigh, Dalton spoke to the stars. "I never wanted to do the commercials. Aunt Darceline pushed me into them. And my mother—the local celebrity—wanted her son to outshine her, so she let Darceline pay me obscene amounts of money. And push. And push."

He stared at the lake.

"And whenever my contract was up, and I thought I was free to go, there she was again. 'You have the easiest job in the world, Dalton. You work ten days a year. You're making millions.'"

A tear rolled down his cheek.

"Push. Push. Push."

Dalton turned toward Win, smiling through tears—six falling simultaneously.

Winston's eyes welled, too. He understood Dalton's pain—more than Dalton would ever know.

Win gently squeezed his arm. "Well, now you're free."

Dalton stepped back, wiping his face. "But I still have a contract."

Win smiled. "If you want out, you're out. No one should do something they hate. Ever."

Dalton nodded, deeply relieved—like he'd been waiting his whole life to hear those words from someone who meant them. He took a deep breath as if ready to speak.

"I—"

But his gaze shifted past Winston, and whatever he was about to say froze on his lips. His expression turned to sheer horror as if Lord Voldemort had just risen from the grave.

Win turned.

Kaitlyn sat quietly a few feet away in a deck chair, lit eerily by the banister lights. Her steely, unblinking eyes locked on them.

She trolled in a gravely, glib tone, "Well, there they are. Our new *patriarch* ... and *I don't wanna be Hoosier Beef no more.*"

Win's hair stood on end. Dalton visibly shivered.

"Hey," Dalton managed, then turned to Win. "I'm gonna go say hi to Grandma and Grandpa."

"Okay," Win said, grateful Dalton seemed all right. Whatever that outburst was—it wasn't Tourette's.

As Dalton slipped back inside, Win watched him go, already thinking ahead.

One of his first acts would be to cancel that damn contract. He'd ask Jasmine about it when he went back in. Then again ... maybe not. Jasmine might've been the one who helped push Dalton into it in the first place.

No. Winston would ask Uncle Phil and Aunt Tami.

Yes, he'd start with them.

Under the Waxing Gibbous Moon

The air grew chillier as the night wore on, and it wasn't just from being outside. Winston leaned against the railing, cigarette in hand, eyes fixed on the family's very own Veruca Salt—Kaitlyn. Equal parts, amused and annoyed, he gave her his full attention.

"I find it rather queer how you show up the day our matriarch dies and so quickly step in to take your place," she said, her voice slick with suspicion.

"What a queer choice of words, Kaitlyn," Win replied, taking a leisurely drag.

Her eyes narrowed with drama practically leaking from her pores. "Any word on the reading of the will?"

"Wednesday. Here. At noon," he answered, utterly unbothered. "Why does that concern you now?"

"How do you even know that already?"

"Leland told me."

"Why are you even here?"

"I was summoned."

"By whom?"

"Aunt Darceline."

"Why?"

"You'll have to ask her."

She exhaled like a raging bull, eyes locked on him. Then she hissed, "You're rather coy."

"I'm being completely transparent."

"I find it suspicious—you show up, Aunt D dies."

"I find it tragic."

"Coming from the man who showed up, and then she died."

Winston tilted his head. "Aunt Darceline and I had an interesting conversation after she picked me up at the airport. She mentioned you."

Kaitlyn's eyes bulged. "I want an autopsy."

"Then ask the coroner."

"I will," she snarled, pushing herself out of the chair and onto her feet.

Win took another drag as she waddled toward him, never breaking eye contact.

"You've always been such a happy man," she said, not done yet. "And I find something wrong with a man who's as happy as you."

Still watching her, Win said calmly, "I believe misery is the worst experience any human being can cling to. You should consider letting it go."

She glared at him, pure venom. Unfazed, he cleared his throat.

"I would certainly hate to see you choke to death the way Auntie D did," she spat.

"She *coughed* to death," Win corrected.

"I know what I said," Kaitlyn scoffed, returning inside and slamming the screen door behind her with a satisfying finality.

Winston returned his gaze to the lake, brushing off her toxic energy with a silent prayer of protection over his mind, body, spirit, and soul. The screen door squeaked open again. If Kaitlyn was back for round two, she'd be talking to his backside—he was done.

But Dr. Funnell stepped out and joined him at the railing.

"Beautiful view," he said peacefully, taking it in. Then, turning, he asked, "Do you have another cigarette by chance?"

Win smiled, opening his case. Funnell took one, and Win lit it for him.

"Enjoying our finer moments?" Win joked.

Funnell exhaled a long drag, then frowned at the cigarette. "I'm actually not."

Win looked at him, attentive.

"Your mother concerns me. And Kaitlyn's disregard for her unborn baby isn't exactly reassuring."

He met Winston's eyes.

"She's overdue, agitated, and irrational. Her blood pressure is probably nowhere near where it should be. She's self-medicating with shots of tequila. None of this is safe—for her or the baby."

"Suggestions?" Win asked.

Funnell took another drag and sighed. "Let the tequila kick in. Maybe she'll calm down. Or go into labor."

"Fingers crossed."

A mischievous gleam sparked in the doctor's eye. "My wife lets me have one cigar a month. Technically, this isn't a cigar, so I won't have to report it."

"Loopholes," Win grinned. "How long have you been the family doctor?"

"Three years."

Winston nodded, enjoying the stillness—finally, someone collected.

Then Funnell asked, "Did you know Darceline made you her Healthcare Power of Attorney?"

Winston blinked. "No."

"She gave me the paperwork when I replaced her former physician. She asked me to inform you only if she became incapacitated." He turned fully toward Winston. "Now that she's passed, I can ask—did she tell you about her cancer?"

"No," Win said, the word heavy with shock.

Funnell looked back at the lake, smoke curling from his mouth.

"Lung?" Win asked.

"Ironically, no," he said, glancing over. "After a lifetime of cigarettes, you'd expect it. But no.

"Darceline came to me last spring complaining of a persistent headache. Over-the-counter meds weren't helping. She insisted something foreign was inside her. She *felt* it."

Win raised his brows.

"She was right. An MRI showed a melanoma in her brain, about the size of a pea. At her age, with her thin frame and her smoking history— surgery was too risky. She refused chemotherapy and full radiation. I convinced her to try a radiation spot treatment regimen.

"That lasted four weeks. Darceline hated it and told me if she was going to die of cancer, she wasn't going to exit this world feeling like she had to vomit on the way out."

Win smirked faintly. He could hear D saying precisely that.

Funnell continued. "You said she coughed to death. But given the tumor and the pressure from a violent cough, it's possible she suffered a cerebral aneurysm. Quick. Painless."

"Jesus," Win exhaled.

Funnell looked at him kindly. "I'm relieved for her. No suffering. And from what you described—it was over fast."

The weight of it hit. Winston's eyes welled. He nodded, voice low. "Thank you for telling me."

The doctor took a short drag and said through smoke, "Your mother's just as stubborn as her sister."

Win chuckled.

Funnell checked his watch. "It's ten o'clock. The ambulance and county vehicle should be here soon."

He took a final puff and looked around.

Winston pointed. "By the door—copper planter turned ashtray."

Funnell stubbed it out, then said, "I'll freshen up and try to get your mother on oxygen."

"Thank you," Win said, meaning it.

Funnell pulled a card from his wallet and handed it over. "In case things get chaotic later. That's my cell."

"I appreciate it, Doctor."

"Please," he said, smiling, "call me Ben."

Win smiled back. "Thank you, Doctor."

Funnell gave a slight nod and stepped inside.

As a falling star zipped across the black sky, it finally hit what Darceline had meant—living hour by hour, minute by minute, with only so many seconds left. He'd brushed it off at the time as the kind of poetic nonsense people in their eighties tend to say. But she was being literal, real. No fluff. No bullshit.

Staring up at the moon, the weight of the day settled on him. It had been long, emotionally draining, bone-deep exhausting. A craving for Jack Daniel's flared up, sharp and familiar. He was over being clean. Done with sobriety. Winston decided it was time to dull the edges and get thoroughly drunk. He stubbed out his cigarette in the ashtray and headed for the bar.

Just then, Willow exploded onto the back deck, appearing playful, obviously several drinks in—sloshing a tallboy in one hand, waving her phone in the other. Win flinched back as she nearly barreled into him. This cracked her up but annoyed him.

"You are not going to believe this," she drunkenly volleyed, eyes wide with mischief. "Jackson swapped out Aunt D's glasses with his sporto sunglasses! It's a scream!"

Win couldn't help but smile. It *was* funny. And that's what he needed: something to smile about.

Then he imagined the household staff losing their minds, which, under normal circumstances, would've meant stepping in to put the fire out. But tonight? Let 'em burn. The whole "don't touch the body" policy was absurd anyway. If someone wanted to give Aunt D a wash and set at the dining room table, hell, let 'em.

His irritation returned.

"Hey! You *gotta* see this," Willow shrieked, eyes glued to her phone. "It's a fartgasm!"

"*A what?*" Win sighed, already regretting asking.

"A *fartgasm!*"

He looked at her cocktail while reaching for another cigarette. "Explain it first. I may not want to see this."

Willow lit up with enthusiasm. "Okay. So, a real fartgasm is when someone actually has an orgasm *and* farts at the same time."

Win closed his eyes, slowly shaking his head, thinking only of sipping on Jack. A smirk came upon his lips, and then he looked at his sister.

"But *our* fartgasms—" she went on proudly, "—are when contestants get on stage, one foot on a plastic milk crate, with a mic up to their butt, and another mic in hand. They let out a world-class fart, then moan like they just came. A fartgasm!"

"*Oh my God,*" Win responded, both horrified and intrigued. "How did you come up with this?"

Willow laughed, searching her memory.

"We can thank our dearly departed Cheri Yoder for that."

"*What?*"

"Oh geez, okay—so one night at the bowling alley bar, Cheri's sitting there midweek, not too busy, just a few regulars drinking. Out of nowhere, she slides off her stool, looks like she's gonna crap herself, lets out this *massive* fart, and moans like she just had the best orgasm of her life.

"The whole place lost it. I nearly pissed myself laughing.

"Then Tom, one of our barflies, stands up and goes, 'I can top that, Cheri!' And *he* lets one rip and groans in his deep baritone voice like he just hit nirvana.

"Everyone at the bar completely flipped and began laughing so hard that people cried.

"Which got me thinking …

"And it took a bit of finagling …

"But I convinced Tom and Cheri to do it on stage—just for fun. Then others wanted in, trying to out-fartgasm each other. It just kind of snowballed into a contest."

Winston stood with eyebrows arched. "Now it's a *thing?*"

Willow grinned. "Now it's a *competition*. He or she with the best fart and moan wins!"

He chuckled over the stupidity of it all.

"Yep. First Wednesday of every month, Balls & Beers has the game on to blow out your farts with gasms galore."

Win couldn't help but ask, "What does the winner get?"

"Ten free drinks and a Balls & Beers T-shirt."

"How many people actually do this?"

Willow tilted her head sideways, thinking. "We have, I'd say, ten regulars but about thirty."

He was speechless, now distracted by *this*.

Smiling proudly, she added, "People come from all over, Win. A guy from Erie, Pennsylvania, shows up every month just to try and knock Cheri off the Fartgasm Champion Board."

Winston winced. "What about the smell?"

Willow swiftly said, "*Well* … now that took some experimenting.

"But! We found the best immediate solution was a good long spray of Febreze right after each blowout. The lemon kitchen odor is the one that works best."

Win gave her a grin with a sigh, relenting. "What the hell … show me."

Willow squealed with delight, setting her drink on the railing. "Yay!"

She queued up a video: "This just got posted—it's a tribute compilation: Cheri's top ten fartgasms."

He leaned in.

There she was, Cheri Yoder: a five-foot-tall, middle-aged woman with a mane of curly brown hair defying gravity and good intentions. Her build was of someone who never turned down pie after dinner, confidently snugged in blue jeans that were gasping for air and a frilly blouse that screamed "festive farm chic." She stood center stage, one foot triumphantly planted on a milk crate like she was about to deliver the Gettysburg Address. A microphone on a stand loomed dangerously close to her ass, like a NASA probe preparing for launch.

With a handheld mic clutched tight, Cheri closed her eyes with fierce determination. Her back arches, her face contorts, and her tension builds. She tapped her microphone three times. And then—**BOOO-Thppt!**—a robust, unapologetic fart thundered out like a tuba solo. She moaned theatrically as if she'd just met Christ Himself.

The crowd went wild. Cheering. Whistling. Applauding like they've just witnessed a small-town miracle.

Cheri stood tall, with hands on hips, and was queen of the stage. Fartgasm royalty.

Willow paused the video.

Win stared, gaping in disbelief. And yet… he couldn't look away.

"Ready for more?" she taunted, but before he could respond, she resumed Cheri's fartgasm collection, which cut from one performance to the next.

Pppsht *OH!*
Blaarp *OH!!*
Pppsht *OOH!!!*

Win giggled, clamping his hand over his mouth.

Pfft *OAH!*
Pfft *YES!!*
Rrrp *OH, GOD!!!*
Pbbbt *OH!!!!*

He giggled harder, shaking his head. This was so, so wrong.

Frrrt *OOH!*
Plllfffftt *OH, FUCK ME!!*
Splop *OAH!!!*

His dam of self-control broke. He exploded in laughter.

Pppprrrrrrttttt *OH, MY GOD!*
Pffft *OAH!!*
Fffft *YES!!!*

Win laughed harder, clutching his abdomen.

Braaak *OA!*
Rrrr *YES!!*
Poot *OH!!!*
Rrrr *YES!!!!*
…
Thpptphtphphhph *OH, GOD!*
Thppt *O!!*
Thppt *OHH!!!*
…
Baphph *YES!*
Braaaa *YES!!*
Aapppppppp *YESSSS!!!*

Now convulsing with laughter, Win passed his cigarette to Willow and grabbed the railing like a drowning man.

Phhhfffrrrttt *OAH!*
Phhreeeeeeeee *OAH!!*
Phut *OAAH!!!*

He doubled over, his laughter burning like wildfire.

"Oh!" Willow paused the video for a quick mention, "*This* is Cheri's *ultimate* grand finale fartgasm!"

Thbtbtbtbtbtbtbppppppssst-zzztt *OH, GOD!*
Pfffffffttttttzzzz *OH, GOD!!*
Ssssss *OH, FUCK!!!*
Ttzztzztzz-t-t *OH, MY FUCKNG GOD!!!!*
Pfffft *YES!!!!*
Pfft *YEES!!!!*

Barely able to breathe, Win's whole body rocked with pained howling laughter. He began to see stars dancing on the deck from the massive rush.

Wildly giggling, Sissy nudged him. "Funny shit, right?"

"*Oh, fuck!*" he yelped.

"That's what *Cheri* screamed!"

Her timing sent him into a new fit—harder, louder, chest burning.

It was exactly what he needed at that very moment—stupid-funny. Seeing Cheri's dramatic human trick … like that … like nothing he'd ever seen before in his life … delivered the perfect release for one helluva day. Gasping, he knew he was a goner.

Willow was delighted, taking a swig from her cocktail.

"I can't believe…" he wheezed, tears running down his face.

Willow giggled, highly pleased with herself for snapping her brother like a twig.

"I can't believe …" he barely squelched again before whine-screaming in pain, *laughing even harder.*

"Are you seeing God yet? Like Cheri did after a can of beans?"

Winston couldn't take it anymore. He staggered away, pacing the long porch like a madman, trying to regain control. He finally returned, touching Willow's shoulders like he'd just finished a marathon.

"*Thank … you.*"

Willow bounced to an imaginary groovy beat in her head. "Any time, bro!"

Win wiped his eyes, replaced his glasses, and watched her take a drag from his cigarette. He lit another, asking what she was drinking.

"Bacardi and Coke Zero."

Barely a second away from reaching for her glass to help himself to a long guzzle, Sissy missed setting it on the railing, and it tumbled off the deck.

"Fuck," Win sighed.

"*Fuck!*" Willow shouted, then laughed. "That's alcohol abuse! Shame on me!"

It was a sign, he thought. An obvious sign not to backslide.

"That video is beyond horrible," he joked, sarcasm as thick as the smoke that blew out.

She beamed. "That's why the bar's packed wall-to-wall on Fartgasm Night."

Win smiled. Despite everything, he was genuinely proud of her. Watching his sister make people laugh—even with something absurd—was special. She'd far surpassed his old "family funny stories." And he was good with that. Even if her brand of humor had clearly crossed into deranged brilliance.

His lungs were sore. The cigarette didn't feel good. He stubbed it out, ready to head back inside.

"Hey ..." Willow said like a warning was tucked inside the word. She leaned in, voice lowered to a loud whisper. "I wouldn't mention the fartgasms. Or Cheri. Especially not inside."

Winston would never do such a thing, confirming with a look stating as much, eyebrows crimped.

Willow's expression shifted. Her voice took on a serious tone. "I hate to say it, but Cheri kind of became the town floozy. A few years back, during her fourth, or maybe fifth, marriage, she had one of her classic drunk confessionals with me. This was just before closing time. She told me—slurring, mind you—that she gave Jackson a little rub-

and-tug at a wedding reception. At the country club. Under the dining table. Full room. Music, dancing, the whole shebang. Right under the draping tablecloth."

Win pointed toward the screen door in horror. "Our Jackson?" he whisper-shouted.

"Yep."

"Our *cousin* Jackson?" he repeated, incredulous.

"Yep. Then she said—and I quote—'If a man can slide his hand up my dress and stick a finger in my pussy, I've got no problem unzipping him for a good rub and tug.'"

Winston's adrenaline high crashed faster than Moe slapping Curly. His face twisted with nausea. "Okay—nope. Stop. None of this is my business. I am officially *done* with the Hicksville gossip!"

Willow bristled. "Welcome to my world of drunks! You have *no idea* how many sad, sick kitty cats belly up to my bar, get wasted, then treat me to a full confessional like it's *The Furball Horking Hour!*"

She turned to look out toward the lake, exasperated but strangely at peace, as though she'd accepted her fate as Hicksville's bartender-slash priest.

Win took a step back, trying to process whether her outburst was a complaint, a badge of honor, or a sign of total professional negligence—being the town barkeep who continually serves until the beans are spilled or blown from someone's ass.

Willow called out just as he opened the screen door, "Oh—and heads up, Sheriff Studly just walked in to get a police report from Uncle Bill over his oopsie-doopsie."

"Okay," Win sighed, stepping inside, closing the door behind him so it wouldn't slam, shaking his head. Turning back, as he reached for his Altoids tin, he said through the screen door to her backside, "What the fuck is wrong with people, Willow?"

She looked to her left, answering, "Exactly, bro. *Exactly.*"

Too Hip to be Dead

Winston entered the Grand Room, his eyes immediately drawn to Sheriff McKay, who was cozied up behind the bar, chatting with Bill and Betsy. Win could still smell Mitch's cologne and practically taste the man's kiss. His heart kicked into a light pitter-patter.

Mitch was busy jotting something down, leaning his head slightly to the right. His gaze lifted to Bill, then popped across the room to Winston. His eyes twinkled, and with the subtle finesse of a man who'd mastered the art of the sly smirk, Mitch sent a nourishing wink Win's way. Winston grinned back and sauntered forward.

And there she was.

Darceline might've been mistaken for a high-fashion grandma on a rebellious shopping spree if she weren't famously dead. Win took the sight of her in—from the white spiky hair to her now sporting surfer-dude sunglasses with shiny bright blue polarized lenses and black rubber arms, casually sitting in her red Chanel dress, appearing chill. Yes, Jackson's single accessory had given their aunt an entirely different vibe.

Winston smiled, finding the sight humorous. He agreed that the shades had a calming effect. As he spotted D's massive black glasses neatly folded on the table, Jackson jumped beside him with a cuddly bump.

"Much better, eh? Dad suggested I put my Maui Jims on her," Jackson said with delight, ever so lightly patting Darceline's arm. "You can keep 'em, Auntie. I love you."

Win suppressed a laugh. "I think she would approve."

Jackson suddenly recoiled. "I'm sorry, Win. I know I'm not supposed to touch her, but …"

Winston looked at Phil's son and was instantly struck by how the more Jackson aged, the more he looked like his father. He lovingly rubbed his cousin's handsome, unshaven cheek. "I don't give a fuck about the no-touching bullshit. It's ridiculous."

Jackson grinned with a relieved sparkle in his eye, reaching for a hug.

In their embrace, Winston glanced at his mother, sleeping, at Jasmine, still in the chair typing on her phone, then at the plate of food on the coffee table he hadn't eaten. He realized he was no longer hungry or crashing—spontaneously energized by Mitch's wink, giving him the boost he needed.

Jackson hugged him tighter. "I've missed you, Cuz."

Winston smiled from ear to ear. "I've missed you, too."

Once they released, their attention returned to Darceline. Jackson immediately teared up, wiping an eye and sniffling.

"This is such a shock," he sighed with profound grief.

Winston said nothing, placing his hand on Jackson's shoulder.

Then, like a sage of the most perplexing wisdom, Jackson faced Win and whispered in a soft, faux-spiritual Keanu Reeves tone, "You're the big kahuna now."

Win looked into his eyes. "Yeah."

Jackson leaned back, studying Winston as though a vision was bursting through. "You don't want this," he softly uttered.

Winston took a deep breath, his lips pursed sideways.

"Okay," Jackson whispered and nodded solemnly like a higher power had a message to relay. He cupped Winston's cheeks with an assuring smile. "It's okay."

Win couldn't help but grin, and when he did, Jackson went in for a second, longer hug. Then, as though the Spirit of Santa Baby possessed him to reiterate his wisdom, Jackson whispered into his ear, "Give it all away, man. Just give it all away."

Winston fully believed in his cousin's gift, knowing it was something very special—an ability, a talent—and he respected it. He squeezed Jackson a little tighter, his emotions joining their tearful reunion. "Thank you."

Jackson whispered, "This is between us."

Win nodded, feeling his body relax in their embrace. Jackson's hugs always had a magical way of physically de-stressing someone. Always.

"Thank you," Win repeated.

Jackson pulled back, looking into Winston's tired eyes with a different, almost relieved expression. "It's a good thing you're no longer in the company of that man-baby Santa Claus who said that to you." His gaze dropped to the green carpeting for a second, seeing something, then returned. "And that's all I have to say about that dude."

The believer, Winston, trusted Jackson and was perfectly fine not knowing what his cousin had just 'seen' regarding the *Campground Swingers* man-whore he met yesterday at Betty's. The repeated guidance was more than enough.

Before Winston could inquire about *his* life, a spontaneous ambush arrived with Jeffrey and Michelle. The cousins tackled them into a group hug like a football team who'd just won the championship. All had loving, affectionate smiles.

"I just love you guys!" Jeffrey declared as though they were about to break into a singalong.

It was apparent their tallboy scotches had kicked in.

Suddenly, Jackson's phone belted out a ukulele rendition of

"Somewhere Over the Rainbow/What a Wonderful World" by IZ. Pulling the phone from his back pocket, he recognized the caller. "I'll circle back," he said, and off to the foyer, he dashed, answering.

Like a flicked switch, Winston watched the jovial expressions on Jeffrey and Michelle quickly fade. With a newfound air of mystery, Michelle glanced at Jeffrey as though she were giving him the green light to proceed. He turned to Win, and in a serious tone, he asked, "You got a second?"

"Sure."

Next thing Winston knew, he was ushered to the Business Suite like a contestant on a game show where the prizes were emotional wreckage of some sort. Leland and Peters were sitting at the conference table. Michelle took Winston's hand, leading them to the library in front of the mansion west of the entrance.

Win spotted Mitch's campaign hat and leather coat on the high-back chair Betsy and his mother sat in earlier, ready and waiting should duty call again.

They entered. The library was empty. Jeffrey closed the doors and then stuffed his hands into his pockets.

"Are you two alright?" Winston cautiously asked, bouncing his eyes between them—curious about the dramatic need for privacy.

Jeffrey and Michelle stood looking at Win, saying nothing. Win looked back, raising his eyebrows. The couple exchanged a glance until Michelle tilted her head towards Win. Winston noted she was the one nudging them into this mysterious get-together.

Jeffrey began. "Since you're the next in line, we thought you should know immediately."

Michelle cut straight to it. "We're divorcing."

Winston was thunderstruck. He wanted to ask why and what happened, but knowing Darceline's three hours were winding down, he didn't have time to dive into all the specifics right then. Instead, he asked, "When?"

The two looked at one another like they were in a pickle. Jeffrey began, "Michelle and I had everything ready, planning to file tomorrow. And now *this*."

"We don't know what to do," she added.

Jeffrey frowned. "It's amicable."

"Amicable" in Hicks's terms usually meant someone's golf clubs had been set on fire.

"Have you shared this with anyone?" Winston asked.

"Only our attorneys know," Michelle replied.

Win took a deep breath, stepped in close, and squeezed each of their hands in his. He nodded slowly and declared, "Don't file yet. Let Aunt D's ashes settle."

They stared wide-eyed at Win, wanting specifics.

"You must update your divorce petition with your inheritances," Win said.

"How do you know we're inheriting anything?" Jeffrey asked.

Winston tried to explain. "I don't. But if either of you do, that changes your assets to divide."

They understood that.

Needing to move on, Win said, "I would like the three of us to talk about this after reading D's will on Wednesday. Okay?"

With a resigned sigh, Jeffrey nodded. "Okay."

With a nod, Michelle was on board, too.

Winston pulled them into another group hug. The three embraced, Jeffrey pulling them in tighter, Michelle pulling them in tighter still. Winston felt absolute love in that very moment of heightened loss. And if he weren't already privately crying inside, Win would have broken into a raging sob.

They parted, opening the library doors as Dano walked from the Great Room. Sally was cradled in his arms like a ragdoll, her head resting against his shoulder.

Dano paused, addressing the three, "Phil texted me she was ready."

Sally was barely audible, sputtering, "Ba ba ba … ba ba ba. Ba? Ba ba ba …"

"My condolences," Dano sorrowfully said, eyes teary. "Miss Hicks was always very kind."

Win nodded, thanking him. "Dano, please join us on Saturday. I know my aunt would want you to attend."

His nod spilled a tear that ran down his brown, round cheek, dripping from his chin onto Sally's pink dress before he quietly left.

As Win, Jeffrey, and Michelle walked the long shotgun foyer, Win asked, "Does Sally always get carried away like that?"

They nodded candidly.

"She's up late tonight," Michelle said.

"Sally's usually out cold by six or seven," Jeffrey added as if it were an everyday occurrence.

Michelle added, "Dano is such a blessing because whenever Sally has reached the point of no return, we can text him, and he'll come and dispose of her body."

Win chuckled over her blunt wit.

He could only imagine what Sally would be like in the coming days, especially if … or when … word got out that she had deceived her online disciples. Leland was right. *That* could be cataclysmic for the family. For now, he decided to black out the thought of it, the way Sally would pass out any minute.

They were back in the Grand Room. Win trailed behind, feeling the last three hours had pulled him into a wretched depth, and he didn't know how to escape. Jeffrey and Michelle returned to the bar, sitting between Phil and Chase, with Stevyn on his right, who grinned like the big man on campus sitting with the grownups. Dalton was standing at the bar talking with Chase. Jeffrey walked around behind the bar to make the next round of drinks.

Mitch was still behind the bar talking with Bill and Betsy. Sissy was stroking Marci's hair with one hand, clutching a cocktail in the other. Jasmine was still in her seat, tapping away on her phone. Kaitlyn was seated between Marci and the bar in a club chair, fanning herself, Dr. Funnell seated by her side.

Then—because the family gathering had gone long enough with-out … or was due for another round of her melodrama—Kaitlyn ex-ploded. "I'm not going to the hospital until my water breaks! *GO AWAY!*"

Though she'd hijacked everyone's attention yet again, it was fleet-ing because the room continued their conversations. No one moved. Not even a glance her way.

The doctor stood, delivering Winston a look of fret before returning to Marci.

Mitch was deeply conversing with his aunt and uncle, so Winston figured it might be his last chance to sit with Darceline. He settled into the chair facing her and placed his hand over hers, as his mother had done earlier. Her skin was cool now, but he didn't care. Win closed his eyes and silently thanked her—from the bottom of his heart—for their conversation earlier that day. He only wished it had happened years sooner.

D had given him the best inheritance he could ever ask for: freedom. A wave of gratitude and love welled up in his chest. He whispered a final thank-you for being in his life. Tears rolled down his cheeks. The goodbye was done. He felt ready to return to his mother.

But as he pulled his hand away, he froze.

Darceline's finger was bare. The magnificent emerald diamond ring was gone!

Winston stared at her bony hand in stunned disbelief. Who would steal from a dead woman? He looked around the room … to everyone … at his family. Taking a breath, he turned to Darceline's body, then leaned back into his chair, mentally paralyzed.

A moment passed before he stood up, dazed, and wandered over to his mother. Squatting beside her and Willow, he whispered in Sissy's ear, "Somebody took Aunt Darceline's ginormous ring off her hand."

"What?" Willow gasped.

"I said it's gone! It was on her when she died," Winston repeated, breathcatching.

"I have it," Marci declared, eyes still closed.

"*You* took it?" Winston frantically whispered.

She nodded.

"Why would you do such a thing?" Sissy asked, startled.

"I took it because … I didn't want … anyone else to have it," Marci rasped between shallow breaths.

"You took it … so no one else could take it?" Winston repeated, trying to keep his voice low and his frustration in check. "So here I am panicking that someone in the family—or the staff—stole the ring, and it was *YOU?!*"

Marci nodded again, still not opening her eyes.

Win shook his head, jaw slack, exchanging a look with Willow.

"Where is it?" Sissy demanded.

"In my right jacket pocket," Marci wheezed.

Willow reached over her mother and yanked the coat from the back of the sofa. She dug into the pocket and froze, her eyes widening as she pulled out the massive diamond.

"Did you find it?" Marci asked weakly.

"Yes," Sissy whispered, sharp and tight.

"Good … it's for you, darling. Darci wanted you to have it, and I wanted to ensure you got it."

Willow and Winston locked eyes. Then, without a word, Willow tossed the coat across her mother's waist, plopped the ring into Winston's hand, and stood for the bar.

"I need a drink," she declared, pissed off.

Winston sighed and began slipping the ring onto his mother's fourth finger.

"Stop!" Marci gasped, lifting her head, eyes wide. "What are you doing?"

"Putting it on you. For safekeeping."

"No! I don't want it."

"Sissy walked away, and I don't know where else to put it."

Marci let her head fall back. "Take it off," she exhaled. After a rattled breath, she added, "My sister appreciated exquisite taste. I preferred the hand-me-downs. She adored beauty. I adored my children. I'm not my sister. Nor is she me. Take it off. Give it to Willow. That's what Darci wanted. And it's what I want."

With a sigh, Winston complied, slipping the ring into his pocket. At that moment, he was tempted—furiously tempted—to let loose on his mother, to tell her how her lifetime of manipulations had messed up both him and Sissy. But he didn't. Instead, he turned to Dr. Funnell.

"What time is it?" he asked.

"We're getting close," the doctor nodded, ready for everything to happen.

Exhausted, Winston drew a long breath. "I'm going for a smoke," he told his mother and the doctor. "I'll be right back."

He stood, his eyes meeting those of Sheriff McKay, who was now by the coffee urn, sipping from a cup. Winston smirked faintly, feeling a small wave of calm from Mitch's steady gaze. As he approached the foyer, Mitch set his coffee down and followed.

Mitch whispered, "Hey."

"Hey," Winston smiled. "I need a smoke."

"Mind if I tag along?"

Winston grinned and led them out the back door. The cool air was bracing. He lit a cigarette and leaned against the deck railing, leering upon everything in the dark.

Mitch stepped beside him, tempted to ask if he was alright—but didn't need to. It was apparent the day had caught up with Win, watching him suck deeply on every drag. His heart fluttered. Mitch couldn't believe Winston was home.

"You've had a hell of a day," Mitch said softly.

Winston nodded faintly, sniffling.

They both stared at the moon, the lake, and the forest silhouette against the sky.

"Let's just stand here a while," Mitch said gently. "We don't have to say anything. If that's okay."

Winston smiled. It sounded like something Chris would've said. He nodded again.

They stood in silence. Win smoked until it was done. He dropped the butt into the ashtray and reached for his Altoids.

"Care for one?" he asked, holding the tin out.

Mitch smiled, taking one. Win popped one in his mouth, slipping the tin into his blazer pocket. There was a strange calm in the air. Something soothing about Mitch's presence—about having this man from his past close again, within reach.

"Thank you," Mitch said, then leaned in to touch the tip of Winston's nose with his own—affectionate, like a kiss.

Neither of them could believe how strong their pull still was.

But for all the chemistry, they didn't know each other's lives. Mitch knew nothing of the messy legacy that had brought Winston home. Winston knew nothing of Mitch's life beyond the bullet points they'd shared in a quick Q&A.

"Is there anything I can do for you?" Mitch asked, watching a tear roll down Winston's cheek. He leaned in and gently wiped it away with his thumb.

"Let me do this," Winston whispered, stepping in for a hug.

Mitch exhaled and wrapped his arms around him, firm and tender. They stood locked in that embrace, heads leaned together, bodies pressing close, relishing how good … how natural it felt.

Pulling only his head back, Mitch looked into Win's eyes. Winston met his gaze, diving into those baby blues.

Then came the screen door, slowly creaking open and slowly squeaking closed.

They both turned to see little Stevyn standing outside the doorway, staring at them, while they still embraced.

Winston broke the moment, smiling. "Hi."

"Hi," the tot replied.

"Hi," Mitch echoed.

"Hi," Stevyn repeated.

The boy studied Winston. "Are you my grampy cousin?"

Winston blinked, thinking it through. "Well … your grampy Jeffrey is my cousin. Your daddy Chase is my first cousin once removed. So, I guess that makes you my first cousin twice removed."

"Okay," Stevyn said as if it didn't matter. Then he added, "My mom screams and cries a lot. Dad and I just learn to live with it."

Winston was taken aback. "When I was your age, my mom did that too. And yeah, your dad's probably right. We all learn to live with it."

"I'm not happy about a baby sister coming soon," Stevyn said next. "I like having my own house."

"One day, you'll be happy to have a sister," Winston replied. "I'm happy I have one."

Then, out of nowhere, little Stevyn said, "I like boys."

"Oh …" Winston popped with surprise, glancing at Mitch.

"Yeah. I like to watch my daddy change clothes and take showers."

"Oh … well …" Winston blinked, trying not to overreact or engage in *that* conversation, casually releasing Mitch and turning to face Stevyn.

He looked at the lad thoughtfully, wondering if the little guy's gaydar was already pinging—drawn, perhaps, to his gay grampy cousin.

Win gently redirected. "Do you like boating on the lake in the summertime?"

"I like tubing."

"Me too!" Win smiled. "Have you tried waterskiing?"

"I tried it but kept wiping out. I like tubing better."

"Both are fun," Winston grinned. "I bet next summer you will be *really good* at waterskiing."

"Okay," Stevyn happily agreed. Then, grabbing the screen door, he said, "See ya, Grampy Cousin Winston."

"Okey dokey," Win replied with a grin, loving his new title. He waited for Stevyn to disappear inside, then turned to Mitch with an expression that screamed, *WTF?!*

Mitch burst out laughing. "Kids say the funniest things. And you …
you look so cute right now."

He leaned in and kissed Winston on the lips.

It's Time

Winston didn't want to be anywhere else. In Mitch's arms, feeling his heat, he ran his fingers through Mitch's hair, around his ear, and along the line of his neck, kissing him tenderly and getting lost in time.

The time!

Reality rushed in. Win pulled away, panic flashing.

"What time is it?" he blurted. Mitch checked his watch.

"Ten thirty-seven."

"I have to go inside. Darceline's three-hour timeout is about over."

"Okay," Mitch smiled, leaning his forehead against his.

"Are you off duty?"

"Yes, but I'm never really off duty. Especially tonight."

"Can I ask you a favor?"

"Anything," Mitch said, his smile unwavering.

"After all this, can you drive Aunt Betsy and Uncle Bill home?"

"Of course."

"And Dr. Funnell will need a lift too."

Mitch lightly laughed. "Anything you need, you got it."

Winston smiled at him—really smiled. He liked this man. This gentleman. He thanked the hot cop with one last kiss.

A commanding "A-Hem!" cut through their moment.

Behind the screen door stood Kaitlyn, arms crossed beneath breasts big enough to nourish an entire maternity ward—and then some—her massive baby bump front and center.

Win didn't budge. He kept his arms draped comfortably around Mitch, giving his neck a soothing pat, then stroked the nape with his finger—the universal sign for 'Play it cool, I've got this.'

"Yes, Kaitlyn?" Win asked, all politeness and poise.

"What's this?!" she snapped, chin jutting skyward like a scandalized soap opera villain.

"We're making out," Win answered, stone-cold nonchalant. "What's up?"

Kaitlyn gasped like she'd witnessed a car crash. But it wasn't the kiss that stunned her—hell, she already knew Winston was gay, and there had been rumors about the sheriff.

No, it was their lack of panic she hadn't expected. There was no shame, flustered apologies, stammering excuses, or begging pleas for her not to tell. She got zilch. And it infuriated her.

Mitch and Win stared at her silently, giving her time *to get to it*.

"The ambulance is here for your mother, and the morgue people are here for Auntie Darceline. They're at the entrance, waiting for you."

"Thank you, Kaitlyn," Winston said with a sunny smile.

Kaitlyn's head cocked dramatically. "For sure," she bit back, sounding suspiciously more like a 'Fuck You!' before waddling off.

Mitch and Winston exchanged a glance before giggling under their breaths.

"Are you okay?" Mitch teased, his finger tracing down Win's nose.

"Right here, right now, with you? Yes."

"Are you okay?" Win asked with a look of concern.

"About what?"

"We're about to become family news in ten seconds."

Mitch arched a brow and smirked. "About what?" he repeated, mirroring Win's faux worry. Then he kissed him, short and sweet, like a defiant period at the end of a sentence.

Win brushed a hand through his hair. "I'll have to address this … us."

"I am so comfortable with you," Mitch reassured, their foreheads pressing together. "I don't know why, but I've always been."

"Are you ready to be outed? Because I guarantee you, Gladys Kravitz at the door has already called a press conference to broadcast her latest discovery."

Mitch's eyes gleamed with a madcap glint surfacing. "Address us however you like."

"You're sure?"

"Absolutely."

"Ready?" Win asked, turning toward the house.

Mitch grabbed his hand, gave it a parting kiss, and let go. "Now I am."

Win's smile returned, lighter, freer.

Inside, a gathering was formed near the open front doors. They crossed the mansion, walking side by side, approaching the small group together. Two male EMTs and a man and woman in black jackets labeled *CORONER* stood by two gurneys, speaking with Mr. Peters, Mr. de Beaumont, and Dr. Funnell.

As they reached the group, Peters turned to Winston. "They're ready."

Winston introduced himself and received polite nods and a "Sheriff" for Mitch.

"We'll be ready in just a few minutes," Winston said, then turned to the coroner team. "Let's have you come in first for my aunt. She has been … her body has been sitting for three hours. I'd like this to be as pleasant as possible. How movable will she be?"

The woman with short, curly yellow hair answered, "Within the first eight hours of rigor mortis, the body stiffens but is still manageable.

We should be able to gently move her from the chair to the gurney quite gracefully."

Winston looked to Funnell, who gave a confirming nod.

He turned to the EMTs. "My mother is on the sofa to the left when you enter the room. She really needs to be in the hospital but refuses to go until her sister's been moved. Once the coroner team exits, please roll in."

"Yes, sir," they replied.

"Thank you," Winston said, then led Mitch, Peters, de Beaumont, and Funnell back to the Grand Room. Halfway through the long foyer, he stopped.

"Mr. Peters," Win said, turning, "would you have the staff begin pouring the champagne? We're nearly there."

"Of course."

"And Mr. Peters," Winston added, "I'd prefer ginger ale in a champagne flute."

"Me as well," Mitch said.

"One more thing," Win continued. "I must warn you both: something has happened. Now, please don't panic. I'm certain her body wasn't disturbed, but … Aunt Darceline is now wearing sunglasses."

"What?" de Beaumont gasped. "But … but …"

"It's fine," Winston said firmly. "With this family, it was bound to happen. It wasn't the staff—it was us. The staff is in the clear."

"But …" Leland stammered again.

"No buts!" Winston cut in. "It's done. We're moving forward. Everything's fine."

Quoting Leland from earlier, he added, "Nod if you understand."
Leland did.

Winston looked at Peters. "Please relay this to the staff. No one is in trouble. Everything is okay."

A bit stunned by Winston's new edge of command, Mr. Peters nodded and turned with Leland toward the kitchen entry off the foyer.

Winston led Mitch and Dr. Funnell to the family, bracing for the main event. With a quick exhale, like a boxer about to enter the ring, he said, "Here we go."

The doctor peeled off to check on Marci.

Win and Mitch moved to stand beside Darceline. All around them, family members began to notice—the room quieting, eyebrows raising, one by one and two by two. In the center of it all, Kaitlyn stood tall, wearing a wicked grin that practically screamed: *I TATTLED!*

Mr. de Beaumont entered from the kitchen, glanced briefly at Darceline, closed his eyes, shook his head, and then looked to Winston, who asked, "Leland, have we honored the three hours?"

He checked his watch and nodded.

"Thank you," Win said, letting his eyes roll slowly across the room, finally landing on Mitch, who gave him a quick wink and stepped closer, brushing their arms together.

Winston breathed, saying, "Ladies and gentlemen, this man and I were high school sweethearts." Turning to Mitch, he continued, "We've reunited—and that's that."

Mitch slid a finger into Win's palm, giving it a tickling waggle. All was good.

"YEAH!" Sissy whooped, leaping from her barstool and starting to clap, drawing the rest of the family into smiling, laughing applause.

Winston looked to his mother—sitting upright, all smiles. Aunt Betsy pressed her hands lovingly over her heart. Bill, Phil, Tami, Jeffrey, Michelle, Chase, and Jackson gave a standing ovation. Jasmine remained seated, gleaming her signature perfect smile, with handsome Dalton beaming his. Little Stevyn stood by his father with a curious grin, looking at everyone's sudden elation. Win scanned the room, watching joy bloom across every face. It was the first time he'd ever seen his family this purely, this collectively, happy.

Then there was Kaitlyn, pouting a severe, downright comedic scowl.

Win turned to Mitch. "You okay?"

"Never better," the sheriff beamed, leaned in, and kissed him—for all to see.

More applause, cheers, whistles. Win turned to Darceline and declared, "That one was for you, Aunt D!"

Mr. Peters appeared from the kitchen. Winston gave him the universal drink signal. Peters nodded and disappeared again.

"ONTO the reason we are here!" Winston charged, pausing to let the room settle, returning to why they *were* there. "The time has arrived for the last call."

He took a breath. Mitch respectfully stepped sideways and back, giving him the floor. Win gave him a thankful smile before turning to the room.

"It is with deep …" Winston choked, folding his hands together. "It is with deep sadness … that we are here to say goodbye to our beloved Darceline. And by honoring her wish … to remain with us for three hours after her passing, I believe we've fulfilled her final request."

He looked at Darceline and let out half a chuckle. "Three hours."

Turning to the room, he repeated, "Three hours.

"We had just sat down for dinner when she died.

"Don't call 911. Don't touch her. Don't help her. Don't move her. Not for three hours.

"I honestly didn't know what to think.

"Then, thankfully, Mr. Peters informed me there were protocols. A plan.

"*Of course there were.*

"But most importantly, per Aunt Darceline, don't do a thing for three hours.

"*Three. Fucking. Hours.*"

He paused, eyes welling.

"I didn't understand why it mattered so much to her.

"But I do now."

He looked across the faces of his family, bittersweet in his smile.

"She wanted us to come together. To be together. And so here we are. Together. For D. Per D."

The room stilled, sniffling, honoring the truth of it.

"We'll toast her before she leaves," Winston continued, softening. "But first, let me quickly walk us through the week ahead.

"Aunt Darceline arranged everything. There will be no viewing. She will be cremated. Her name will be added to the family mausoleum plaque.

"Wednesday at noon, right here, Mr. de Beaumont will read her Will, followed by lunch.

"Friday at 4 p.m., a board of directors meeting will be held here.

"Saturday at noon, a private luncheon at the club for family, friends, and business associates. At 2 p.m., a procession to the cemetery for the public to pay their respects. At 6 p.m., another private dinner at the club for family and close friends. Then, at 11:30 p.m.—just us, the family— we'll meet here at the docks, where her ashes will be taken by boat and spread at midnight.

"Our beloved Darceline Hicks shall be laid to rest."

He paused, then casually asked, "Any questions?"

"YOU'RE DUMPING HER BODY IN THE LAKE ON HAL-LOWEEN?!" Kaitlyn indignantly shrieked.

Before Winston could respond, Leland stepped in calmly. "Miss Hicks' instructions are specific: her ashes are to be spread across the family lake at midnight, five days after her death—holiday or not. That was her choice."

Kaitlyn grimaced but said nothing more.

Winston nodded to Susan, who stood by the kitchen doors with a tray of champagne flutes. She began serving, starting with Mitch and Win, whispering which were ginger ale.

Once she had made the rounds and returned to the kitchen entryway, Winston approached Susan. "Please bring the entire staff out to join us for the toast—with champagne in hand."

She gave him a surprised look. He smiled, "Please."

Susan obediently nodded, returning to the kitchen.

Soon, Darceline's team slowly filed into the Grand Room, glasses in hand, appearing bewildered by the request. Susan stepped out last, holding a flute of bubbly, giving Winston a pleased grin.

Win slightly raised his glass to her and mouthed, "Thank you."

He turned to his family. A tear slipped down his cheek. Win looked at Mitch, at his mother, and around the room. Then, raising his glass toward Darceline at the head of the table, he said, "To Darceline!"

The room echoed, "To Darceline!"

Glasses clinked and clinked. And everyone sipped.

Winston stepped back into the foyer, waving the coroner's team in. As they approached Darceline with the gurney, he made another announcement.

"My dear family …"

All eyes turned to him.

"The time has come for these fine folks to take our guest of honor on her final ride down the lane.

"So please, let's keep to the bar or the lounge."

He caught Willow's eye across the room and tilted his head toward their mother. She headed that way.

Marci had reclined again, eyes half-closed, panting harder than she had all evening. She silently watched her sister lifted from the chair and gently placed on the gurney. Dr. Funnell sat nearby, elbows on knees, chin resting on folded hands as if counting the seconds until he could get her to the hospital.

Sissy sat beside her. Winston settled on the coffee table to avoid blocking her view of D's departure.

Dr. Funnell stood. "Marci," he said gently, "the EMTs are here and will bring in a stretcher as soon as Darceline is moved."

Marci didn't respond. She remained focused on the now-empty chair.

Funnell left to bring in the EMTs.

"Mom?" Sissy whispered lovingly.

Marci's eyes fluttered, and she looked up at Willow. "Hi, honey," she said, her voice soft and distant.

She looked at her son and cooed, "You're my beautiful baby boy."
Winston smiled.

She turned to Sissy. "You're my beautiful baby girl."

Willow smiled warmly.

Marci reached out for Sissy's hand, then Winston's, and said with quiet absolution, "I have loved you two souls more than I ever possibly could in this world. I am so eternally grateful for that.

"And I have failed as much as I've succeeded at being your mother. I hope you can forgive me … and love me."

Sissy leaned over and kissed her cheek. "I love you, Mom."

Marci closed her eyes.

Winston leaned in and kissed her cheek, too, but noticed her huffing and puffing had stopped. Marci's hand slipped from his, falling away. Willow immediately shot Win a look. Win locked eyes with her, and grief struck them both in that exchange. They turned back to their mother, her face peaceful and calm.

Winston slowly reached for her neck, feeling for a pulse.

She was gone.

"Oh my God," Sissy exhaled, breaking into a quiet sob.

Shattered, Winston pressed his lips to his mother's cheek, trembling, crying, "I … love … you … too, Mom."

Dr. Funnell, positively relieved he could finally get Marci to the hospital, hastily led the two EMTs in with a stretcher to chipperly announce: "Shall we go, Mrs. Clarke?"

The Key

Bucks Peak lay in eerie silence as Winston stood in the open front doorway, smoking, watching the last vehicle disappear into the night.

The family had departed—utterly devastated, shattered, in complete shock. Their sobs still lingered in the air, haunting the hush. Sissy had left just after the EMS took Marci to the morgue. Jasmine drove Bill and Betsy home. Mitch was returning Dr. Funnell to his wife.

Leland approached in his overcoat, briefcase in hand, his shoes sounding quietly against the limestone flooring. He paused beside Winston.

"We should include Marci's passing in the press release," he said. "The twin sisters died three hours apart. That's the kind of detail the media will seize and should be framed properly, controlled." He adjusted his grip on the briefcase. "I'll email a proof once the draft is ready."

Winston nodded, then hesitated. "Okay ... no, wait."

Leland lifted his chin to listen.

"This is a private family matter," Winston said. "I don't want it becoming some tweaked-out human-interest story. Don't mention her siblings. Don't mention my mother. Just write a short release about Darceline's passing." He made air quotes. "She died."

He looked down at the floor for a beat, then asked, voice raw and quiet, "Can we do that, Leland? Can we just … keep the family out of it?"

Leland gave a solemn nod. "Yes."

"Thank you," Winston said, pulling out his phone to check the battery. "Leland?"

"Yes?"

"Text me the release, will you? I don't want to dig through emails for it."

"Of course."

With nothing more to say, the two nodded, and Leland left.

Win tucked the phone back inside his blazer, extinguished his cigarette, then slowly closed each of the heavy front doors. He turned to face the long, empty foyer. The grandfather clock tolled. He leaned against the door, feeling as crushed as the two buried cars outside. His head gently rolled back until it met the wood, and his eyes lifted toward the darkened triangle skylight as the chimes echoed all around.

A fitting finale, he thought. The Grim Reaper gonging twelve. The End.

Mr. Peters emerged from the kitchen corridor, his movements slow, his expression heavy.

"The front gate has been closed," he reported, voice low and drained.

"Thank you," Winston sighed, the words barely audible.

"This has not been a good day," Peters added quietly.

"No."

Winston studied the older man's face—deeper wrinkles now, more age spots than when Win had left for college. Time had weathered them all.

"Cleanup is complete. The staff has turned in," Peters continued.

"I've left the lights on so you can find your way. Help yourself to any-thing."

"Thank you," Win said again, barely above a whisper.

"I'm deeply sorry for your losses today," Peters said, sincere and soft.

"As I am for yours."

They exchanged a somber nod.

"Can you show me how to buzz the sheriff through the gate?" Win asked.

"He's got the keypad code. All emergency personnel do."

"Okay."

"Good night, Winston."

"Good night."

Peters' footsteps faded into the depths of the house, eventually swallowed by silence.

Win stood there, the weight of solitude settling in. The air was thick and stifling. Though the temperature had dipped slightly since he'd opened the doors earlier, the heat still clung stubbornly. He realized he didn't know where the thermostat was. With a resigned shrug, he opened one of the front doors again, letting the stagnant warmth spill into the night.

If critters wanted to wander in and pay their respects—or shit on the floor—so be it. He didn't care.

He drifted into the Grand Room. His eyes found the empty chair where D had died. Then, the loveseat, where his mother had passed. He turned, meandering to the BS entryway, pausing to stare across the room at Darceline's desk. The shadows seemed heavier there.

His fingers grazed the pendant on his chest.

Her legacy now rested with him.

Winston entered the office, slipping out of his blazer and draping it over the back of her empty desk chair. He unfastened the top three but-tons of his shirt, removed the pendant, and studied it in his palm.

An odd impulse stirred—an urge to follow where it led.

He circled her desk, approaching the mysterious door. His eyes locked on the chrome light switch plate, its small, deliberate hole waiting.

He froze.

County Road 800 flickered across his mind. *She won't be taking me there tomorrow*, he realized.

The thought hollowed him.

His lips trembled. He pressed a hand to his mouth to keep the grief from spilling out.

Shaking his head, Winston forced himself to move. He took a slow, deliberate breath. Then, trembling fingers, he raised the pendant, aligned it with the hole, and slid it in.

A soft electronic chime—*be-ba*—sounded. The wooden door clicked free and edged open.

Win hesitated for a heartbeat, then pushed the door wide.

Lights clicked on automatically, revealing a narrow concrete stairwell, like a stripped-down subway entrance descending until it curved out of sight to the right. The steps were gray, clean, and cold-looking—stark and sterile. The descent was not warm or welcoming, but it was spotless.

With a short exhale, Win stepped in.

The stairs were steeper than usual, almost theater-like in-depth, spiraling down two or three stories. Wherever this led, it was genuinely subterranean.

At the bottom, he found himself face to face with a massive silver vault door. His hand instinctively touched his chest—still in the slot, he'd left the key upstairs. He glanced left, then right. No switch plate this time. No keyhole. Just a large, black, three-spoke safe handle at the center of the door.

He reached for it, expecting resistance—but it spun easily, like the dial on a car radio. After four smooth rotations, the door softly clicked and popped open a few inches toward him.

Winston pulled it wider and watched as rows of ceiling lights flickered on—one after the other—revealing what looked like an underground warehouse. The air hit him immediately, twenty degrees cooler than the stifling manor above.

Inside, rows upon rows of industrial shelving like at a Costco—smaller in height, more like eight feet high versus two stories tall—stretched to the right and left. Beside the entrance on the right sat a gray utility cart, and above it, a folded stepladder. Three brand-new, clean black garbage bins with hardtop fold-over lids—just like the ones he rolled out to the street for pickup on Mondays and Thursdays back home—lined the wall just beyond the cart. To the left, more shelving ran the concrete wall, and the floor to the ceiling was stocked with five-gallon water jugs.

"What the hell is this?" Win asked aloud, staring at an underground otherworld.

He stepped into the central aisle, moving slowly, eyes scanning left and right at countless wooden boxes that appeared to be roughly 24" x 18" x 12" in size. Two were neatly placed on each row of shelves, six shelves high, that ran both sides of the aisle.

Win approached a box to his left, leaning in for a closer view. It appeared to have been handcrafted. It was made from traditional milling techniques with precise box-joint joinery and finished with a clear coating that enhanced the wood's natural grain and rich tones. It was a beautiful, articulate box with a custom sliding wooden lid. A small, aluminum frame centered on the front of each had an index card neatly tucked in with its contents labeled, typed from an old typewriter. His eyes first went to *EGYPT 1927*. The box to its right, *EGYPT 1928*. The boxes on the shelf above read *EGYPT 1921* and *EGYPT 1923*.

Each shelving rack was roughly four feet wide, and every shelf had a slight lip with a small handle in its midpoint. Win reached out and pulled, and the shelf glided effortlessly and easily on rollers or ball bearings.

The box's wooden lid was designed to slide open smoothly. Win slowly pushed back the top of *EGYPT 1927* halfway. A burst of cedar wafted out with a hint of something aged and quite old. Inside were mysterious shapes wrapped in aged linen and fine, ancient-looking cloth. He returned its lid gently, sliding the shelf to its place.

He walked the aisle, feeling bookended and towered over by countless more wooden boxes, each the same size, each appearing ominous. At the end of the aisle, he counted—nine rows of shelving to his right, eight to the left.

Turning right, Win walked to the end of the vast chamber and began scanning the wooden boxes. Two stacks in, he pulled out and opened an unmarked box. Inside were tightly wrapped bricks of U.S. $100 bills in cellophane, eight inches thick. Further down, another unmarked box held wrapped blocks of €100 Euro bills. Another was filled with hundreds of physical cryptocurrency coins in protective cases. A shelving section held stacked silver bars beside stacks of gold bars, lining shelves from bottom to top.

In the next aisle: boxes labeled *BASEBALL CARDS*, *COINS*, *STAMPS*. At the end, a single shelving unit, floor-to-ceiling, filled with more boxes labeled *JEWELS*. He opened one—inside were jewelry boxes from Cartier, Van Cleef & Arpels, Harry Winston, and Sterlé. Reaching into his pocket, Win pulled out Darceline's emerald ring and gently set it atop a Tiffany necklace box. He closed the lid and slid the shelf back in.

The following aisle was chronological, marked *1791, 1792, 1793*—each year following the next, aisle after aisle, through *2035*.

As he walked the length of this collection, three boxes stopped him cold: *1948.1-CR800*, *1948.2-CR800*, and *1949.1-CR800*. Win stared at them, uneasy. A vague queasiness crept in, and he decided to move on.

He noticed a different open corner at the far end of the vault—less warehouse, more workspace. A desk. A chair. It caught his interest. He slowly approached it, passing aisle after aisle filled with more wooden boxes.

The fourth-to-last aisle was filled entirely with hundreds of water jugs.

The third-to-last drew him in: a survivalist's dream of canned goods, stacked cases of vegetables, fruits, meats, rice, powdered milk, and even hygiene products like shampoo and Clorox Wipes.

The next aisle stocked spirits, beers, and cases upon cases of cigarettes and cigars.

But the final aisle held a surprise: a narrow open loft apartment built right against the concrete wall. It was carpeted and fully furnished—like a room from a Home2 Suites. A full bathroom, bedroom, living room, kitchen, and dining area. The desk and chair he'd spotted earlier were here, too.

This wasn't just a vault. It was a fallout shelter.

Overwhelmed and exhausted, Winston walked to the king-sized bed, quilted with a handmade cover of antique patchwork. He sat at the edge, then fell back into its softness. It cradled him, and he didn't want to move. He removed his glasses, reached over to place them on a nightstand, kicked off his shoes, and shifted toward the center, pulling his legs onto the bed.

And then it struck—a jolt of realization down his spine.

He was stuck now. Cocooned in silk. Caught in the sticky web of his family. And his 'out' was nowhere in sight.

He stared at the concrete ceiling, pitted lines, and ventilation ducts crossing overhead. He couldn't believe they were gone—his mother, his aunt. He hadn't felt this alone since the day he collapsed on his bed after Chris died.

The dam broke.

Tears began to fall … and then they gushed.

Winston grabbed the edge of the quilt, pulling it tightly around him. It smelled old—like history itself. Curling into a fetal position, he pulled a pillow beneath his head and buried his face into it.

He howled. A long, wounded cry, like a lone wolf mourning under a full moon.

And he kept howling.

Every ounce of pain poured out—minute after minute, or maybe an hour. He didn't know. Time meant nothing down there.

H

Winston heard a tender, familiar voice softly call out, "Hey ..."

He pulled his face from the damp pillowcase and looked up. Mitch was standing at the side of the bed, watching him.

"How did you find me?" His throat was dry, voice-catching.

"When I came back, you were gone. I searched everywhere—upstairs, downstairs ... until I checked the office and saw your jacket draped over a chair. Then I heard a faint cry through an open door.

"I followed it down here—to you."

But Win didn't want this right now. He was too deep in it. So, he rested his head back on the pillow, one eye half-open, watching this beautiful man standing before him, looking utterly wrecked. Mitch's face fell in silent sorrow, as if he could feel the grief radiating off Win's body—like he was sinking with him, soul to soul.

Winston watched as Mitch slowly removed his leather coat, which he draped neatly over the back of a nearby chair. He unstrapped his holster and laid it gently on the nightstand. He untucked and unbuttoned his uniform shirt one by one, folding it over the coat. His belt dropped to the floor, and his shoes came off.

Winston kept watching.

Mitch climbed onto the bed in just his undershirt and navy uniform trousers. Gently, he wrapped his arms around Win's curled-up body, pulling him close. Then he laid his head on the pillow beside him, their faces inches apart, gazing into his tear-swollen eyes.

Mitch held him tighter, cradling him, pressing Win's folded shape against his own. Then came the softest kisses—forehead, left cheek, right cheek—and finally, he rested his nose against Win's.

Win stretched out his legs, slowly unfolding to lay fully against Mitch's solid frame. He tucked his face beneath Mitch's chin, breathing him in, feeling safer. A broken cry escaped.

Mitch pulled him in tighter, his whole body a shelter.

And into Win's ear, he whispered:

"It's okay …
"It's okay …
"Howl on my lone wolf.
"Howl … and howl away …"

Destination Unknown

Winston jolted awake. Something compelled him to get up.

Flat on his back, he squinted—the lights were still on, glaring overhead. Rolling his head on the pillow, he saw the sheriff fast asleep, a soft snore purring from his lips.

Win slid off the bed with practiced care, as he would when he was with Chris, trying not to wake him when he got up to pee.

The bunker was cold. A chill crept over him as he reached for his glasses. He slipped them on, picked each shoe up, and quietly walked through Darceline's subterranean Costco and up the stairs.

Stepping into BS, Winston spotted his blazer and immediately thought of Irene—maybe she'd texted him the passwords. Then he wondered if Leland had texted him the press release to proof. He had no idea what time it was. He picked up the jacket and pulled out his phone.

No texts. No calls.

It was 3:33 a.m.

He set the phone down on Darceline's desk.

The mansion was now comfortable—not sweltering like when he first arrived. Still carrying the bunker's chill in his bones, he slipped on the blazer and reached for his cigarette case. It was empty.

Without a second thought, he pulled out the chair at D's desk and sank into it. He took off his glasses, rubbing his eyes. When he opened them, he first saw Darceline's crystal cigarette box. He put his glasses back on, reached for a filterless Chesterfield, and lit it with the heavy crystal table lighter beside it.

His gaze drifted across the Business Suite as he exhaled a long plume of smoke. He reflected on all that had happened … and wondered what the hell he was going to do.

Before he could fall into a depressive state or break into another cry, his phone vibrated on the desk.

Snapping to—maybe it was Leland—he grabbed it and saw: Unknown Caller.

Is Irene on a satellite phone? Win answered.

In the faintest of whispers, he heard:

sh sh sh sh shh shh shh shh shh shh shh shh shh shh shh

He asked, "Irene, is that you?"

shh sh shh sh sh shh sh

"Irene, this is Winston. We must have a bad connection—I can't hear you."

shh shh shh sh sh shh shh shh shh shh shh shh shh shh shh

"If you can hear me, text me your number. I'll call you back."

There was a beep, and the screen went black. Dropped Call.

Win stared at the phone, took a long drag, and waited.

Then it vibrated again. A new text arrived.

....- ----- ----- -----

-.-. .-.

---.. ----- -----

What the hell?
The phone vibrated again. New voicemail notification.
He opened it.

Transcription
".…- ----- ----- ----- .... -.-. .-. .... ---.. ----- -----"

What the fuck?
He hit Play.

sh sh sh sh shh shh shh shh shh shh shh shh shh shh shh. shh sh shh sh sh shh sh shh shh shh sh sh shh shh shh shh shh shh shh shh shh shh

Winston set the phone on the desk and stared at it, perplexed, thinking:
That must have been Irene.
It was a bad sat call.
That's what it was.
She'll call back.
He leaned into Darceline's executive chair and took another long drag from the cigarette, his eyes never leaving the phone—until something in the air moved.

Every hair on his body stood on end.

It was that unmistakable sensation, primal and electric—another presence was in the room. Watching.

He looked up. And froze.

A gray alien stood between the long conference table and the seating area. Just under four feet tall, its frame was slender, almost delicate, with limbs just a bit too long for its body—giving it an eerie, spider-like grace. Its skin was smooth and uniform, a matte gray that shimmered faintly—not with light, but with a strange, anti-reflective stillness as if it absorbed illumination rather than reflected it. No shadow fell from its body, as if it didn't quite belong to this reality.

The visitor's head was disproportionate—an elongated teardrop shape with a broad, domed cranium and a tapering chin. No hair. Not even the suggestion of it. Just more of that same gray, stretched taut over a skull that hinted at an evolved, maybe even overdeveloped, intelligence.

But the eyes. That's what held Winston.

Massive, almond-shaped, and bottomless black—locked on Winston's with calm, unwavering intensity. There were no whites. No iris. No pupil. Just obsidian darkness, glossy and unblinking, drinking in everything around them. They weren't eyes designed to communicate. They were made to witness.

The rest of the face was crowded out: a mere suggestion of a nose—two narrow slits—and a thin, lipless mouth, more seam than a feature. No ears, either. Only faint indentations where they might have been—or never were.

Its fingers were long and spindly, with an extra joint, giving the impression of delicate precision over strength. It didn't breathe, didn't fidget, didn't sway. It just stood there. Perfectly still. Perfectly calm. As if waiting. Calculating. Recording.

But it wasn't cold. There was a familiarity—an unspoken message that whispered:

I know you.

A presence that said, without a sound:

It's good to see you again.

Winston didn't flinch. He didn't speak. He just sat there, relaxed, the cigarette still perched between two fingers. No tension in his shoulders. No alarm in his eyes. Just recognition, settling over him. It was like seeing a childhood friend no one else remembered—one he'd half-convinced himself he'd imagined. And yet, here it was, looking back at him with that same unreadable gaze like no time had passed.

They stared at each other like that for a long while. The room was peaceful.

Then, without warning, a fresh and vivid memory surfaced as if the being was projecting it into his mind, playing it back like an old home movie on a screen only he could see.

Win was four. Burning with fever from an intense, strong cold. Tucked into a narrow bed beneath heavy blankets, his slight body sweating, caught between sleep and something stranger. He looked toward the foot of the bed—and saw it. The same little, gray being. Motionless. Watching him with those enormous, black eyes. It stood just to the left of the bedpost, still as stone.

He hadn't felt fear—just calm—the strange kind that only children know when something unknowable is happening and simply accept it.

Even then, he had sensed something more profound—a presence not just physical but mental. A connection. Not words, exactly, but something telepathic. A transmission. It was not understandable, not in any clear language, but unmistakable to *him*. And that was enough.

He remembered sinking back into the pillow. Blinking.

And it was gone.

His mother entered moments later, concern on her face as she smoothed his hair and placed a cool washcloth on his forehead. He told her what he'd seen in the earnest way only a child can.

Marci tilted her head and smiled softly. "Winston," she said, "when we have a fever, we can imagine things that aren't really there."

He remembered believing her. Letting her words comfort him. But even then, deep down, he'd known.

He *had* seen it. He still believed it.

The memory dissolved.

Winston's cigarette had burned slowly, forgotten, its ember inching ever downward. The ash clung stubbornly, arching longer and longer until nearly two inches of it dangled at the tip. He finally moved only when the smoldering heat crept dangerously close to his fingers. He leaned forward and dropped it into a crystal ashtray.

Then he looked up—

And the alien was gone.

No sound. No movement. No sign it had ever been there. Just the fading warmth of something ancient, impossible … and oddly comforting.

It was like the moment just before a dream fades forever.

Winston leaned back, the weight of the moment pressing in. Smoke from his dying cigarette curled lazily in the air. It wasn't just memory anymore—it was presence. That steady gaze, quiet and unmistakable, like the one that had once stood beside his childhood bed ... and had just been here again.

He floated in a space between *here* and *not here*, absorbing an understanding that required no thought, no analysis—only acceptance.

Oh, my God ...

Now, it made sense. The dots and dashes were Morse code.

He sat forward and tapped his phone awake, diving into Messages. He reopened the one from the Unknown Sender.

He'd learned it at Camp Ottertail the summer he was eleven, though it took him a moment to recall the alphanumeric equivalents. It had been years since he'd thought about Morse.

Squinting, he read aloud as he decoded: "Four. Zero. Zero. Zero. C. R. Eight. Zero. Zero."

His gaze lifted, landing precisely where the being had stood.

"4000 CR 800," Win said under his breath.

"You want me to go to 4000 County Road 800."

Yes.

The word pulsed telepathically through Winston.

"Okay," he replied with a strange acceptance that he was talking to something *else*.

Then another pulse:

Alone.

"Okay," Win said again—like it was an order.

He exhaled.

Wow.

And ... *WOW!*

Win pulled another cigarette from the box and lit it. He was too tired to completely freak out, yet wired from the surreal, adrenaline-fueled *whatever-that-was.*

He sat bewildered, blinking, shaking his head.

"I think I'm going insane," he glibly said in smoke to himself before he spiraled back into wondering what the hell he was going to do about *everything*, including *that.*

Knowing he was sleep-deprived and already jet-lagged from the time change, and the only real meal he had the day before was a sandwich on the jet, Win's entire body ached, including his brain. He needed food. He needed rest. He was thirsty.

Winston got up and walked to the bar for water. His eyes immediately locked upon the crystal decanter of bourbon. He reached out and ran his index finger around the circular edge of the stopper, longing for a pour.

He took a drag from his cigarette, snapping back to why he was standing at the bar in the first place. Reaching for a water bottle, he opened it and turned to lean against it as he guzzled half, pausing for a breath. His mental mindfuck was interrupted by Mitch emerging from Darceline's subterranean wonderland, looking half-asleep, his eyes wincing from the lights.

"Hey," Win said, relieved to see him.

Mitch entered with his arms wrapped around his chest, clearly chilled from the vault air. Spotting Winston across the room, he replied, "Hey."

Win grabbed a second water and crossed BS, handing it to McKay.

"What time is it?" Mitch asked.

Win returned to D's desk, tapping his phone to wake up as he sat. "Four forty-four."

The sheriff ambled to a club chair across from him to sit.

Winston's mindfuck returned:

Wait!

What happened to the time?

He couldn't have been up there for an hour and eleven minutes.

Where the hell did an hour go?

What the actual fuck?!

And then Win sighed, remembering.

Oh shit ... it's happening again ...

Watching Win seemingly go deep in thought, Mitch asked if he was okay, then cracked open the plastic bottle and drank until he polished it off.

"Yeah," Winston answered automatically, more like an email autoresponder than someone genuinely fine. He puffed on his cigarette and added, "I just had the strangest thing happen."

He hesitated.

"Aunt D's assistant is on a cruise to Antarctica. Leland placed a call to the ship to reach her. My phone buzzed when I came upstairs, and I thought it may have been her calling on a satellite phone."

"Hmm," Mitch hummed, trying his best to sound interested.

"And then—"

Heed caution.

The voice stopped Win cold, skidding him into a mental U-turn.

I can't say what really happened, he realized. *Not yet.*

"I hear you," he thought silently in reply.

Good.

So instead, Win said, "And then the call dropped."

"Hmm," Mitch repeated, screwing the plastic cap on the empty water bottle, looking like he could fall back asleep.

Winston took a long drag, gazing fondly at Mitch.

The tired sheriff caught the look and winked.

Their eyes locked. The energy between them stirred—something unspoken, like the soft flicker of faery dust spiraling through the air.

But Winston was sitting with two gaping holes in his heart and soul where his mother and his aunt were anchored just hours ago. Two. Gone. In one day. One hundred eighty minutes apart. The craters of loss were sudden, unexpected, deep, and profoundly painful.

"Is there anything I can do?" Mitch asked with an early-morning frog in his throat, sitting heartfelt, like a man who found his long-lost prince charming … yet powerless to heal his anguish. He'd felt the core of Winston's spirit profoundly cry out in great agony as he cradled him in his arms. And he knew all he could do was simply be there for him.

At that moment, Win felt something click, like a missing piece of his soul had slipped effortlessly back into place, making a part of him whole again. He was paired. And whatever came next, he had a real, honest man by his side.

"You already have," Win said, his voice thick with gratitude.

They lingered in each other's gaze until Mitch stirred, waking up more fully. He stretched his arms high, leaned right, then left, twisting at the waist like he was wringing the night from his body. His eyes landed on the mysterious door behind him as he twisted to the left.

He turned back to Win, curiosity kindling in his face. "What is this place?"

Win shrugged and looked around. Then, at the chrome light switch plate and the necklace chain dangling from the inserted key.

It was so much more than a house on a hill under the watch of a satellite. Or where a trove of artifacts was stashed below in a cold, cavernous vault. Or where two crushed cars were entombed. Or where something popped in to personally invite him to a private party happening on County Road 800, where *something* was waiting.

There was history here. Childhood memories with the family. Like hopping on a golf cart with Sissy to cruise the grounds and down to the lake, Thanksgiving dinners around the crowded dining room table in the Great Room, sleepovers, endless ice cream sundaes specially made by Penny, crawling under the BS conference table with Jasmine and Jeffrey in a game of floor-tag when they were little, July Fourth barbeques and fireworks on the beach, playing cutthroat in billiards with Uncle Bill and Aunt Besty in the basement game room, Christmas Eve when Uncle Phil would be nowhere in sight just as Santa rang the doorbell with a large bag of presents to hand out, laying on the second-floor skywalk staring at the night stars through the pyramid skylights on a cold spring night, and getting a scolding alongside Jackson for taking turns joyriding inside the dumbwaiter up and down from the basement to the second floor. Growing up at Bucks Peak was a haven … no, heaven.

Winston didn't know how to answer. He wasn't even sure he could. "I honestly don't know."

Mitch tilted his head. "I mean—what *is* this place?"

Win's eyes drifted back to the spot where the alien had stood. A slow smile crept across his face. He looked at Mitch.

"Let's find out."

Sinking into the chair from his words, Mitch exhaled with a hopeful feeling of wonderment. "You and me?"

"You and me."

"Together?"

Winston could feel his puffy eyes from crying squish as he grinned. "Together."

Mitch grinned, too, his eyes glistening with a trusting warmth. He felt the love in his heart for Win begin to open once again.

Suddenly, telepathically, in a voice that sounded distinctly like a child who missed out on the last piece of birthday cake, Winston heard:

What about me?

ALSO BY Scot Rogers

Welcome to the Shitshow introduces Winston Clarke in the series, *My Family of Hicks*.

This insanely funny comedy is free to read at Scot's website. It's also available in paperback and Kindle media at Amazon.

Simply scan the QR below, to see where the hilarity begins …

ScotRogers.com  @theScotRogers

Did you enjoy *My Family of Hicks*?
Your review makes a difference.

Follow Scot Rogers
across social media for details on the upcoming sequels to
My Family of Hicks.